# The SIGN
## of the
# SEVEN SEAS

# The SIGN of the
# SEVEN SEAS

## by CARLEY DAWSON

*Illustrated by Lynd Ward*

1 9 5 4

HOUGHTON MIFFLIN COMPANY BOSTON

𝕿𝖍𝖊 𝕽𝖎𝖛𝖊𝖗𝖘𝖎𝖉𝖊 𝕻𝖗𝖊𝖘𝖘 𝕮𝖆𝖒𝖇𝖗𝖎𝖉𝖌𝖊

To

Rafael Fernández del Castillo

who first told me of

The Sign of the Seven Seas

and without whose help

I could never have seen it

# C H A P T E R 1

*ASTER CAME EARLY* that year, and with it, Christopher Mason's Easter vacation.

On the first day of it, school behind him and what always seemed, at the start, such a long spread of freedom, Chris woke early, from habit. Then, as he realized that school was out, breakfast would be later, and the whole day lay fresh and empty before him, he gave a long sigh of relaxation and turned over in his bed. A luxurious sense of time to fritter away, instead of hoarding it to use for the too many things there were to do, filled his mind as if he looked out over a vast plain. He clasped his hands behind his head and gazed peacefully around his room. Well as he knew it, it always looked just a little different to him in vacation time.

Outside the sunny window, trellised with leaf shadow from the maple trees that lined O Street in Washington, D.C., lay the old brick houses of Georgetown. The quiet streets and pleasant doorways mirrored the Georgian towns that first English settlers of 1751 had called home. Beyond Georgetown's small circumference stretched the ever-widening growth of the capital city. Chris knew its white domes and colonnaded buildings as he knew his own street. He loved his city, but to Chris, Georgetown seemed the best part of it.

With the spring, the many gardens of Georgetown were gay with flowers. Everything was out at once. All the flowering trees — cherry, crabapple, and white pear blossom; and spring flowers — tulips, narcissus, daffodils, and hyacinths. Some of the old elms, like the one on the next corner at 28th and P streets, had their roots wreathed with violets, pushing up through the uneven brick pavements. The maple trees that along Chris's street formed a green tunnel of shade in the summertime, were now fragile and palely green.

Chris smiled in a dozy way and blinked drowsily. This time last year he would have been content to fish on the rocks above the Potomac River, or go on day-long canoe trips up the Canal. But this was springtime, and a new year; a year as yet unstamped by adventure, a year when it was time to call on Mr. Wicker once again.

How many times during the long winter had he recalled, lying awake in the dark, the fabulous, unbelievable adventure he had lived upon the *Mirabelle!* Unbelievable except that it had happened, for all his life he would keep a small white scar on his jaw, and a long delicate whiplash, faded and hair-fine now, across his shoulder blades. Those things were real, but without their living testimony it might sometimes have been difficult for Chris not to have doubted his own memory.

Could it hapen again? The old antiquarian Mr. Wicker, in the cozy sitting room Chris remembered so well, had told him he could come back. *That* he could do; and remember his past

8

adventure. But all through the winter that was now gone, Chris had been unwilling to strain his luck by going back too soon. For when he went back, into ancient Mr. Wicker's shop on the corner of Wisconsin Avenue and Water Street, down near the factories and the river, then Chris wanted to be able to stay. He had long been homesick for a sight of his dear friends, Rebecca Boozer, Amos, and Ned Cilley.

Not forgetting Mr. Wicker. He had missed Mr. Wicker most of all, his dark smooth head of chestnut hair, the finely modeled face, lean and strong, and the vividly piercing eyes — black, or brown? — that told Chris so much that was never said. Time without number Chris had journeyed back in his mind to that sun-filled sitting room where the fire crackled, and looked out through the small-paned Georgian windows beyond the long curtains of ruby damask to the neat rows of Mr. Wicker's vegetable garden. Mr. Wicker would be sitting in his high-backed red leather chair, the brass-headed nails that outlined it winking in the firelight, and he would be tapping his fingertips together as was his habit. Chris could almost hear his resonant deep voice that held a smile hidden in it, saying, "Well, my boy?" when he saw a question large on Chris's face.

Chris flung an arm over his eyes and squeezed them up, to shut out the present and bring back the past.

It seemed more than a year ago that Chris had first opened the door of Mr. Wicker's shop near the glinting Potomac River. It had been on a bleak late afternoon when he had seen hanging beside the bow-fronted, small-paned window of the old antiquarian's shop a sign in Mr. Wicker's fine legible hand. Chris remembered it well: "Boy Wanted," it read, and Chris had applied with his friend Mike, asking that the place be given to a schoolmate who needed the job more than they did. Then, like all his friends who had also wanted the job, Chris recalled how he too had been met by the incredibly wrinkled, wizened old man dressed in black who was William Wicker. Chris had been given, as had the others before him, the strange command, "Look out the window and tell me what you see." Chris knew as well as any other Georgetown boy what lay outside Mr. Wicker's bow window. There was the slope of the hill going up Wisconsin Avenue, the tumble-down brick warehouses opposite, the surge of traffic between, roaring overhead too on the freeway. The river was close, at the left, but almost entirely hidden by factories. Yet — and Chris grinned again with a return of the old excitement — when he had looked out that bow window the traffic was gone. So was the freeway. So, too, was even the People's Drug Store, high up on the corner of Wisconsin and M Streets. He had found himself looking back into the past — as it used to be in 1791. He alone of his friends had had the ability to go back in Time.

As the traffic and freeway had vanished, so too had the factories. The river lay extended in all its early beauty before his astounded eyes, holding on its blue palm a forest of masted sailing ships of every description. Of all the things he had known in his own twentieth-century time, only Mr. Wicker's house and the warehouses across the way remained. Everything else, including, surprisingly, himself, was in another age.

Mr. Wicker, too, had changed. This had taken place the next day in front of Chris's unbelieving eyes. From a bent, fragile old man, Mr. Wicker had taken back his eighteenth-century form — that of a man in the prime of life, vigorous and strong.

10

Chris remembered how he had doubted what was happening to him. How could he, he demanded of Mr. Wicker, be
back in 1791 when he had been born in the twentieth century?
Mr. Wicker had answered his question by asking another. He
had asked Chris how television worked. Chris, furrowing his
forehead, had searched his mind, but it had proved too complicated for him to understand and explain, and he had had to
give it up. Mr. Wicker had seemed pleased, for, he explained,
the ability of people to move backward or forward in Time

11

was a knowledge and gift granted — so far — only to a few. But the discovery and mastery of this seemingly fantastic possibility — even as the discovery of television had not been achieved until recently — lay in the future. To be able to move back and forth in Time would come to pass. In the meantime, Chris was one of the rare ones who had this power, together with Mr. Wicker himself.

This was the beginning of the wonderful adventure of a year ago; the discovery that Mr. Wicker was really a magician of unusual force, able to teach Chris much that he knew. The difficult voyage Chris later made on the *Mirabelle* would have seemed impossible to him — except that it had really happened.

The thought of the journey made Chris jump out of bed. He tore into his clothes, pausing only long enough to give his morning glance at the model of the sailing ship *Mirabelle*, safe and snug within the bottle where Ned Cilley had painstakingly built her, years ago, on the way home from "the Chiny Seas." This too, was a reminder to Chris that his adventure of the year before had been real and no dream, for Mr. Wicker had given him the model of his merchant ship, taking it out of the window of his antique shop to put it into Chris's hands.

His mother eyed Chris with a faint smile as he gobbled his food and winked at her with his mouth full.

"You're in a great hurry this morning," she said. "You're never in as much of a hurry on school days, it seems to me."

Chris swallowed. "No — you bet! Say, Mum, could I spend the night away, maybe? I might *not* be that long — " he considered — "and then again, I *might*."

"Where, Chris?" his mother asked. "With Mike?"

"N-no," Chris answered, "with Mr. Wicker, down at his shop. He just *might* take me on a trip — but I'd be all right."

"That tottery old man who has an antique shop?" his mother asked, incredulous. "What in the world can you find of fun in him? He looks a thousand years old, poor soul."

Chris grinned. "Could be, but I don't think so — not quite. He knows an awful lot. You'd be surprised."

His mother was losing interest and returning to her newspaper. "I suppose I easily might," she said and then murmured over the top of the women's page, "what sort of trips do you go on?"

"Boat trips," Chris replied, grinning from ear to ear at the back of the newspaper.

"That's nice," said his mother absently. "Better take a sweater, dear — "

Chris kissed his mother on the cheek and went quickly out the door.

Standing on the top step, the whole world burst on him green and gold, gay as a parakeet, and cool, still, because they were in March. The sunlight flecked the street like a shower of golden coins, and as Chris began to run down the long hill toward Wisconsin and M Streets, he already seemed to see Mr. Wicker's house before him, and hold the sound of his friends' voices in his ears.

# CHAPTER 2

*PRING SUN RE-*bounded in white flashing chips of light from the distant Potomac at the foot of Wisconsin Avenue. Panting from his run down the hilly street, Chris did not even see the stiff-legged trestles of the freeway, nor the smokestacks of the factories that so nearly blotted out all the shimmer of the river. He saw only the low brick house far down at the corner of Water Street and Wisconsin Avenue; the last house on the left-hand side.

This particular morning it seemed to Chris that he saw the familiar house for the first time. Its long reversed L-shape ⌐ with the back door opening onto Water Street and the front door beside the bow window of the antique shop seemed to spring to his sight with all the freshness of the unknown. The flowers and box shrubs beyond the white picket fence that filled in the long wing of the ⌐ looked brighter than they ever had as Chris walked downhill toward the house. Scarlet geraniums and red and white striped tulips were vivid against somber clipped box and warm rosy brick. Chris saw someone moving about beyond

14

the starched curtains of the kitchen window and he thought he knew whom it might be. His boy's heart thudded with pleasure and anticipation as he looked at the familiar house. Moving back from the garden he stopped as he had uncounted times, in front of the bow-fronted window of Mr. Wicker's shop.

"W<u>llm.</u> WICKER, CURIOSITIES," read the faded gold sign over the window. Chris, delaying the longed-for moment of his return to his friends, stuck his hands in his pockets and stared into the window as he had hundreds of times before.

The display was half gone — had he not used the Rope? And the model of the *Mirabelle* was now his own. As for the carved figure of the wooden Nubian boy, Amos was now alive and released from this stiff form to be his companion and friend.

Chris's heart took a leap, and he turned to go up the step. His impetuous affection carried him to the top step and brought his hand on to the worn brass doorknob. Then his spirit quailed for the first time that spring morning.

That unknown shadow moving behind the curtains in the kitchen — it had been only a glimpse — was it really Becky Boozer? The shop seemed so dusty and deserted — could it be that in the intervening months something had happened and Mr. Wicker was no longer there? Perhaps for all he knew, strangers now occupied the house, and his friends, living in another year and time, were lost to him forever.

Seized with a terrible misgiving Chris went cold with dread. This was something that until that moment had never occurred to him, but its probability seemed only too possible. Mr. Wicker was so very old — in Chris's year and time.

The boy stood hesitant and then took heart. There was only one way to find out. As he had once before, Chris opened the door and the same tinny distant bell jangled persistently at the back of the house.

Chris shut the door behind him slowly, without looking around, so frightened, all at once, that his power to return might be gone that he was incapable of making any further movement. It seemed an unconscionable time before he heard a door opening, and sunshine from a window long familiar to him outlined a wispy fragile figure dressed entirely in black. Seeing the frail old man advance so slowly toward him, Chris found his throat to be in a vise of emotion so that he could not speak, and his eyelids smarted. The old man, wrinkled and faded with endless years, buffeted by time and worn thin by the rough careless hands of passing days, stood hesitant in the path of light that followed him like a friend from the door he had left open behind him. He came forward uncertainly, as if it was all his thin old legs could do to hold up the thistledown of his body, and the nimbus of gold that sunlight or firelight always made about him outlined him against moving particles of dust in the air.

"Christopher?" the thin cracked voice asked finally. "It *is* you, is it not? I have been expecting you."

Chris forced his voice out but it did not sound like his own. "Yes, sir, it's me. I had to come — it's been so long — "

"It has, my boy, it has," the old man agreed earnestly. "It was time you came again, and here you are. What troubles you?"

Chris swallowed, intensely conscious of the bow window at his right and the street onto which it gave.

16

"I'm afraid, Mr. Wicker, sir. Afraid I haven't the same power — "

"The power to see back into the past?" croaked the old man. "Well, turn and look, my boy," Mr. Wicker said, his voice stronger and with a command to it. "There is much to do and little time for shilly-shallying — "

Some sound behind Mr. Wicker's voice, and a part of it, gave Chris the courage to turn and look out through the crescent window of the shop.

There it was, that other view, the view, now, of 1792, one hundred and sixty-two years before. There were the muddy ruts of the earlier street; gone was the traffic, the freeway, and the factories. There was the view Chris loved of the Georgetown of a younger time, with masted ships lying at anchor on the river, and all the bustle and commotion of the wharfs. The first time he had looked out that window, and through it, seeing back into the past to what it had originally looked on, the passing scenes its Georgian panes had reflected, Chris had been overcome and had fainted into a rush of darkness. But now he looked out Mr. Wicker's window not only with awe — that would always be in his emotions — but also with a sweep of relief. For he was reassured that all was as it had been, and that he would find his friends again.

"Is it all there as before?" Mr. Wicker's voice enquired, a chuckle underlying the quiet words.

Chris turned with a smile. "It's all there," he answered breathlessly.

The tottery figure of the ancient old man turned at once, going toward the open door through which the sunlight streamed so generously.

"Come then, my boy," he said over his shoulder, and Chris followed eagerly.

There ahead of him was the sitting room of his remembrance, everything the same. On his right, the spiral staircase ascending to Mr. Wicker's bedroom above, and past it, the deep fireplace where a fire snapped against March coolness. On either side of the hearth stood the two red leather wing-backed chairs, and Chris took a step forward to put his hand on the smooth polished leather. There, in the corner by the window facing him, stood the grandfather clock talking to itself, and past the two windows in the facing wall, beyond the welcoming ruby red of their damask curtains, lay the box-edged rows of herbs, the pleached fruit trees of Mr. Wicker's vegetable garden. Between the two windows still stood the well-remembered desk with the quill holder at one side, long goose-quill pens standing stiff and white as sails in a breeze.

The center of the room was occupied with the polished table Chris knew well, with on it the china bowl of flowers, the silver pitcher, and the hand-blown glass, while the floor under his feet was gay with the bright colors and intricate design of the East Indian rug. Finally, near the window at the far end of the room that gave a view of the pasture and hill behind the house, stood the carved wooden cupboard where Mr. Wicker kept his magic books.

Friend that he was first and foremost to Chris, Mr. Wicker was, after all, a worthy follower of Merlin; a magician without peer. All that Chris had learnt from him in that room a year ago had been left there too; wiped from his knowledge and remembrance by Mr. Wicker's power, for every period has its own kind of magic, and that kind had to remain in the

18

past. Now his eyes lit and his face glowing with the deep happiness he felt at his return, Chris turned about at last to face his old master in the strong spring sun.

The man watching him closely with a half-smile was no longer the ancient who had led him in. Mr. Wicker stood before his hearth in all the rugged health of his eighteenth-century age, and as he had one other time, a year before, Chris gazed and marveled. For the frail old man had vanished into the twentieth-century which Chris too had now left, and Mr. Wicker stood before his fireside vigorous and tall.

For in 1792 Mr. Wicker was forty-one and in his prime. He stood well over six feet; the width of his shoulders made his height seem less. His skull was no longer bald and fuzzed with white but well capped with chestnut hair caught at the nape of his neck with a neat black bow. His face, not parchment-pale and withered as before, was tanned and smooth, and his quick smile showed strong white teeth. His eyes, dark and penetrating, echoed his smile, and his hands, strong with slender fingers, hinted at his exceptional abilities. Standing before Chris in his knee breeches, white muslin stock, and full-skirted coat, his feet in silver-buckled shoes, and his well-shaped legs in black stockings, he laughed at his pupil's dazzlement and held out his hand.

"Well, Christopher, still amazed? Welcome back, my boy! It does my heart good to see you here!"

Chris clasped the offered hand, looking up with a grin. "And does mine good to be back, sir!" he answered warmly. "It feels like home, the way it always did!" He looked about him again and enquired, "How are the others, sir? Amos, Becky, and Ned Cilley? And Captain Blizzard and Mr. Finney — and the *Mirabelle?*"

19

His master held one hand up. "You shall see, for that is the best reply to questions." He gestured to some garments folded on a stool close to the fire. "But first, leave off your modern clothes, my boy, or you will sadly affright your friends, who would never understand it. There are your clothes, all waiting, as before."

Chris looked down, hesitating.

"What is it, Christopher? Will you not put them on?" Mr. Wicker asked.

"Yes, sir, but please — I think I've grown," Chris said, embarrassed.

Mr. Wicker drew a hand over his face to hide a smile. "And have you forgot me in a little year? Would you think I should forget? How now, lad, try them on!"

Chris shook his head at himself. He might have known, he thought, and while Mr. Wicker busied himself at his desk, Chris took off his clothes and put on those awaiting him. Then he too stood dressed as Mr. Wicker was, only his coat and breeches were of blue-gray wool. They fitted him as if they had been made to measure, his silver-buckled shoes even more comfortable than his own had been.

"I'm ready, sir," he said, his eyes shining. As they swung toward the door a booming voice Chris knew from long ago came rolling down the passage from the kitchen. It was Mistress Becky Boozer singing, "Farewell and Adieu, to you, Spanish ladies."

Mr. Wicker looked down at Chris and dropped a hand to his shoulder. "You see," he said, his eyes twinkling, "we do not change."

*A*T A MOVEMENT from Chris, the man and the boy stopped within the shadow of the corridor before going into the kitchen. Standing so in the dusk of the narrow passage they could watch the scene before them for a moment without being observed themselves.

Chris thought it might almost have been a moment after he had last left it, for there was Rebecca Boozer standing in the familiar room before the fire. Yards of sprigged cotton still made up the dress of the enormous woman, tall as a man and buxom into the bargain. Her white muslin fichu circled her neck as before, to be tucked into the top of her bodice. Becky, brawny of arm and as round as a barrel, rustled cheerily about in her white apron, while on her head still bounced and trembled her outrageous and unremovable hat. Twenty-four roses and twelve waving black plumes trimmed the swaying brim of her fabulous bonnet, which reposed — forever, thanks to a remark from the Devil himself — on top of a white turban which bound Becky's hair. Stirring her kettles over the fire, turning pigeons or wild duck upon the spit, or scrubbing away at laundry at her wooden tub; at whatever task Becky Boozer was occupied, her flower- and feather-trimmed bonnet must nod above her head, keeping its own sly rhythm.

Before them now, she was evidently in the last stages of preparation for the midday meal. Chris knew all the signs, and his mouth began to water of its own accord at the double force of remembrance joined to many present appetizing smells. It was with a swelling heart that Chris watched the big woman at her tasks, so light of foot and deft of hand. The light from the fireplace — deep enough for three men to stand upright inside it, shoulder to shoulder — lit Becky's face, matching the roses on her bonnet. From time to time she went to the high open cupboard against the side wall, from whose shelves she took down a blue and white plate or cup and saucer.

The wall at the opposite end of the big room from the huge fireplace was just as Chris remembered it too. The back door that led to Water Street was flanked by its two wide windows, each with their window seats and gay curtains. Before the right-hand window stood the gate-legged table Chris remembered, with chairs drawn up to it to face the street.

As Chris was glancing out the window toward the distant view of the harbor and its many ships, the door was flung wide and a colored boy dashed in. Chris made an involuntary movement toward his friend, for the sight of Amos, who had shared so many adventures and dangers, was one he had been longing for. But this time it was Mr. Wicker who held him back a moment more.

Amos was no longer dressed in the clothes Chris had known. Before, he had worn what had been carved on him as a wooden

figure — full scarlet trousers of a Turkish look; embroidered jacket and white turban, and shoes of an Eastern design with curled-up pointed toes. Now Amos was dressed as was Chris himself, only his suit was a becoming dark red cloth and his stockings a bright canary yellow. Otherwise, his clothes were patterned as Chris's were, and Chris approved the change. He listened as Amos called out happily to Becky.

"Here I am, Miss Becky, and my hunger's mighty sharp! Ned Cilley's on his way, says to tell you, and for you not to count too much on his appetite, he says, for his stummick is right peevish and delikit today. That's what he *says*," Amos added with a chuckle and a grin, "but did I have ary money to bet with, I'd declare he'd do your dinner justice."

"Now Amos," Becky admonished him over her shoulder as she stirred, " 'tis not kind to mock poor Master Cilley, for he did ever eat like a sparrow, the poor dear soul," and Becky went on with her cooking. Amos peeled off his jacket and rolled up his shirt sleeves in order to help Becky turn the spit, where roasting wood pigeons sputtered as they turned a delicious brown.

"That sparrow you says he eats like's a buzzard sparrow, if he's a bird!" Amos muttered, smiling to himself, and Chris had to put a hand over his mouth to stifle his own laughter.

A hearty stamping and heavy footfall were heard outside, to be followed by what Ned Cilley accounted a gentle knock on the door. The house shook and the door rattled and jumped on its hinges, while Becky, instantly flustered, wiped her hands and face upon her apron, smoothed her fichu, and trotted to the door with her best effort at a mincing walk.

Into the kitchen marched Chris's old friend Ned Cilley, looking for all the world as he had a year before. Just as red of face, just as ruffled of sandy hair, and with as rolling a sea gait. Ned, gnarled of hand and bandy-legged as of old, was, Chris suspected, still ready and willing for Becky's sumptuous meals, for all his "delikit stummick." Certainly he was not an inch taller; it was quite a stretch for him to chuck Becky Boozer under the chin. Becky, blushing like a schoolgirl, simpered and tittered, overcome with giggles and delight to see her gallant.

"Eh, God's truth!" cried the sailor, "you do good to a man's eye, my roguish lass! Sweet Boozer, I salute you!" And whisking out a footstool Ned jumped up on it to clasp Mistress Becky and reach up on tiptoe to kiss her cheek. He held her off at arm's length to admire his demure sweetheart, who towered high above him, and was about to salute her other cheek when Becky became overcome with embarrassment and at the same time smelled something burning. She disengaged herself rapidly.

25

"There now!" she exclaimed, bustling away, "such ways, Ned Cilley! Get along with you! How's a body to do any work with such gallivanting as you go in for? Alack and alas! I will be bound you do have a lass in every port. Woe, us pore females, with such a heartbreaker about!"

"Nay, sweet Boozer," objected Ned, seating himself in a chair and straightening out his legs with a comfortable air of familiarity and a look of anticipation, "Amos, there, will bear me out — I do no such thing. Come now, Amos, where's your charity? Tell the lady that I'm faithful."

"He is that, Mistress Becky. At least, *seems* like he is —"

Becky turned ominously. "What do you mean, 'seems like'?" she demanded, her hands on her huge hips.

26

"Well —" Amos parried, ducking his head, "I don't keep a close watch on him. All I can say is, I don't know how he could like those Tahitian ladies — they don't wear too many clothes. Of course, the weather's warm — 'stremely warm, but it don't seem hardly proper." He cogitated further while Becky waited sternly. "An' the Chinee ones — they only eat rice and old nestses and such-like. 'Tain't savory."

"Humph!" snorted Becky. "Seems to me I should go on your next voyage, Master Cilley, for they do say, 'Out of sight is out of mind' — "

"No, ma'am," Amos said, his eyes wide and sorrowful, "that isn't so. Not with me. For Chris — he's out of sight, but not out of *my* mind, no, *ma'am!*" and his eyes were overbright as he thought of his friend.

"Ah — " sighed Becky, resting her hand on one vast hip, a ladle standing out at right angles from it, "in his case absence makes the heart grow fonder, is that not so, Master Cilley?"

"Aye," Ned agreed, giving a gusty sigh, "and would you had not mentioned the lad, for now me appetite has clean left me, and all me vitals filled with sorrow and with missing him!"

Chris could bear no more. "Then hail your appetites back and set another place at the table, for here I am!" he cried, rushing into the room.

Becky dropped her ladle to the floor with a clatter, clutched at her heart, and then opened her capacious arms. Chris was enfolded in Becky's tremendous embrace, his face buried on her fichu that smelt of clean laundry and lavender, with Becky's happy tears falling on his head.

Next came Amos, who squeezed his friend until the breath left them both, but who could not trust his voice to speak, so amazed and overjoyed he was. Last, but not least, came Ned Cilley, whose iron handshake left Chris's hand numb, and who pounded him on the back with such welcoming gusto that Chris coughed, staggered, and burst out laughing.

What a scene, forever to be remembered! Mr. Wicker stood in the corridor observing it and smiling, while Chris's friends, so often yearned for and dreamed of, gave him a welcome worthy of their friendship. At last Becky's tears were dried and some measure of calm restored, and with Amos hastily resetting the table and looking over his shoulder to be sure Chris was still there, Mistress Boozer hastened to set a few viands before the company.

"Now calm yourselves and be seated," she said, "for sure

and the joy of this lad's return has so unsettled us all that I doubt that any can eat more than a morsel. How say you, Master Cilley?"

"Aye, you speak truly, Mistress Becky," Ned replied, wagging his tousled head. "I am that churned in my innards with the unexpectedness of it all that if I can swallow a crumb I shall count myself fortunate."

Amos and Chris winked heavily at one another and stifled their laughter, while Ned took on a dubious air, held to with difficulty as the dishes began to pile on the table. Becky Boozer, concerned and comforting, moved from table to fire and back to the table again.

Chris watched the table's surface disappear under roasted pigeons and broiled ducks, a beef pie and mince tarts; an apple cake and four kinds of cheeses; vegetables, savories and pickles, all side by side in happy plenty. The two boys and the man sat holding their knives and forks, gazing in wonderment and admiration at the bounty before them.

"Fall to if you can," urged Becky. "Just a taste, Master Cilley, a trifle; a wee crumb."

"To please you, sweetest Boozer," thundered Ned, his eyes sparkling, and glancing across to the boys he lifted his bushy eyebrows in a sort of signal.

"Every man for himself!" shouted Ned Cilley with gusto, as he reached out with both hands.

Chris was indeed back again.

# CHAPTER 4

*W*HILE CHRIS AND HIS friends were busy with their meal, a young girl was full of very different plans from those Mr. Wicker contemplated. She lived in the fashionable part of the Georgetown of 1792, and Susan Moffit was her name.

Above Water Street and Wisconsin Avenue — that in 1792 was called High Street — rose the gently sloping hills that gave from their crests a panoramic view of the Potomac. Off a narrow street on the lower level of those slopes ran Duck Lane, and from it sprang Cherry Alley, along whose winding ways stood the best buildings of that time. Here rose quaint houses of two stories made of brick brought from England as ballast for the merchant ships. Their roofs were peaked with strangely shaped gables, and rows of dormer windows jutted above the eaves. On the ledges of the dormer windows, the housekeepers were used to set out their pickles and preserves to sun, and those of the local boys who were quick and quiet enjoyed many a taste on the sly.

Susan Moffit had just returned to her house, followed by the inevitable and annoying presence of Miss Theodora Teackle, her governess and chaperon. Anyone who could have watched their return might have been entertained by it, a look of radiant expectation on the young girl's face, and prim-mouthed disapproval of all things young and lively all too plain on Miss Teackle's.

Susan was the image of her dead mother, and was therefore the apple of her father's eye. Her small slight figure seemed constantly in motion, so quickly did she move, and with a natural grace. Her hair, neither dark nor fair, held autumnal lights of gold and russet, and her fair skin set off her startling eyes which changed from grey to green, depending on what she wore. Her hands and feet were small; none could surpass her in the dance, and no other young woman of her age could bake or sew as well as she. Above all, she held herself proudly, as befitted one of as old and respected a family as were the Moffits.

The Moffit house on Cherry Alley stood in its own well-ordered grounds. The front of the brick house was covered with English ivy, spreading its glossy tendrils toward the roof and luring many birds to nest in its vines. Ivy thickly encircled the windows too, and it was on the window to the left of the front door that Susan Moffit's large grey eyes moved as she and Miss Teackle turned in at the gate and walked sedately down the path.

Usually Miss Teackle, rigidly wrapped in her cloak against a possible spring chill, made Susan walk before her. In this way Miss Teackle fancied she could prevent the giving of signs and smiles, or any unseemly behavior from Susan toward the handsome young men they might pass while shopping. Alas! there was never made by God or other powers a Miss Teackle strong enough, vigilant enough, or wily enough to prevent young people from meeting and falling in love. Her thin angular presence only added to the fun of the game which, a few months before, and entirely without her knowledge, had ceased to be a game for Susan and had become the most serious and absorbing object of her life.

For Susan was in love, and with a perfectly suitable young man, David Russell. They had met at one of the many Georgetown balls, and saw one another frequently, since David was a close friend of Susan's brother Tom. There was — or would have been in any other family — nothing against such an excellent match, had it not been for Colonel Moffit and Susan's mother's will.

Before she died, which she had when Susan was small, Mrs. Moffit had bequeathed her not inconsiderable fortune to her daughter on the condition that she would inherit it only if she were unmarried at the age of eighteen. In the eighteenth century young girls married young; sixteen was by no means an uncommon age to become a wife. But, too, the hazards and dangers of life in the new and scarcely settled country meant that all too frequently the father who was left to guide and protect his children might be killed in some hasty skirmish of war or duel, or drowned at sea in a foundering sailing vessel. Mrs. Moffit, prudent even on her deathbed, considered that at eighteen her daughter would be sufficiently mature to be able to choose between those of her suitors who loved her for herself and any whose interest lay chiefly in her fortune.

Colonel Moffit, Susan's peppery-tempered father, agreed with his wife's wishes, and had long ago laid down a dictum

that he would never give his consent to any marriage before Susan had reached eighteen. Susan and David, however, discreet in spite of the strength of their feelings, determined that it should be otherwise.

Weeks before, David had hit on the plan of leaving notes for Susan, hidden in the thick ivy near the window, and when Susan came back that spring morning, she stepped politely aside for Miss Teackle to go into the house before her, and as the front door was opened for them by Uncle Borb, the colored houseman and coachman, Susan's slender hand flashed out like a bird, and slipped back under her cloak holding a neatly folded paper.

Nothing was ever lost on Uncle Borb, any more than it was on his wife Aunt Abby, who had been Susan's nurse. Uncle Borb bowed as Miss Teackle swept haughtily by, and his old eyes flickered to Susan's hand and then away again. A smile shone on his face at sight of her and he said softly:

"I conjure you found what you wanted this mornin', didn't you, Miss Susie?"

"How *do* they always know?" snapped Miss Teackle, pursuing a completely different line of thought, her hand on the polished curl of the bannisters. Susan smiled a confederate's smile at Uncle Borb.

"Uncle Borb has known me since my beginning, haven't you, Uncle Borb? I grew up with his children, Juno and Jonah. He and Aunt Abby know me better than I know myself."

But her eyes said other things to Uncle Borb, and Uncle Borb's told her in reply that he was glad the note was there, and that no one but himself had seen it being left.

34

She ran up the curving staircase as if she flew, and safely in her room threw off her cloak and flung herself in a chair, after locking the door against any sudden invasion by Miss Teackle.

*My own darling Susie [she read], I have urgent and somewhat frightening news, and dare not put all my thoughts upon this paper. Can you not come to the Reverend Balch's church, opposite Suter's Tavern, at three this afternoon? At that time it should be empty. I shall see to it that the small side door is left unlocked, and shall wait for you there for one hour. Failing this, try Mr. Wicker's shop at Water Street and High Street. Our meeting is of the utmost importance. Ever your own —*

DAVID

Susan folded the paper after reading it several times, and with a heavily moving heart, hid the note where she had hidden all the others. She wandered to the window, from which, far away to the left and down, the Potomac glittered like an irregular blue shield, its emblem or device the white sails moving upon it. Without knowing it, Susan was tearing her minute lace-edged handkerchief to pieces, her young face troubled and her eyes made twice as large by the tears they held. An ominous feeling of danger oppressed her, and her mind turned on what she could say to Miss Teackle, and how she could get away. But at last she gave up the problem and rang the bell beside her bed for Aunt Abby.

In a few moments Aunt Abby's ponderous footsteps sounded on the floor boards of the hall, and Susan ran to let her in. The broad-bosomed colored woman came in slowly, because of her unwieldy size, and shut the door majestically behind her. Instantly Susan was in her arms; the dark head turbaned in flowered muslin was bent above the young one, as Aunt Abby rocked the girl who was still but half a child.

"There now," she crooned, "what ails my baby? Now don' take on so, child, we'll work it out. Hush, quiet yourself. Be still!"

At length Susan's trouble was eased on Aunt Abby's bosom, as it had been times without number, and with her head in her nurse's lap, Susan began to talk as the loved hand lovingly smoothed her hair. Aunt Abby listened to what she had to say, and then she said quietly:

"You eat your dinner, like a good girl, and then, I'll tell you what — Juno's ailing."

Susan lifted her head quickly. "Juno's ill? What's wrong?

36

Why didn't you tell me?"

Aunt Abby threw back her head and laughed, a low fat laugh that shook her all over.

"Law, child, I just *say* she's ailing. Never was a stronger girl nor my Juno. Tough as a plow horse, she be. No — for Miss Teackle, and your pa, she's ailing, but better not let your granny see you when you say so — your grandma's shrewd. You an' me'll take some soup and dainties to poor Juno, and leave this house at half after two, taking the little lanes — "

"Oh Aunt Abby! What would I do without you!" Susan cried. "You always know what to do!"

Aunt Abby smiled down at her. "I loved your mammy, and she was good to Uncle Borb and me. She wouldn't want her child to be upset, all living with older folkses like you do. She'd like that nice young man who loves my Susie." She rose, dignified and calm. "Now wash your face and straighten down your hair, and at the table, just let the news fall easy outen your mouth, that Juno's ailing. Nothing particular. Just ailing. Nothing *catching*, mind you don't let on." She gave Susan a broad-handed, forceless smack. "Get moving!" she said.

Susan laughed.

# CHAPTER 5

$S$USAN,      CHEERFUL
and herself again, hurried
to such good purpose that
she came down early for
the midday meal. Looking, in her full-skirted cotton dress, de-
tached and fresh and without a care, she went straight to her
father's study.

This room, with its own entrance opening at the side of the
house beside the orchard, had been a wing added to the main
building after the death of Susan's mother, for her father could
not bear, then, to be in the sitting room that too poignantly
evoked his wife.

The study on the outside was made of alternate blue and red
English bricks, wainscoted inside in well-polished pine. Directly in the center of the room, following a whim of Colonel
Moffit's and a not unusual fashion of the time, a spiral staircase rose to the room above. The windows gave onto the orchard on one side, and toward the garden at the back of the
house on the other, with a fireplace in the back wall that cor-
responded with the fireplace in the dining room behind it.

Here, in this agreeable room, Colonel Moffit received his fellow officers and friends for a glass of hot mulled wine and a game of cards in the evenings, the smoke of their pipes and sound of their discussions or hearty laughter remaining beyond the main part of the house.

It was a household habit that Susan's grandmother, old Mrs. Moffit, should come to her son's study for a glass of Madeira wine before meals, and to discuss the affairs of their distant plantation in Virginia. Here Susan found them when she came down for lunch.

Old Mrs. Moffit looked up briskly as Susan came in. Susan had a great respect and admiration for her grandmother, and had inherited some of the old woman's remarkable qualities. For it was largely due to Martha Moffit that the Moffit plantation was as well organized and self-sustaining as it was. Mrs. Moffit had been left a widow early, but like other women of the time she had put her energies and commonsense into the managing of her wide estates. As a result, not only had her numerous children been properly brought up and wisely launched into the world in different spheres, but her lands were so well run that other landowners came from far to ask advice and note her methods.

On the Moffit estate whatever the family consumed or needed had been furnished from their own lands. They had their own turning mill and gristmill, as well as a wool factory and blacksmith shop, all manned by Mrs. Moffit's slaves. Cloth of various kinds was woven on the place and dyed according to Mrs. Moffit's instructions, and all manner of preserves and jellies made in season. Mrs. Moffit taught her people the trades for which they seemed best fitted, and was never long "in

town" away from the many duties she felt bound to oversee.

Now, in her sixties, a good age in 1792, she was plump, alert, and nearly as quick-moving as her granddaughter. She resented the fact that her eldest son had not remarried, for Susan and Tom, in her opinion, needed a woman in the house, and Grandmother Moffit had little patience with her son's choice of Miss Teackle as a guardian.

As Susan came into her father's study, she knew that her grandmother and Colonel Moffit had been arguing again. The air of the room was charged with their disagreement, and although Susan heard nothing as she came forward, she knew by long experience that the two who were closest to her had been in some altercation. Her grandmother's cheeks were pink with agitation and her keen eyes flashed with the residue of her quick temper. Her father and grandmother had evidently heard her step before she appeared and had governed and silenced their words before her entry. When she came in, her grandmother made an attempt at casual conversation.

"What is that frock you have on?" she asked. "Ah yes, the morning-glory blue. That dye came out very well. I must try to get that shade again. It suits you, Susie dear. I like it better on you than I do the green."

She sipped her Madeira, her white cap bobbing gently. Colonel Moffit, his red face shining with pleasure at the sight of his daughter, set down his glass to put his arm around Susan's waist.

"There now! The prettiest girl in Georgetown!" he exclaimed. "What has my puss been doing all the morning?"

"Out with Miss Teackle, Father, to see what had come in on the *Southern Star*," Susan replied. "Some fine taffeta and satin,

41

and lace from France." She paused, a faint grimace brushing her face. "Miss Teackle needed pins and needles."

"Humph!" snorted old Mrs. Moffit in disdain. "She would! How you can stomach that pickle of a woman in your house, Alexander, I shall never know," she went on indignantly. "It fair spoils my appetite to see her peck at good food the way she does. All that she knows is to find fault with everything."

"She is an intelligent woman, Mother," Colonel Moffit replied carefully, "and cares for Susan as she should."

Mrs. Moffit was not appeased. "But no spark of fun to her, that is only too evident!" she snapped.

"Our Susan and Tom provide plenty of that, may I bid you

remember!" her son retorted. "A rein is needed on a spirited filly!"

"Hold a race horse too long on a check rein and you will have a beast fit only for the fields!" contended Susan's grand-mother, who always insisted on having the last word. Her son was bound in respect and politeness to let her have it, so Susan took advantage of the moment.

"Grandmother, Aunt Abby tells me Juno is ailing. May I go with her after dinner with some herbal teas and meat soup? We should not be gone long."

"*I* see nothing against it!" her grandmother said with energy. "A relief to be with a congenial soul, I should say," she pur-sued, nodding her head. "So long as Juno has nothing catch-ing, dear. What are the symptoms, did Aunt Abby say?"

"She said, just poorly. Maybe a strained back. The poor girl works hard enough," Susan answered demurely.

"Humph! I hope she does! It will keep her out of mischief, as it would you, my pet! Well," and Mrs. Moffit rose as Uncle Borb announced, "Dinner's on the table," "you ask your father, girl, but be sure Juno has nothing you will bring home. What say you, Alexander?"

But Colonel Moffit, fiery though he was, knew when to hold his tongue, and winking at his daughter, gave his arm to his mother to escort her in.

# CHAPTER 6

*A*UNT ABBY KNEW well how to reach Georgetown's first church without attracting attention. Carrying a basket covered with a white cloth, she and Susan started out as soon as lunch was over, for the Georgetonians of the period "dined" late and rarely left the table before two o'clock.

The old woman and the young girl turned at first in the direction of Aunt Abby's and Uncle Borb's cottage, but as soon as a twist of the lane hid them from view, Aunt Abby doubled back, taking an overgrown grass path that skirted the fields of adjoining properties but ran parallel to Bridge Street. In no time the white walls of the simple church appeared before them, and going in first to make sure no neighbors were there to see and speak of the meeting, Aunt Abby reappeared in the doorway beckoning for Susan to follow.

The interior of the church seemed cold and dark after the warmth of the sunlight, but before Susan's eyes could accustom themselves to the dusk, two strong young hands held hers and she was pulled close into a young man's arms. She looked up into her lover's face, so tender above her own, admiring, as she never failed to do, his straight nose and brows, his wide-set eyes and humorous, smiling mouth.

"Dearest Susie!" he was saying, "I was so afraid you would be unable to get away. Your father — or grandmother — or worst of all, Miss Teackle!"

Susan laughed. "I am not here at all, dear silly boy! I am taking soup to poor Juno, who is ailing — or so Aunt Abby suddenly decided. Is she not wonderful, to find a way?"

David Russell glanced smilingly toward the dusky corner where Aunt Abby sat at a distance for propriety's sake. "It is you who are wonderful, Susan. Lovelier every time my eyes see you — "

David's words drifted away, his thoughts and eyes lost in Susan's face.

"Tell me what you meant in your letter, David," Susan urged. "You frightened me!" And the two young people sat down close together at the end of a pew.

"It is this, Susie," David began. "My father and uncle intend to make a survey of the land beyond Charlottesville," he told her, "and they insist I go with them. They may be gone for months — the terrain is unknown, and a map is needed of it. I thought — " he broke off and raised one of Susan's hands to his lips — "if we could go to Williamsburg, we could be married. I have an aunt and cousins living there. You would not be alone — "

He lifted his eyes to study her face, his own troubled and uneasy at how his plan might be received, but Susan's glowing happiness almost made a light in the somber, silent church.

"Oh — David! If we only could! Could we ever manage it?" she asked.

"Then you will, Susan? You really will?"

"Of course! Of course! You knew the answer before you asked!" she cried. The words were scarcely out before her face clouding she added breathlessly, "When would it be — that we should have to start?"

"This very night, my darling, for Father means to leave day after tomorrow. We should have to take back roads, for they would follow — "

Susan, not at all daunted at the prospect of riding across country in the dead of night, reflected.

"We should have to take Aunt Abby, you know, somehow," she said.

"Aunt Abby?" David's voice rose with dismay and his forehead puckered. "Why? She's so fat she would never stay long on a horse, and a carriage is out of the question!"

"Nevertheless," Susan persisted, "she will have to come. Don't you see — if we become confused or somehow go the wrong way, Aunt Abby always knows what to do. I would not be here now, David, had it not been for her. If we got into a pickle she would surely get us out. Besides — " she added solemnly — "it would not be seemly for me to go alone, and Juno, while younger and spry on a horse, has very little sense. No," she shook her head, and a faint cool smell of camomile brushed David's face, "no. I am afraid it will have to be Aunt Abby," she said with finality.

David closed his fingers even more closely over Susan's. "This makes it more difficult, but I will do what I can," he told her. "I can sell my watch for a horse for you, but some-

thing big enough to hold Aunt Abby — " He shook his head in despair.

Susan's eyes sparked. "You will do no such thing, David Russell!" she declared with spirit. "I have my own horse that I can ride, and as for Aunt Abby, she is a part of our family. It is up to me to find her a mount!"

David had to smile when Susan's father showed in her voice and actions as clearly as he did then. With it all, she was so feminine, so pretty, and so young. He laughed softly.

"Dearest! If you entrust yourself to me it will begin *now*," he announced with firmness, and Susan's manner changed at once. David might be young, but there was that in his voice as he spoke that made her know he would care for what was his own. She became docile, her face all smiles.

"Very well, sir," she mocked him lovingly, "as you will. But do me the service to sell this pin" — and she undid a brooch that held her muslin fichu — " for necessities that Aunt Abby or I might need on the journey. I have not a penny, as you know. Miss Teackle holds what Father gives out for me."

David took the pin doubtfully. "If you wish me to, Susan," he said, looking at it as it lay in the palm of his hand. "It is not one that belonged to your mother, is it?" he asked.

"No, of course not. It was a Christmas present from Father last year, and has some value. Please do this for me, David," Susan asked, and as she spoke she rose, putting a hand lightly on his arm. David got up reluctantly, but he knew, from the direction of the sun through the high windows, that the afternoon was advancing.

"I will come for you tonight at eleven o'clock," he said. "At the gate beyond the orchard. *Eleven*," he stressed. And then, tipping up her face to look into her eyes, "Is this what you truly want, Susan? You are not afraid?"

"Only afraid without you, David," she replied. "And it is what my heart truly wants, now and forever."

The two young people walked hand in hand down the aisle toward the side door where Aunt Abby waited, passing under gold blades of sunlight, high-slanted, as if they walked under the upraised swords of wedding friends. And Susan, reaching the door and looking up into Aunt Abby's face, knew there would be little to tell the old woman that she did not already know or guess.

48

# CHAPTER 7

IN MR. WICKER'S study, a large, varied, and entirely satisfactory meal under his belt, Chris leaned back in the winged leather chair he remembered of old, and grinned in a luxurious way at Mr. Wicker. Mr. Wicker's eyes looked back at Chris with as much happiness and content- ment as there was in the boy's face, and he stretched his long legs in their silver-buckled shoes to the blaze of the fire, look- ing affectionately at the lad in whom he felt a father's pride.

"So — " he began, "our Becky's cooking has improved, has it, in the year? It must be practice that does it, for our Ned and Amos are bottomless pits that she never entirely succeeds in filling! Well," and he gave his rare chuckle, "your return makes this a red-letter day, Christopher my boy, and not a moment too soon. For as I began to tell you a while back, the *Mirabelle* is set to sail tomorrow."

"She *is?*" Chris exclaimed, starting forward in his chair, his after-dinner somnolence gone. "Where to this time, sir?" he enquired.

"Ah, this time 'tis an ordinary voyage, I am afraid, young man. No such adventure as the one you went on last." Mr. Wicker turned to the fire, and the coppery light touched his finely chiseled features and long-fingered hands. "This time I intend to go myself," he said, arching an eyebrow to see how Chris took this bit of news, and then, encouraged by the pleasure he found in his pupil's face, he went on. "What do you remember of me, Christopher?"

Chris looked at him for a moment, puzzled. Then he understood the question. He remembered the last time he had been in that same room, over a year ago, when, laying his hand lightly on his eyes and his head, Mr. Wicker had caused to be wiped from his recollection all knowledge of the magic he had so painstakingly learnt months before. But Chris remembered too that he had been given one quality that he could retain, and which he had had to choose.

He recalled, staring across at his master, lean in his black clothes before him, how he had hesitated on whether he would retain the power, which he had held and enjoyed, of being able to turn himself into various forms — a dolphin, a fly, a mouse, a bird. Or whether he would wish to make things with the magic rope, which had been so hard to learn to manage, flicking it into the air to form a boat, a camel, an elephant, or an eagle.

Yet in the end he had chosen the best power of all — the power to return, to re-enter this past time that only he and his master could straddle, as one can leap a barrier, going over into the past or back into the present time. For Chris loved his eighteenth-century friends almost more than those he knew so many years ahead of Amos's and Ned's time. He loved the impossible things that could happen, all those years back, just as — had they been able to pierce into the years ahead — Amos and Ned Cilley would have been fascinated and agog at the life of modern times. They would have thought it magic — the machines and carriages that ran along by themselves without the aid of horses; ships that crossed seas more quickly than any vessel with sails; airships that flew distances in an hour or two that it took Ned months to sail; and television, which would be, for Ned and Amos, the wildest, most fantastic kind of magic of all.

So Chris had chosen to go back, since his friends could not come forward through the years to him. He recognized — as one admits that one has blue eyes instead of brown, or an ability to run better than some other fellow — that he possessed the knack of being able to go back in Time. It had been explained to him quite understandably by Mr. Wicker, that other year, and now it seemed no more strange to him than that his skin was pale while that of his friend Amos was dark. It was simply a difference, that was all. So now he understood Mr. Wicker's question and replied.

"Why, sir, I remember all you taught me — except that I can't do it any more. You took that memory away, right there — " he pointed to a spot on the brick hearth — "I was standing right there."

Mr. Wicker nodded, pleased. "Quite so, Christopher. And you elected to come back. Very wise of you, very wise. For a moment there, last year, I was afraid you might choose something else by way of remembrance, but I had no cause for alarm. You are a sensible boy, as your adventure on the *Mirabelle* proved, time and time again." He looked keenly at Chris

51

where the boy sat on the edge of his chair across from him. "Would you like to have those powers back, my boy, that you took so long to learn?"

Chris's eyes lit up, then a frown put out the light in them. "That depends, sir," he said cautiously.

"Depends?" Mr. Wicker's eyebrows went up, his face impassive. "Depends on what, Christopher?"

"That depends, sir, on whether — if I have the powers of magic again — I could still come back here. I should never want anything to interfere with that. I would rather not know the magic ways, or else, learn them all over again." His face creased with concern, he looked up, his hands gripping the arms of the wing chair. Mr. Wicker sprang to his feet and clapped the boy on the back.

"I might have known it!" he cried, jubilant. "You always choose aright! Come back you shall, my boy, and have your magic too — at least" — he amended — "for a time. You shall know all your magic again, if you wish, but the practising of it shall be for another moment. Let us speak now of the voy-

age the *Mirabelle* is to make."

Walking to the end of the room he pulled forward a globe, set on a carved mahogany stand which permitted it to be spun as it was examined. Chris, going nearer, saw with interest how many empty patches and unfinished parts there still were on the world map at that time. Mr. Wicker, bending over the globe where he had stood it before a window for the benefit of the light, turned it until North and South America came into view. Whole parts of both continents were still uncharted. He put a long forefinger on what was later to become Washington, D.C.

"Here we are, Christopher," he began, "and from here we shall descend, along the Potomac, down the Chesapeake and finally to sea. Along the coast here" — the finger traced the course — "and much the same way for a while as the *Mirabelle* took a year ago. Past Cuba and along the South American coast. We intend going around toward Mexico, you see."

"Well, sir, isn't that the long way round?" Chris asked. "Wouldn't it save time to cut through the Panama Canal?"

Mr. Wicker smiled, his dryest smile. "It *would* save time, my boy, to 'cut through' as you suggest, except for one small hitch — the Panama Canal has not yet been 'cut through.' That is nearly one hundred years away."

Chris smiled too, no longer embarrassed, as he would once have been, at such a mistake.

"I forgot for a moment where I was, sir," he said. "I'm at home here in myself, but not quite, in my thoughts!"

"So I perceive, my boy," commented Mr. Wicker, and went on. "We sail around the Horn and up, but instead of veering across the Pacific as you did before, we continue up to Mexico. It might interest me to begin trade with the owners of the silver mines of Taxco." He paused. "There is much silver in Mexico," said Mr. Wicker thoughtfully.

There was a pause, and Chris filled it in with visions of how Mexico would look. Jungles and cockatoos? Beaches or arid plains? Or marshy morass and flocks of flapping birds? Impossible to tell but fun to ponder on.

"Then where?" he finally asked. Mr. Wicker came back from wherever his thoughts had led him, and looked down once more at the globe.

"Perhaps up farther, Christopher. California is now almost deserted, but gold is there, and possibilities which, if they knew of them, would stagger the quiet minds of eighteenth-century men. Yes, that is where I should like the *Mirabelle* to proceed, but there are times when I wonder if we shall ever get there. . . ." He frowned, then turned more briskly. "Come now. Let us waste no time. Let me put my hands on your head to help your memory, and then we shall see how well you remember how to become a fish, or a fly, or a mouse!"

# CHAPTER 8

*W*HAT ARE THE forces that weave the crystal webs of our lives? Tough as jungle lianas, they can nevertheless be hacked by the hatchets of good or bad events, yet are delicate as shreds of spider silk, swaying in a gale and unable to be torn apart. Had it not been for a well-meaning and too-observant colored boy — Jonah, Aunt Abby's son — who can tell what direction the lives of David Russell and Susan Moffit might not have taken? Like looking down the lane one always intends to take to see where it goes, and somehow never follows, it is idle to speculate since it will remain forever a dream and unknown.

What was important, as it turned out, both to Chris and Mr. Wicker, as well as to the two young people themselves, is that Jonah was sent to the Fountain Inn, or Suter's Tavern as it was then popularly known. On the northeast corner of Bridge and Congress Streets, the Fountain Inn stood directly across the street from the Reverend Brother Balch's church. Houses along Bridge Street were sparse at that time, and many were the fields and trees with which they were separated.

Jonah took a message for an expected guest, a friend of Colonel Moffit's. As he stood, hat in hand, at the side door, the owner of the inn, John Suter, came to the doorway, speaking over his shoulder to someone inside in the shadow who remained unseen. As he reached the place where Jonah stood waiting to give his message, John Suter held an object up to the light. It flashed a brilliant dahlia red, and Jonah saw in the innkeeper's heavy fingers the brooch he had seen many a time on his childhood friend's dress; Susan Moffit's pin. John Suter was saying:

"Well — 'tis a good brooch, no doubt of that. I will oblige you, and the price shall be as we agreed — twenty pounds ten shillings." Then, lowering his gaze from the pin flashing in the afternoon light, he caught sight of Jonah standing before him. "Well, boy?" he asked.

Jonah gave his message, as had been required, and went back posthaste to his father, Uncle Borb, where Uncle Borb sat in the sun outside his cabin door.

"I seen it right before me!" Jonah exclaimed breathlessly, as Uncle Borb, smoking his pipe, listened, puffing. "Indeed, I know that pin! The Colonel, he gave it to Miss Susie last year, Christmas time. Weren't we all there to get our presents when she cried out so pretty at it? Red stone in the middle, and pearls all around. So big — " and he leveled finger and thumb to show the size. "Somebody's done gone and stole that pin," Jonah went on indignantly, "and sold it to Mr. Suter, sure as I'm a-standing here!"

Uncle Borb brought the tipped-up front legs of his wooden chair down from their comfortable position with a snap, and aid his clay pipe carefully along the cabin window ledge.

"I believe you, boy," he said slowly. "The Colonel, he's in his room now, goin' over the accounts. Come on with me and tell him what you just said, every word the same."

Pulling his clothes smooth, and giving a sharp glance at his son's jacket and shoes before they should confront the Colonel, Uncle Borb and Jonah, who still carried his hat in nervous hands, marched with stately tread to Colonel Moffit's study. On being admitted, Uncle Borb gave a gesture of his hand toward his son. The Colonel, interrupted, looked up over his spectacles from behind his desk at the old man, and at the young one, standing a step or two beyond.

"Well, Uncle Borb and Jonah?" he demanded, eager to resume his task. "You have something on your minds? Speak up. You have my attention."

Uncle Borb gave his slight ducking bow, that always merely succeeded in adding to his own dignity, while conveying his respect to the Colonel.

"Colonel, sir," he announced, "Jonah here just seen something troubles him. He just come back from Suter's Tavern, where he takes your message, an' there he see what seems like you should know."

Colonel Moffit's eyes grew keener, and he took off his glasses. "Step forward, Jonah. Let me hear what you have to say," he encouraged.

And that is how, one filament of circumstances leading to another, as the spider weaves its intricate and symmetrical design, the Colonel unraveled, bit by bit, his daughter's plan of escape that very night. And that is why, when night had drenched the Moffit house and gardens with dark and made

into large black parasols every apple tree of the orchard, a
young girl going quietly over the grass with Aunt Abby toward the gate where she heard the chink of horse's bits, went
no farther. A hand she knew only too well fell on her arm, and
her father's angry voice thundered suddenly from impenetrable shadow.

"So! It is thus that I am repaid for my care and my love,
Mistress Headstrong! Go to your room at once, and you, Aunt
Abby! For shame do I find you here at such an hour and with
such an intention! Let me not see your face until I so choose,

lest I cannot govern my hand nor my words!" The outraged man turned again toward his terrified daughter. "You, miss, go before me, for I hold the key to your room here in my hand, and I do surely purpose to lock you therein, so that I shall know where my only daughter is, and not a-wandering in the dead of night!" And as poor Susan turned, speechless, beginning to tremble with shock and fright, he bellowed behind her, "That young gallant of yours has escaped us but I shall catch him yet, never fear of that! And if it be not I, then sure his own father will, for my good friend Russell feels as I do in this matter! So now — go forward where you belong, my headstrong lady! An you will not be managed with a light hand, then needs must I use stronger methods!"

But as Susan turned, her long hooded cape trailing after her on the grass, she caught Aunt Abby's eye. While startled and guilty, as Aunt Abby felt, to be found leaving her good master's house in what she knew would be an act against his every wish, her sharp eyes had glimpsed something that had escaped the rest. As Susan looked toward her, Aunt Abby rolled her eyes upward toward a neighboring apple tree. The persimmon glow of lanterns held by Uncle Borb and Jonah did not spread far, and as Susan's surprised glance followed her nurse's look, she saw what Aunt Abby's quick sight had seen: the gleam of a silver shoe buckle high up among the leafy branches.

So that is where he is! Susan thought, and her heart, from feeling like a stone at the bottom of a well, was light as a bird in the sun. She hid her relief and her half-smile in her hands, as, seemingly grief-stricken and quite subdued, she followed her father's pointing finger, and preceded him humbly into the house.

# CHAPTER 9

*C*HRIS AND MR. Wicker, their feet comfortably stretched to the fire in Mr. Wicker's study, were going over old times, as good friends will. Supper was long past, but the heat of the fire and the satisfying meal he had eaten were combining to make Chris drowsy. He was about to ask leave of Mr. Wicker to go to bed when a sudden brassy pounding clattered from the direction of Mr. Wicker's front door.

Master and pupil sat up straight and looked at one another questioningly. As they did so, their words and thoughts scattered and jolted from their calm ways, the imperious knocking sounded again. Mr. Wicker sprang to his feet, hurrying to the study door.

"Who comes so late?" he enquired of no one in particular. "Come, Christopher, run before me and light the lantern with this taper. Someone is in great need to see me, that is sure!"

Chris was already thrusting a twig-thin wax taper into the fire, and Mr. Wicker was scarcely beyond the study door before Chris ran after him, lighting the lantern as he went. Its warm light made straw edgings to Mr. Wicker's hurrying shoulders; lit the tip of Chris's nose and caught the eager curious expression in his eyes. As the two reached the front door, Chris held the lantern high above his head as, a third thundering clatter deafening their ears, Mr. Wicker bent to unbolt the door.

Against the blackness of the street, for Georgetown of 1792 boasted no street lamps, a second lantern outlined with yellow the sweep of Colonel Moffit's cape and the set of his hat on his determined head. His red face was redder than ever, and his eyes gleamed in Chris's lantern light with anger and with purpose.

"Ha!" he cried, as soon as Mr. Wicker opened the door. "At last! Mr. Wicker, sir, I bid you good evening, and do excuse myself for so disturbing you at this late hour. May I entreat entry, nevertheless, to discuss a matter of urgent business with you?"

"Most certainly, Colonel Moffit," Mr. Wicker answered, stepping aside and swinging the door wide. "I pray you to come in and follow me." He turned to Chris. "My boy, please be so kind as to let the Colonel's man in to the kitchen. Becky may have retired, and the night grows chill. There will certainly be some fire covered against the morning, where Uncle Borb, here, can warm himself."

It was not surprising to Chris that Mr. Wicker knew at once who his visitor was, nor even that he knew Uncle Borb's name. Georgetown was then like a small village where everyone knew everyone else. Even had Mr. Wicker been an everyday man and not a magician, he would have known the names of all his neighbors as well as those of their servants; being a magician, Chris recognized, he could know these things without ever having laid eyes on either of the visitors before.

Chris therefore lit his master and their guest to Mr. Wicker's study, and left the two men alone. Running to the back door across the silent kitchen empty of Becky's ample presence, he unbolted the door to let Uncle Borb in. He had heard Amos speak of Uncle Borb and Jonah, and Chris and the old man talked softly together as Chris uncovered the hot coals heaped over with ashes by Becky to keep a glow for her morning fire. Adding chips of dry wood, Chris soon had a blaze going in the deep kitchen fireplace.

Meantime, Mr. Wicker, taking his guest's cape and three-cornered hat, offered him one of the red leather chairs, and poured out a glass of port to ward off the night airs. Colonel Moffit, calming himself somewhat, seated himself ponderously and accepted the glass held out to him. The firelight catching rich gleams of ruby in the wine, however, seemed to remind the Colonel of something else, for he frowned sharply, sipped, then smiled, and leaned back at last in his chair looking across at his host searchingly.

"Mr. Wicker," he began, "I do excuse myself once more for so disturbing you, but I am sorely distracted by an event that has just taken place, and — not for the first time — I am come to you for counsel. Also" — he looked at the small glass of winking red wine — "with a proposition I hope you will agree to, and indulge me in."

Mr. Wicker, at ease in his chair, said nothing, his eyes alert and his intelligent face intent, waiting until his guest should speak in his own good time. After a moment's reflection

Colonel Moffit began again.

"You know I have but one daughter, Susan? It is hard for me to understand that the years of her childhood are gone — gone so soon and so fast — and that she is near the time when she should have her own life. Yet, owing to the terms of her dead mother's will, and which I shall respect to the letter, Susan can only have her dowry if she. marries after the age of eighteen. Now," and he set down his glass on the table between them, "the dowry is unimportant, for I should always see to it that the girl lacks for nothing. What is important to me, sir, is her mother's last wish. Mrs. Moffit considered eighteen

63

the proper age to wed — not before. That this event may be as my dear wife wished it, I am determined shall come to pass. Yet my obstinate daughter has traces of my own poor character, and wants her own way when she wants it." He sighed. "Well — " he shook his head at Mr. Wicker — "we were both young, you and I, and I'll warrant you, perhaps, remember those times more clearly than we could wish." He looked across at his host with a twinkle in his eyes, and his face relaxed for the first time. "What my young gal needs is a distraction for her mind, Mr. Wicker, and I have heard that you do intend sailing on some voyage shortly. What I wish to ask, as a favor to me, and in some measure as a favor to my young miss so that she may calm her mind and her heart, is that you agree to take her and her lady companion on board."

He looked sharply at Mr. Wicker and Mr. Wicker returned his scrutiny with his usual imperturbable gaze, tapping his fingertips together, pondering. Colonel Moffit hastily began once more to further urge Mr. Wicker, taking his silence to mean a refusal.

"Come now, sir, do consider my request. I shall make it worth your while, on my honor. I will go so far as to charter your ship — there, that is fair, is't not? And bye the bye, for where is she bound?"

Mr. Wicker rose slowly, pacing the room, his hands behind his back. At last he spoke.

"You take me by surprise, Colonel Moffit, and I do not know how to answer you. My ship, while as new and fit as any at the quays, was not made for ladies to travel in. And our voyage will be a long one — around Cape Horn, to Mexico and perhaps beyond, for my intention is to explore that territory," he said, his voice taking on an edge, "and not even your generous offer can dissuade me from the purpose of the journey."

He eyed his guest, but Colonel Moffit seemed satisfied, and to be still awaiting an answer.

"I propose to lift anchor tomorrow night," Mr. Wicker went on firmly. "The tides are right, and I have been otherwise delayed. This may be too soon for your daughter to make her preparations. However, those are my plans."

He stopped before the Colonel, who looked up steadfastly and took a sip of his port wine.

"You are the owner of your ship, Mr. Wicker," Colonel Moffit said, "and hold the highest respect among us all here in Georgetown for your sagacity and honest dealings. As to your captain, Captain Blizzard, and first mate, Mr. Finney, they are well known to be loyal, and first-class seamen of long experience. My daughter could not be in better hands unless she was in yours."

Mr. Wicker continued to look down into the face of the man who looked up at him so earnestly.

"I do purpose, this time, to go on the voyage myself, Colonel," he said quietly. "There are certain matters I wish to see to, outside of the need I have for a change. It is long since I left Georgetown. So, whether or not you wish to charter the *Mirabelle* for the journey, she is — no matter what your wishes — to pursue her course in any event. I will care for your daughter as if she were my own." At the sweeping relief he saw in the Colonel's face, Mr. Wicker held up one long hand. "However, I do suggest that you come aboard my ship at your earliest convenience tomorrow, Colonel Moffit, to see the quarters that I could put at your daughter's disposal. The

*Mirabelle* is not large; Miss Susan would be obliged to share a cabin with her companion, I am afraid. You may feel that she would not be satisfactorily settled. I should prefer that you approve the quarters available."

The Colonel rose to his feet, his face once more wearing its jovial look.

"As you wish, sir, as you wish. And if it suits you, I shall at the same time put down the charter money. You shall either consider the ship chartered for her voyage to Mexico and back, or else the sum shall be in payment for my daughter's, and Miss Teackle's, passage."

At mention of Miss Teackle, Mr. Wicker's face was brushed as by a grey cloud.

"I have in my employ a most excellent woman, Colonel," he said thoughtfully. "Rebecca Boozer is her name, and it is my intention to take her along as cook for these ladies — and for myself. She could care quite adequately for your daughter — "

Colonel Moffit waved his hand as if fanning away some large and troublesome fly.

"No doubt, no doubt, Mr. Wicker, sir, but Miss Teackle knows and understands my daughter's ways. Added to this, she acts in the capacity of tutor, and is coaching my young miss in bookkeeping and mathematics, for — should Susan be fortunate enough to have a plantation of her own someday — this sort of thing is highly necessary. Needlework, and a knowledge of the arts, is needed too, and Miss Teackle is skilled in the teaching of both. A young woman's accomplishments are more complicated than they were in our day!" snorted Colonel Moffit, and laughed. He clapped Mr. Wicker genially on the shoulder. "So. We understand one another,

66

sir, and I am heartily relieved that you are so kind as to help me in this matter. The young lady shall come aboard your ship at whatever time is convenient to you, with her luggage, and if it sets your mind at rest, I shall come to see her quarters early tomorrow morning — say, at eight o'clock?"

Mr. Wicker went slowly beside him to the study door, and, holding a candle, rang a silver bell for Uncle Borb. His face was reflective, and Colonel Moffit noticed it.

"You are uncertain on something, Mr. Wicker?" he enquired. "Some matter troubles you?"

Mr. Wicker looked up with his quick smile. "The sailors will not like it, Colonel," he rejoined. "They are a superstitious lot, sailors, and as you have no doubt heard, will consider the presence of women aboard ship an ill omen for the voyage. If I may suggest it, be so kind as to refrain from the mention of who the passengers are to be. It may be wise to get them aboard secretly. My crew, this trip, is an especially good one, but they are quite capable of leaving in a body if they hear that I intend taking women along." He smiled again, a disarming smile so fleeting it was scarcely seen. "It *has* been a curious fact, sir," he said, "how often women bring disaster to sailing ships. I shall have to ask you to sign a paper absolving me of any harm that may come to your daughter regardless of my strongest efforts on her behalf."

Colonel Moffit's face, now, was grave, and then, as at some recent recollection, it broke into a smile as winning, almost, as Mr. Wicker's own.

"You are a cautious man, Mr. Wicker, sir, and I commend you for it. It would almost seem that you know how head-strong a lass my daughter is, to require such a surety from me, but begad! and you shall have it! For I know you to be the shrewdest among us all, and your ship well manned. I have no fears for Susan if she is with you, and so it shall be in every detail as you wish it. The girl must be out of harm's way for the better part of a year. Then she shall see if her choice is still the same. If so — well — I shall have carried out her mother's wish. More I cannot do." He clapped Mr. Wicker once more on the shoulder and stepped out into the night, where Uncle Borb's lantern blossomed like a yellow flower at the end of a dark stalk. "You there, Uncle Borb?" bellowed Colonel Moffit, his face happy and red with port and firelight, and he turned to Mr. Wicker and Chris, who had by then joined him. "I thank you, sir, for your hospitality and help, and bid you good night until we meet in the morning. All right, Uncle Borb! Go on ahead!" And the two figures their capes wrapped about them, tugged at by the night wind, disappeared toward Cherry Alley.

The cold wind whipped into Mr. Wicker's house, and still he stood looking after the bobbing yellow light. Chris waited, and at last, his handsome face brooding, Mr. Wicker turned with a sigh and shut the door.

"Our voyage on the *Mirabelle* will not be quite as I planned, Christopher," he said, almost sadly. "We have new passengers."

# CHAPTER 10

COLONEL MOFFIT'S house in Cherry Alley was in an uproar all of the following day in more ways than one. Not only was Miss Teackle in a frenzy of organization, ordering, and direction over the packing of Susan's and her own effects into a variety of brass-studded leather trunks; but poor Aunt Abby and her daughter Juno were trying to carry out her wishes amid a flood of tears. Aunt Abby felt to a great extent responsible for Susan's attempted flight of the night before, and her tears were those of guilt and sorrow. Juno's were tears of rage toward Miss Teackle's arrogance, and sadness at her friend's departure on what she considered a very unsafe means of transport.

Below stairs, no sooner was the Colonel back from his inspection of Susan's cabin on the *Mirabelle,* than old Mrs. Moffit, her muslin cap trembling with rage and emotion, seized hold of her son's lapels and stared furiously into his face.

"Alexander Moffit!" she exploded, "I should never have believed it! First, that while I slept as peacefully as a lamb in the fold, my own granddaughter was trying to elope — and a good thing if she had, say I! — and before I've scarce et my breakfast, I hear she's to be sent off to sea in a sailing vessel — a merchantman no less! Are you gone clean daft, man, my own son? Answer me!"

The Colonel made a gesture with his hand to show he would have liked to but could not get a word in edgeways, for his mother rushed on without drawing breath.

"The very idea!" went on the indomitable old woman. "Why, that the girl's in love is the most delightful, natural thing in the world, and David Russell is the catch of Georgetown! How you can be as obstinate as you are, will or no will, defeats me entirely." She drew breath long enough to glare at her middle-aged son. Then, taking up her forces again, she gave him a push that sent him back a pace or two. "Pshaw! Let it be known by all that I have no part in this. Why — the girl may be shipwrecked and never wed at all, who can tell? Your own daughter drownd-ed, sir, and by your own wish! And who to care for her — let me ask you that?"

She glared again, and the Colonel, his face purpling like grapes in September, opened his mouth to reply, but his mother gave him no time.

"Cared for by a pickle on two feet, that's who!" she spluttered. "Imagine that! Why, Aunt Abby has more sound sense in her big toe than that woman Teackle will have in fifty more years! Pshaw, man! I am that contrarified that I shall absent myself from this house until my granddaughter shall be brought back to it, and — given my age — I hope this shall not be overlong, for already I feel I have seen too little of her." She turned from her speechless son, her skirts rustling over the pol-

ished oak floar in an echo of her anger. "My trunks are being packed, Alexander," she said, "and when my granddaughter leaves this roof which is her own, so shall I. If my grandson desires to see me, he well knows the way to the plantation, but you, sir, will only be welcome if you bring good news of my poor little Susan," she snorted, settling her spectacles back on her nose with one capable forefinger and glancing over the top of them at Colonel Moffit, standing before her in the hall of his own house like a small boy caught stealing jam.

"Had you the sense you were born with, my poor Alexander," Mrs. Moffit wound up, her tone softening briefly, "you would have married again, and a good woman would have guided our Susie through shoals which now you yourself have made into a dangerous passage." She stalked off down the hall, her back stiff with indignation. "Kindly notify me when Susan is to leave, and be so kind as to let me see the child before she goes," she said.

Colonel Moffit shook his head as will a horse beseiged by flies, hopelessly, wearily, but with annoyance. Upstairs, down the airy spiral of the stairwell, he could hear Juno's whimper and Aunt Abby's alternate soothing tone and wail of misery. From Susan he heard no sound, neither a word nor a broken phrase. Miss Teackle's occasional commands to Juno or to one of the house maids he could hear: "Do not forget these — " or, "Did you pack my medicine chest?"

A sudden quailing of his own determination and will beset the Colonel, and with a flashing foreknowledge of how silent the house would be with no sound of Susan's laughter, no trip of running feet on the stairs, no sight of a young smile, the colonial American had a devastating and black misgiving. He went into his study and with bent head, shut the door.

# CHAPTER 11

*I*T MUST HAVE BEEN that the whole series of events had left young Susan numb. The excitement of the elopement, and after her stealthy preparations its sudden failure, there in the dew-drenched orchard; then, being locked in her room only to hear in the morning that she and Miss Teackle were to set sail on a long sea voyage far from home. Too many things happening too quickly left the young girl in a daze. She had never been farther from Georgetown than to her grandmother's, or some other neighboring plantation. To be so abruptly cut off from familiar and well-loved people and scenes, with a woman she detested and otherwise among total strangers, was enough to shock anyone, even in our faster-moving time.

As it was, she later scarcely remembered kissing her grandmother goodbye, and saw Martha Moffit's kind face as through a wall of smoked glass that half obscured images as well as stifling sounds. Mrs. Moffit looked intently into Susan's face, stony and expressionless under its charming blue traveling

hood, the long blue cape trailing along the well-waxed floor boards. The old lady shook her head, patted Susan's cheek, and all at once took her by the shoulders and gave her a sharp shake. Susan blinked, and the wall between her and what was happening to her cracked for a moment. Her grandmother saw the change in her eyes and spoke briefly.

"Susie! Are you paying attention to what I say?"

"Yes, Grandmama."

"Then remember two things, do you hear? *Two*. One is that I love you. And the other is — remember at all times that you are a Moffit." The eyes that had seen much waited, watching, to see if this had reached Susan, who was slipping back behind her wall where she felt protected from the outrage of leaving her home and her country, as well as David, and then said quietly, "Kiss me, Susie!"

It was old Mrs. Moffit, too, her own luggage piled around her, and her own carriage waiting for Susan's to go first, who put her hand on Aunt Abby's arm as the massive nurse came forward to bid Susan goodbye. Mrs. Moffit's voice was low, but it reached through Aunt Abby's and Juno's distress, and

even reached to the ears of Uncle Borb, who missed nothing,
as he bent to hand out the boxes and direct Jonah's handling
of the trunks.

"She's got all that a human heart can bear, Aunt Abby,"
Mrs. Moffit said. "If you love her, you and Juno will go
quietly away where she cannot see you. Just a little more and
that young heart will break!"

So it was that with the later afternoon sun lying flatly gold
on the orchard grass, a young girl stepped past an ivy-framed
door toward the carriage where Uncle Borb sat high on the
box. As she passed Jonah, his arm held out stiffly for her to
lean on as she stepped up, she pretended to pause to gather her
skirts together. Her head bent, her lips barely moved, but
Jonah heard.

"Were you able to deliver the note, Jonah?"

"No, Miss Susie. Not anywhere."

"Keep it, please, and try again after I am gone. If it cannot
be delivered, burn it. Promise?"

"I promise, Miss Susie."

A small foot went up to the carriage step, and Susan settled herself next to Miss Teackle. Colonel Moffit followed, the carriage door slammed to, and Jonah moved back as the wheels began to grind. Old Mrs. Moffit stood erect in the open doorway, her hands folded tightly over her stomach and her mouth a straight line, while behind her, Juno and Aunt Abby's turbaned heads inched forward to strain their eyes after their dearly loved Susan. But before they could join their voices and their tears, Mrs. Moffit clapped her hands and turned to them.

"I am now ready to go home, Aunt Abby. Where's that good-for-nothing coachman of mine? Hurry! I want to stop by the church on my way!" Her eyes snapped with anger and the effort to hold back her own tears. "Aunt Abby!" she said sharply, "and you, Juno! You shall both come along with me to Mr. Balch's church. I shall expect you to say a prayer for Miss Susie every day, as I shall, until she is safely home again. Come now, help me into that ill-made carriage and get in with me. It will do none of us any good to see that ship's sails spread!"

If Aunt Abby remembered all too keenly the last time she had been in the Reverend Brother Balch's church, she said nothing of it. Three heads were bowed in the dusk of the little church. One, Mrs. Moffit's, in a white muslin cap, was bent alone in the center of rows of empty pews, and above her in the slave gallery, two turbaned heads were leant on dark folded hands.

But the prayers were all the same.

# CHAPTER 12

*C*HRIS KNEW THE *Mirabelle* from stem to stern, and he and Amos were old hands at letting out sail. Nevertheless, the springy feel of the gangplank under his racing feet gave Chris a thrill the twentieth century would never possess. The sight before him as he set foot on the deck of the *Mirabelle* was of graceful soaring masts shining in the clear spring air, the mist of rigging, and all about, the hum of voices; the activity that surrounds a sailing ship in her last moments close to shore.

What adventure would there be this time? Chris wondered. For adventure he felt sure there would be. Mr. Wicker, consulting below him on the docks with tubby Captain Ezekial Blizzard and the *Mirabelle's* first mate, Elijah Finney, seemed as relaxed and at ease as if in his own sitting room. The tall spare figure, neatly dressed in black, far from seeming in any way sinister or depressing to Chris, warmed his heart with affection, pride and wonder. For he might, as an apprentice, have learned many things from Mr. Wicker, but he knew —

and sensed even more than he knew — that Mr. Wicker's knowledge surpassed, in all probability, that of any other man then living on this side of the Atlantic.

Chris was delighted that, for this journey at least, he would have his dear friends with him, even Becky Boozer, and as he swarmed up a mast, watched from the deck below by Ned Cilley, he looked out far and wide over the Georgetown of 1792 that he was soon to leave far behind on the seas of the past and the unknown.

His old friend, the sailor Abner Cloud, perched near him, and they paused in their work to look out over the scattered roofs of the little town. Chris did his best to bring before his inner eye how the Washington D.C., of his time would look, with its crowded streets, lack of trees — compared to the time in which he now found himself — and distantly, the giant hum of the airfield. It all seemed too far away to recall.

Instead, he and Abner saw the few streets — little better than muddy lanes in wet weather and dust traps in dry — sloping down to the wharfs. Acres of wooded hills rose where a town would one day lie, and down the incline of what was now High Street rattled a carriage in a cloud of dust. Its top was piled high with barrel-topped trunks, and as it slowed among the crowds of the wharfs, Chris saw that it was headed for the *Mirabelle*. At the same time, another smaller dust cloud farther up on the hill showed by its direction that a second carriage was making for the church. Chris's attention centered on the coach then coming to a standstill far below him at the end of the dock.

He watched as a colored man hopped agilely down and gave the reins of the horses to one of the sailors of the *Mirabelle*,

who came forward for the purpose. The old coachman, his three-cornered hat in hand, opened the carriage door for, first, his master, who stepped solemnly out. Then followed a woman so tall and so thin that Chris thought the length of her would never have done, unfolding from the interior of the coach. She issued out by degrees, cautiously, and with infinite displeasure, setting first her skirts and then her very ugly bonnet to rights. She glanced about her with her nose in the air in such a way that Chris, from his perch high above her, could not be sure if it was the sights or the smells of the dockside which most drew forth the lady's disapproval.

Last but best, a small white hand was put out to take that of the coachman. It disappeared completely in the large dark fingers of the manservant, whose expression had changed completely and whose face radiated affection. Next a neat foot shod in a silver-buckled shoe came down on the carriage step, and there followed, gently, and as if with regret, the charming figure of Miss Susan Moffit. Simultaneously with her appearance, work seemed to be held up in all quarters nearby that were within eyeshot. Sailors rolling hogsheads up into the hold, merchants on their way to a neighboring ship; Captain Blizzard, dour Mr. Finney, and perhaps even Mr. Wicker, drew an unexpected breath and were interrupted in the train of their thinking. What was the more striking was that the poor young lady was entirely unaware of the sensation she was making, and stood looking vaguely at the *Mirabelle*, and then at her father, and last at Uncle Borb, as if she were a sleepwalker.

Chris watched the three people confer with Mr. Wicker, who, bowing, escorted Susan up the gangway as handsomely as any other young person could have wished, while Captain Blizzard and the lean Miss Teackle made a very ill-assorted pair, the one so short and squat, the other so tall and spare. Captain Blizzard was chortling in his usual good humor, in anticipation of a pleasant voyage; Miss Teackle looked down her long shiny nose, which meant looking down a very long way indeed.

Chris glanced about at the sailors, for he knew the superstition they held to, that to have women on board was an ill omen, but Mr. Wicker sang out in a moment to the ship's cook that the ladies would take some refreshments before the ship set sail. This, Chris knew, was intended to be heard by the men, and to lead them to believe that the visitors would be going ashore before the *Mirabelle* lifted anchor.

Smiling to himself, Chris bent once more to his task, yet, half listening to Captain Blizzard roar out to "bring the gentleman's boxes aboard," Chris found himself wishing that, pretty as she was, Susan Moffit was not to be of their number. The sea, and a long voyage, was not easy on what Ned Cilley referred to as "delikit females," for not only were ships in the eighteenth century uncomfortable, but the *Mirabelle* had not been designed to carry many passengers. Chris wondered as he worked how the angular Miss Teackle would stand the journey, and then caught sight of a procession weaving through the bustling longshoremen and stevedores that dashed all else from his mind.

It was no less a personage than Mistress Rebecca Boozer, complete in her Sunday best. Her famous hat, spreading far enough over her ample person to shade even that grandiose bulk, waved its twelve black plumes and twenty-four roses as if in constant hilarity. Mistress Boozer held her reticule in one hand and a large brass cage with a gaudy parrot in it in the other. The parrot, given to Becky by Ned and named after George Washington, was usually addressed as the General, and was, after Ned himself, the apple of Becky's eye. The General had learnt quite a few of Ned's phrases, some polite and some not. Now, as Chris and Abner Cloud looked far down from the mast top to the docks, they were able to laugh without offending Becky, for she was too engrossed in picking her gigantic way, and in cheery replies to the sallies of the sailors, to be aware that she was in any way out of the ordinary.

Most of her remarks were addressed to the General, for Becky felt keenly that the journey might go hard with the General and that he might, as she said, "catch some furrin sickness" and be lost to her forever. So as she moved ponderously forward, Amos staggering behind her with her trunk on his back, she and the General kept up a brisk conversation.

"Hold tight, dear General, we shall soon be there!" Becky

advised; "We shall soon be there."

"By me cap and buttons! Avast there, ye lubbers!" shrieked the General, and sailors, merchants and dockmen fell back to leave a wide passage for Becky and her bird.

"Easy does it, dearie. Rely on me," said Becky.

"What I need is a small quart or two of ale, to keep up me strength and spirits, Becky, me love," sang out the General.

"Hush now!" Becky warned. "What sort of talk is that!"

"Tush! How can I go on 'thout a kiss from my Boozer?" queried the General, mimicking Ned's voice until one would have sworn that that good soul stood there in person.

"Hist! Whatever next! Fie on you, General George Washington! You're making Becky blush and behaving all unseemly!"

So, with roses and plumes all a-bob, Becky reached the gangplank of the *Mirabelle*, where she was greeted by Ned Cilley. Ned rushed down to help his lady love aboard, but after repeated tries, it was found — to the consternation of the crew, hanging over the ship's side to look on — that the gangplank was too steep to allow Becky to board the *Mirabelle* unaided.

Here was a pretty kettle of fish! Becky stood puffing on the dock, arms akimbo. Ned stood rubbing his chin to help his thoughts on how to overcome this unexpected dilemma. Captain Blizzard and Mr. Finney appeared on the bridge. The Captain looked and pondered, and called Ned up to him. There he bent and whispered a few words in Ned's ear. Ned's face broke out in a wide relieved grin. Taking up one end of a rope he called the nearest of the crew into consultation. Smiles and laughter, that were quickly suppressed in deference to Mistress Boozer, touched all Ned's friends. They stood eady, and Ned shouted up to where Chris sat high on the crosstrees above the deck.

"When I give the signal, Chris — you understand me?" he called, between cupped hands.

Chris waved his hand in assent and yelled down, "That I do, Ned. I follow you. I can see fine from here."

Ned again rushed down the gangplank and explained his plan to Becky, who nodded so hard in agreement that her stupendous hat shook and quaked. Ned thereupon tied the end of the stout hawser twice around Miss Boozer's barrel waist and tested the knot with all his strength. It held. He looked up then to where Chris and Abner Cloud could scarcely hold to the rigging, they laughed so much. Chris, coughing and laughing and wiping his eyes, saw Ned's raised hand, and signaled below him to the waiting crew. These good men had wound the hawser around the capstan as if Becky was the anchor of the *Mirabelle* itself, and when Chris called: "Ready!" they bent to the bars.

As Ned dropped his hand, Chris sang out, "Walk her up, boys!"

"Up she comes!" shouted the crew, in high good humor, and bowing their backs, began singing in unison as they walked around and around, winding up the rope, just as they did when they walked up the anchor. Singing gave a rhythm so that the rope was wound evenly, and made the task seem lighter.

*"Oh — what shall we do with the drunken sailor?*
*What shall we do with the drunken sailor?*
*What shall we do with the drunken sailor —*
*So early in the morning!"*

They sang at the tops of their lungs, and the crowd watching from the wharf, joined in in a mighty chorus of laughing voices.

With a jerk, Becky, with her reticule and the General in his cage, swaying one on each side of her, was — willy-nilly — hoisted up the gangplank of the *Mirabelle*. A crowd of enormous proportions had gathered to watch this unique feat, and all those on board the *Mirabelle* who were not engaged in walking Becky onto the ship came running to the side. Becky, far from being uneasy, took the whole matter as a great joke, and as she was finally heaved to the deck, Susan Moffit came

84

o the rail in time to see what was going on.

At first flabbergasted, then, before she had time to think, so amused that her natural gaiety and youth asserted itself, Susan burst into peals of laughter. Becky set foot on the deck of the *Mirabelle*, her face red with her own effort at helping the hawser. Looking about her with an air of triumph, glancing at the sailors who stood laughing and wiping their perspiring faces with the backs of their hands, she cried:

"You are me own dear boys for this grateful act, that you are by me faith, every man jack of you! I thank you most kindly, gentlemen!"

That did it. Never had sailors been addressed as gentlemen before, and far from being a jinx to them, Becky in that instant won them over completely. From that time on she was the mascot — though a massive one — of the *Mirabelle*.

Looking about her further, and fanning herself with a large handkerchief, Becky caught sight of the laughing Susan, and throwing her own head back, laughed with her. The infection spread, and in a moment not only were the whole of the ship's company laughing and holding their sides, but the watching crowd below had joined in, ending at last with a roaring cheer for "Mistress Boozer."

"Eh, upon me soul," ejaculated Becky, well pleased with her reception, "sure, lads, you need have no fear at losing the ship's anchor, for all you need do is to throw me overboard at the end of a rope, and not a foot nor a furlong shall your ship move!"

And so saying, as firmly ensconced in the hearts of all the crew as she was in that of her devoted Ned Cilley, Mistress Boozer descended majestically to her cabin.

85

# CHAPTER·13

*I*T WAS BLUE DUSK when the *Mirabelle* lifted anchor. Such a deepening dusk that the hooded figures who went ashore escorted by Colonel Moffit scarcely needed to bend their cloaked heads and sniffle into their handkerchiefs to hide their faces from the glances of curious sailors. The three blended with the thinning wharfside crowd; the waiting carriage wheeled away. Then — or so it seemed — Colonel Moffit boarded the *Mirabelle* and the Captain, standing on the bridge with sad-faced Mr. Finney, gave the order to "cast off." The "Colonel," with a fly clinging to his low-pulled hat, went down to his quarters, where he became who he had been all along — Mr. Wicker. Chris, who had taken the part of Susan, to fool the crew into imagining the two women passengers had gone ashore, changed from the form of a fly — one of his favorite and most useful disguises, and in which he had returned to the *Mirabelle* unseen. Laughing, he went off to see how Becky Boozer was faring.

Becky was obliged to have a cabin to herself, since she took up the space of two people, and had changed from her silk Sunday gown to her more usual sprigged cotton. As Chris stood talking with her at the door of her cabin, the neighboring door burst open and Susan ran out. She was white-faced, her eyes burning, and she ran toward the door leading to the deck. With a quick rush Chris barred her way.

"I'm sorry, Miss Susan," he said politely, "but you remember that it was agreed with you and Miss Teackle that you would not be seen by the crew until we are well to sea."

His voice was gentle, for the poor girl looked wretchedly unhappy. Behind them, Becky moved forward to see what was going on.

"Let me pass!" cried Susan. "Please — you have to! I must see Georgetown slide away, at least, and Miss Teackle will not let me. She wants to look out the window herself. Please — don't you understand? There might be a friend on the docks whom I have to see — "

She attempted to push by Chris, and Becky, whom Susan had not noticed, spoke up.

"Come, my little dear, look from my window. Hurry, for we are getting out into the river!"

Susan flew past Becky, not even distracted by her hat whose roses and ostrich plumes waved and gesticulated their own sly farewell.

A widening interval of water, flecked with the colors of sunset, already lay between the side of the *Mirabelle* and the wharf. A sparse crowd, mostly of loiterers and members of the sailors' families, were still watching the departure of the ship. In those days when ships came and went daily, their sailings were nothing new to the colonials.

Susan, on tiptoe, peered out and along the wharf, her glance darting from group to group, searching, hoping. But the figure she longed for was not to be seen. Although darkness was descending rapidly, Susan would have known David Russell's tall figure anywhere, but he was not there.

Becky was now alone in the room behind her, for Chris had run up to stand on the bridge where Amos was already chattering with Mr. Finney, and at one side Mr. Wicker and Captain Blizzard held a low, friendly conversation. As Susan, below, turned at last, despair on her charming young face, Becky, observing, said not a word. As the girl faced about, with a simple human gesture Becky opened her arms wide, and Susan, bursting into heart-tearing sobs, ran into them, putting her arms around Becky's neck as she had around Aunt Abby's, crying as if this time her heart would surely break. Becky, like Aunt Abby, was even more portly and comforting to cry on, and she rocked Susan, crooning, so that in a while Susan dried her eyes and drew away, exhausted by her grief. Becky sat down, and Susan, blowing her nose on a scrap of lace and linen, sat on the cabin floor in a billow of blue skirts. Becky patted her shoulder.

"There now! I'll warrant the tears are for a young man, and a right handsome one he must be!" she ventured. Susan did not trust her voice to reply, so Becky went on. "He will wait for you, Miss Susie dear, never doubt it. 'Tis hard to be separated when you be young, there's no denying that. But the time will pass."

Susan looked up, the tip of her nose pink from weeping. "So many months! I dare not think how long! How shall I ever make the days pass, Mistress — Mistress — "

She hesitated, not knowing Becky's name. Becky filled the gap with a chuckle.

"I am Rebecca Boozer, dearie," she said, her blue eyes warm. "But I feel we are something of friends already, so why not call me as do all my good friends — Becky?"

Susan smiled uncertainly, and put her small hand on Becky's work-worn one.

"Thank you, I shall," she said.

"As to the length of the journey, miss," Becky went on, "have you considered what a wonderful opportunity this can be?"

"Opportunity? This?" Susan asked derisively. "A voyage of months far from home?"

"Why yes," Becky said, bending toward the upturned earnest gaze, "for consider: if you apply yourself to the things Mistress Teackle is able to teach you, you will be well fitted to be a capable, good wife when you reach home again. And should you wish it, you and I shall do some cooking together, for that is what I am here for." She winked at Susan and smiled broadly. "For let me tell you a secret, dearie. The old saying is true, and the way to a man's heart is through his stummick! I shall prove it to you shortly. You should see my friend Ned Cilley eat, and he does make so bold as to say he loves me!"

At this point the General, who had been sulking in his cage, came to life and in Ned's very tone announced: "Pass the pie! Pass the cheese! Who et up the gammon, by me cap and buttons!"

Susan burst out laughing, her spirits somewhat restored. "Ah there!" cried Becky, delighted, "it's a pretty face and no mistake!"

"A pretty face and no mistake!" mimicked the General, hopping about in a frenzy of gaiety. "Awk! Avast! Walk 'er up and give me a kiss! Awk!"

Becky and Susan laughed at the silly bird, and the General, fancying he was being admired, minced along his perch and blinked coyly. Susan turned to Becky as she rose.

"Dear Becky! I am indeed fortunate that you are aboard, for I can see that my life on this ship will be quite different with you here. I had thought myself without a friend, but" — and she smiled her most enchanting smile, "I see it is quite otherwise. Bless you." She laid a hand on Becky's cheek. "Indeed, if you have time, I should be most happy to learn cooking secrets from you, for, God willing, I intend making David Russell the best wife in Georgetown!"

"So you shall, dearie, so you shall! Now, go wash your face, for old tears are not becoming, and you shall eat a bit of supper, for I shall bring it to you."

So saying, a lighter-hearted young miss, and Becky, her frondy bonnet a-wave, went their different ways. Under their feet the planks of the *Mirabelle* creaked as she moved down the Potomac, and up on deck, a solitary man in black stood with his hand on a boy's shoulder, under the white bloom of the high-filled sails.

# CHAPTER 14

*T*HE FIRST TWO DAYS of the journey of the *Mirabelle*, across Chesapeake Bay and into the first waves of the Atlantic, were not steady ones, and Miss Teackle felt very ill indeed. Moaning and holding smelling salts to her long nose, she kept to her berth. Susan, feeling a sense of freedom now that her jailor was herself a prisoner, was allowed by Captain Blizzard on the second day, when the *Mirabelle* dipped and rose on the open sea, to come to the bridge. The salty rush of wind winding and unwinding her cloak about her, the blue whipped water, the creak of masts and boards were a tonic to Susan, in spite of the soreness of her heart. The sun dazzled her eyes and spun its mysterious gold in her hair, and her cheeks blossomed with a new rose they had not held for many a day. Mr. Wicker, leaning against the side of the ship, found that his eyes seemed rested when his sight was filled with Susan's youth and beauty.

Chris and Amos, also on the bridge, were learning how to take the ship's bearings from Mr. Finney and had no interest

in a girl, pretty or otherwise. Chris remembered his manners enough to come forward as Susan came onto the bridge to ask if she had slept well and how Miss Teackle did.

"She does very poorly, I thank you," Susan replied with a wry smile, wrinkling her nose.

"And you do well?" Mr. Wicker smiled at her, coming forward in his turn. Susan's twinkling eyes were on him.

"Indeed, I thank you, Mr. Wicker, sir, I do extremely well as long as Mistress Teackle does so ill, heaven save me for an unkind wretch!"

Mr. Wicker's dark eyes glinted and his calm face relaxed at the amusement reflected in the face below his. Susan went on.

"Is this windy blow likely to remain a while behind us, Captain Blizzard?" she asked. "I do pray so, for not only will it hasten us on our way, but seems to suit us all — all but Miss Teackle." She looked around with a smile.

Captain Blizzard considered. "Aye, that it may, Miss Susan,

and roughen too, but winds, we sailors say, are contrary things, like women, ma'am, saving your presence. Not even the best of us know for certain what they will do next."

There was a good feeling of friendliness among the group standing there on the pitching bridge that windy morning. It was well that it was so, for they were to be close company for a long time to come. Chris, looking over once or twice as he and Amos applied themselves to understanding a sextant, thought Mr. Wicker's brooding eyes watched Susan Moffit overcarefully, even if he was her guardian. And all at once it struck the boy what a fine-looking man his master was, lean and strong, his dark hair held neatly, even in that strong wind, by his habitual black ribbon at the nape of the neck. His profile, against the tossing sea, was sharp and clear, and his eyes, usually so somber, were fired now with whatever thoughts sparked there behind their diffidence. In a short while Susan began pacing the deck for exercise, and Mr. Wicker joined her, putting out a steadying hand when a sudden movement of the ship tended to throw his charming ward off balance.

"How long will our voyage be, Mr. Wicker?" Susan asked, as her small feet and his, black-shod, kept rhythm up and down.

"That will depend on the winds, of course, Miss Susan," he replied, "but — all being favorable, perhaps a year or more." Mr. Wicker's keen eyes watched the girl's face for the effect of his words.

" 'Or more'!" Susan stopped short and her distress was plain. "Oh, sir, why should my father treat me so — and I thought he loved me!" The large eyes, as changeable in color as the sea, filled with stormy tears. Mr. Wicker looked away.

"Indeed, Miss Susan," he said, "it is precisely because he loves you, and your mother before you, that he sends you on this voyage." He looked down at her gravely. "I remember your mother, perhaps, better than you do, for you were very small when she died." Mr. Wicker looked back at Susan with a pensive smile. "There never was a lovelier, gentler lady than Mistress Moffit, and her death was a loss to all who knew her. There is nothing easier to understand than that her last wish would be followed to the letter by her husband."

Susan's tears still hung at the rims of her eyes, but she listened to Mr. Wicker intently.

"Your mother was not only beautiful but wise, Miss Susan," Mr. Wicker pursued. "She wanted your happiness in a life she knew she could not watch over. She who had such a tender one herself knew that young hearts are sometimes like twigs aflame — soon fired but soon burnt out. She wanted you to have the certainty, in yourself, that what you felt was for a

94

lifetime. If it is, then time will only better it, and fan a flicker to a steady blaze. If not, then wiser to discover any weakness now."

There was a pause, while Susan bent her head and watched her silver-buckled shoes go in and out at the hem of her blue skirt. At last she said:

"I think I see. You've made her seem nearer, all at once; almost within sight and touch." She hesitated, lifting her head. "How strange! I never felt before that I knew what Mother looked like — even though I have her picture in a medallion, and another portrait hangs in my father's study. Yet as you spoke I had a picture of her in my mind as if I were before her, looking at her." She turned wide shining eyes to the dark man at her side. "I could see her as a living person — not something in a frame! I shall hold to that image always, now, and seeing it, feel closer to her."

The young girl stopped and looked out over the sea across which she was being carried to who knew what shore?

"I am grateful to you, Mr. Wicker," she said, "for, hard as it is to be away from home and kin, I am now willing to do as she would have wished, for I see that she knew best and wanted only good for me." She looked up with a sad smile and a shake of her head. "But that will not help to shorten the journey, I am afraid!" she confessed.

Just then a commotion took place on the deck below. Two sailors were dragging a third figure up from the hold, and Abner Cloud ran up the ladder to the bridge to stand before the captain breathlessly and say:

"Sir — we have found a stowaway!"

# CHAPTER 15

*M*R. *WICKER LOOKED* down at the man held fast between the two sailors, and sighed. There was a great deal in that sigh, but knowledge and resignation were foremost in it. As for Susan, her breath was caught tight, like a silk dress on a briar, and her hands gripped the rail as she gazed down.

"It can't be!" she murmured, as if to herself, "but it is! It *is!* David — oh, David!" she called, holding out her arms and leaning forward.

The young man straightened, his white face turned to where Susan stood. His dry lips cracked in a smile of joy and triumph, and his eyes shone. Ned Cilley, hurrying up, as usual, to see what was going on, hit his head with his hand, thunderstruck.

"By me cap and buttons!" he exclaimed, " 'tis no ordinary stowaway that ye have there, lads, but young David Russell, whom ye know well. Look, Captain, sir, 'tis David Russell, here!" he shouted, turning his face up toward the bridge which David's eyes had not left since he first saw Susan.

Captain Blizzard put a hand over his mouth to mask a smile, and as he spoke, attempted to look severe.

"Well now, young Mr. Russell!" he thundered, "you a stowaway! Do you intend to delay us by making us return to port to put you safe ashore?"

Susan whirled quickly around. "Oh no, Captain, please, do not turn back!" she pleaded. "He will work his way — won't you, David?" she appealed, swinging back.

Captain Blizzard appeared to consider this, and spoke to the sailors who still held David Russell's arms.

"Let go of him, lads, for though he be a fine swimmer, yet is the shore far distant, ahead of us, and astern." The plump Captain of the *Mirabelle* clasped his hands behind his back in a habitual gesture. "How long have you been aboard, Mr. Russell?" he demanded.

"These three days, sir," David replied, "for I boarded the *Mirabelle* the night before she sailed." He turned to where Mr. Wicker stood beside Susan, looking down at the young face with tolerance and wisdom. "I owe you an apology, sir," he said, "for I listened at your study window, while Colonel Moffit was with you, and thus knew what plans were afoot."

Mr. Wicker smiled, a smile that gave Chris, who watched his master's face closely, the impression that this knowledge was by no means news to him. Captain Blizzard, standing as solid as a boulder on the bridge, was pondering.

"Well," he said at last, "here you are, and I do not feel inclined to put back to shore, for we are making good headway with the wind in this quarter. But since you have elected to come aboard, young man, as a stowaway, even though I know your gentle birth, yet must you work your way and make

97

yourself useful, for such is the reward of anyone who seeks passage on board ship unlawfully." His blue eyes slid over to Susan's troubled, anxious face, and as quickly slid away. "I therefore commend you to the attentions of Ned Cilley, here, who shall endeavor to teach you how to rig and furl a sail, how to splice a rope, and in short, how to be a true addition to the crew of the *Mirabelle*." The good Captain drew himself up to the fullness of his short, rotund height. "For look you, men," he said, raising his voice, it might have been, against the wind, "we want no repetition of an incident many of you may remember, a few voyages back, from young Zachary Heigh. *There* was treachery as bald as a buzzard's head! No. This is a fair ship, that any of us will allow, and here are we all on a fine voyage, carrying with us no less a personage than the owner of the ship himself. Let us all, severally, still be of one heart. And so this good ship will go forward even more smoothly."

"Yet do we have women aboard!" cried a voice from the back of the crowd that had by now gathered to see the stowaway and listen to the Captain, who was universally respected. "And all know that women bring bad luck to a voyage and a ship!"

Captain Blizzard turned eyes that were abruptly stony toward the voice, but before he had time to speak, an apparition appeared at the door to the ship's galley. Feathers and roses all a-flourish in the wind, Mistress Boozer looked sourly at the crew before her.

"By your leave, Captain, sir!" she cried, planting her hands on her wide-jutting hips, and before the good Captain could so much as say, "Granted," Becky Boozer had taken the floor.

"What be ye?" she demanded resoundingly of the sailors

packed before her, "men or squeaking mice? Can ye not trust your Captain, who has sailed this ship these many years, and ever brought you safely home? Must you coddle a legend, as a mother a babe in arms, that you keep it so warm?" She gave a disgusted gesture, as if chasing them all away from her sight.

"Fie on you all, for being babies yourselves! Did you not always put a carved woman on the prows of your ships? Where is the ill luck in that? Now you have a beauty on the bridge, and me in the kitchen to bake you cakes such as a crew never had before! Fie and for shame! Where would any mother's son of you be without us, the women, answer me that!"

At this point General Washington flew out from his perch in the galley, and clinging to Becky's wind-blown shoulder shrilled:

"For that you owe us a kiss, my sweet Boozer!"

The assembled sailors broke into a roar of mirth, but the same doubting voice sounded out above the din, shouting above the laughter and the wind.

"Indeed, we may have a mascot and a beauty on board, but sure and we have a pickle, too!" it called.

But laughter again drowned out more, and when it subsided, Becky was equal to the last word.

"Surely!  And who says there was ever good without some bad to make it seem the sweeter?  Now let the poor young man come to Becky for some food and drink that I'll warrant he'll not say 'no' to. And any man that is dissatisfied to be of the crew of the *Mirabelle* need not come to the galley door for my new-made cakes!"  And with an air of triumph that she had richly deserved, Becky Boozer, with her parrot on her shoulder, withdrew, with feathers and roses a-bob, into the galley.

And Captain Blizzard, smiling to himself, was wondering who had charge of the *Mirabelle*, himself, or Becky Boozer?

# CHAPTER 16

*A*S ON HIS FIRST VOY-age aboard the *Mirabelle*, Chris devoted the mornings to study. Not the kind of studies he was used to at school, but the practising of magic. Though fun to Chris, it needed all his attention. This time, however, he had the help of his master instead of having to work alone.

Every morning, therefore, before the sun was far above the horizon, Chris would knock at the door of the owner's cabin. Mr. Wicker would call out from where he sat with his black-coated back to the window, and on going in, Chris knew he should always turn the key, so that their concentration should not be disturbed by Amos or a member of the crew. Then he would work at the fantastic tricks that Mr. Wicker had taught him long before; tricks that the magician had also erased from Chris's mind when Chris had last stepped back into his own century and time.

Chris would practise turning himself into a mouse, or a fly; or, as upon that particular morning, into the design in the rug on the floor, repeating within himself the words of the Incantation 73, Book I. The old sensation of a humming inside himself would fill his head as if a new kind of machinery had been set in motion there. The giddiness that followed, Chris knew, would disappear as he became once again more adept and quicker at the changes. Then, as he persevered, would come the feeling of faintness, the sickness, and the lurch, as he concentrated on the words and on whatever form he had chosen to become. All at once, there he was, feeling flat, and looking up at Mr. Wicker from the level of his master's feet. He was, sure enough, the blue design at the corner of the rug, and the desk above him, the raftered ceiling of the cabin, the swinging lantern that would be lit at dusk, his master's neat bunk against the wall: all these things seemed gigantic and miles above him. Mr. Wicker would get up from behind his desk where he had watched his pupil make the magic change, his white quill pen suspended above the long sheets of paper on which he had been writing, and slowly move around the carpet.

"Yes," he would say, examining the design in the carpet intently, "you have made a very exact change, Christopher, my boy. The design has been very well followed. A trifle fuzzy, just here" — and he would put a slender forefinger on a spot on the carpet — "but nothing anyone but Claggett Chew would notice." He would straighten himself at the name of his enemy. "*That* is why you must be perfect in all your disguises, Christopher, for you have nothing to fear from an average man — only one who is not average — and Claggett Chew is *not*. His powers of magic are strong — very strong — and it is against his *knowledge*, more than against his sight, that you must be able to defend yourself."

From across the cabin he would wheel from where he had been gazing at the restless and ever-moving sea.

"Very well, Christopher. Now make The Return. Incantation 74, Book II."

Chris, feeling as flat as he indeed was, would repeat to himself the magic formula that restored him to his own shape, and with a jolt, there he was once more, standing on the very carpet of which he had been, only a moment before, a part.

It was a great strain. No human can leave his own shape and return to it, without a major effort of will and knowledge, and for many weeks Chris felt faint, and would have to sit down for a moment until his normal strength returned. But as he persisted, he was able once again to become so skilled in the magic that Mr. Wicker knew how to teach him that soon his changes of shape were almost as lightning fast as Mr. Wicker's own. In a breath, Chris could turn himself into a host of different objects. Yet even magic has its limits, and there were only a certain number of changes that he could make.

Still, there were many other kinds of magic to relearn and practise. The use of the magic rope was one of these. This apparently ordinary length of hemp, rough-looking to the eye but surprisingly silky and pliable to the touch, could, when Mr. Wicker had once more taught Chris the twists and turns of arm and hand that were necessary and how to draw with the rope in the air, become a boat, an eagle, or an elephant. Chris learnt for a second time how to outline a rowboat to float in the room, and never failed to be fascinated as the magic rope coiled back and forth in mid-air. It became at first the skeleton of a dinghy, with only the essential keel and ribs. Thereafter, almost faster than the eye could follow, the rest of the spaces

103

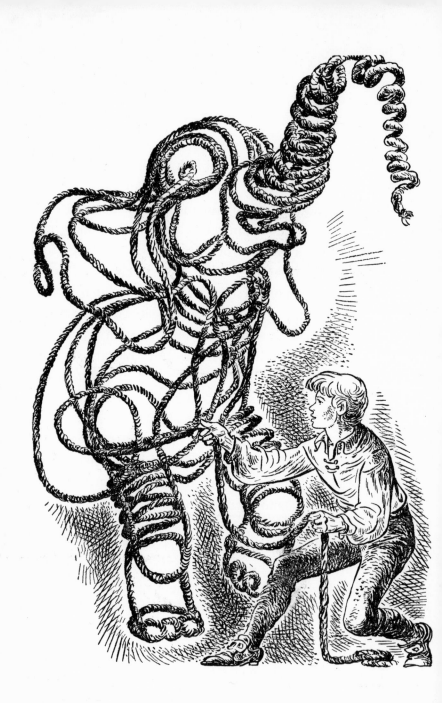

would be filled in until the two rope ends were left dangling on either side. These became oars when Chris stepped into the now solid boat and picked them up.

Or an elephant could be made, but it had to be, as Mr. Wicker had once said, "quite a *small* elephant, because of the size of the room. . . ." This magic animal, its trunk and tail the two rope ends hanging at front and back, could move at Chris's touch as any live elephant could. And last, there was the eagle made of rope, its great beaked head thrust forward, and broad stiff wings outspread for ever-ready flight.

Yet, one morning, Mr. Wicker had new magic to impart. Chris, as usual, knocked at the cabin door. By this time many weeks had gone by, long sea weeks for Susan, even though she and David Russell could be together when his sailor's duties were over. Shorter weeks for Amos, who busied himself working with the crew, or learning all he could of navigation from the patient, if dour, Mr. Finney. Shortest weeks of all, perhaps, for Chris, who not only had a great talent for learning magic, but was so absorbed with this game, so far removed from his usual boy's life, that the hours and days seemed all too short for everything he wanted to know. Therefore, he invariably hurried through breakfast in order to be a little earlier, to have more time to perfect this or that bit of magic.

One morning, some time after the *Mirabelle* had rounded Cape Horn and was moving toward Mexico, Chris woke to a brilliant day that heralded the tropics into which the ship was sailing. The sea, calmed of its storms, sparkled under a hot sun. A brisk breeze whipped the crests of the waves into white, and dappled the troughs of the swells with a changing pattern of spume. Chris's face was lit with eagerness as he came into Mr. Wicker's cabin.

"Good morning, sir! Such a fine day! If only there were some new magic to learn, this would be the very day to learn it in!" he cried, standing before Mr. Wicker, who stood looking out over the sea. The glare from the sunny water outlined the black-clad figure of the magician in front of the wide cabin window, until for a passing second Chris imagined that the familiar figure of his master was rimmed with tiny flames.

Mr. Wicker turned from his contemplation of the water to look at Chris. The finely chiseled face was in shadow, but the eyes still seemed to hold a light from the sea, and burned steadily at the young novice.

"Good morning to you, too, Christopher, and indeed you are right. It is an uncommonly fine day, and as it so happens, I *had* a new bit of magic I wanted to work on, and have been waiting for you to arrive so that we could do it together."

Chris's breath came faster, and he was silent, waiting.

"We are approaching Mexico, Christopher," Mr. Wicker began, "and I have reason to know that we are soon to be faced with trouble. We must take all the steps at our command to minimize it, and time is already short."

The handsome dark face was stern. Chris felt a needle of fear, and his own expression changed.

"Trouble, sir?" he asked. "What sort of trouble?"

Mr. Wicker shook his head and turned away once more to the sunny sea.

"Almost the worst trouble we could have, Christopher," he said. "Claggett Chew."

# CHAPTER 17

*F*AR *AHEAD OF THE* ship that plunged with all sails set into the warmer seas lay the dry shrubby hills and blanched sweeping shores of Mexico, and at a certain point on the coast, past an island set like a sentinel at its watch, opened the beautiful harbor of Acapulco. High mountains rose behind and around the blue bay. Its blazing white beaches were of the finest coral sand, and the graceful shores, empty of houses, rustled with slender palm trees.

A small cluster of whitewashed adobe huts formed the village of Acapulco. The low one-storied houses were grouped like a crescent of pale-dressed children around three sides of the central square of the little town. The fourth side, open to the beach and the bay, gave the villagers a view of the harbor mouth and any ship that might sail in, and into the edge of the surf stalked the tall spiny legs of the few rickety wharfs where incoming ships unloaded their cargoes. Here, on these barnacled docks, were lifted out treasures of silks and jewels, fine furnishings and costly church relics from all corners of the

Europe of that time. The ships that brought them had come from Spain and France, England and the Philippines. For their return, they were filled with ore from Mexican mines, gold and silver, for the lengthy journey home.

Mexican peons, speaking in the ancient dialect of their district, mingled their voices with the resounding phrases of Spanish grandees and the coarse jokes of sailors from all over the world. Arriving travelers could see, beyond the sparse docks, the half-moon of houses surrounding the square. The town seemed like arms opened wide to receive men tired of the sea.

The far side, where the church stood, facing the advancing sailor, was partly hidden by trees of great age that offered shade and coolness for the townspeople. Ilex, hibiscus, palms, and broad-leaved bananas spread a green shadow; cashews and feathery tamarisks rose above tropical shrubs. Flowering vines laced the trees in colorful festoons and made the square seem what in fact it was: a remainder of the jungle. Above this tossing green rose the dome and tower of the church, and behind this, still, were piled the craggy steeps of the mountains, rising to the range that made a rough barrier along the coast.

Streets broke, right and left, into the farther corners of the square. The one to the right led toward the straggling outskirts of the town. This street became the highroad to Taxco and its silver mines, while the street to the left ran unevenly along an ill-kempt row of houses that soon petered out entirely, as if ashamed of their slatternly appearance. One by one they dissolved into the fringe of the jungle that waited, a green beast, where the houses faltered. The few streets of eighteenth-century Acapulco, indeed, were no more than alleys, uncobbled and evil-smelling, along which the wary traveler must pick a devious way.

Centered among the houses on the west side of the square stood a prosperous-looking building. Its tiled roof was in better condition than those of its neighbors, and it even boasted two stories, for shuttered windows above the front door opened onto a balcony of graceful Spanish iron. The stout door below, of greater width than was common, was held by boldly scrolled hinges that showed their Spanish and Moorish inspiration. The door was, at that early hour of the morning — a little after three, before first light — firmly closed; no doubt bolted from inside. So too, were the shutters on all the windows, for the air of Acapulco by night was not considered healthy, built as the village was close to swamps and brackish inland water. Then, too, closed shutters took the place of curtains, and shut out not only curious eyes, but roving thieves, bats, and a host of stinging creatures.

The adobe of this building was washed with a deep apricot tint. The black shutters closed over the tall windows on either side of the entrance, and those forming a double doorway for the apartment opening onto the balcony above, gave the house a look that was both rakish and sinister. Its well-kept appearance was strikingly at odds with the other houses round about, whose cracked walls and broken doors advertised their poverty.

Outside this more prosperous building, the sidewalk was worth a second glance. It was raised three feet above the muddy edge of the town square. Its uniqueness was in the material used to make it, for it was entirely made up of gaily colored and varied tiles of different designs. Narrow steps at intervals allowed anyone walking in what passed for a road

around the edge of the square, to get out of the way of wallow-
ing carriages or overladen donkeys to the easier and cleaner
walking above, and passers-by walking on the tile sidewalk
were perforce on a level with the windows on the lower floor
of the yellow building. Years of wagons and the feet of pack
mules had long since churned the roadway below into a foul
mess of stinking mud. The raised walk was a necessity, and
the Mexican imagination and natural love of beauty had transformed a commonplace into something that delighted the eye.

Somnolent as the square was at that hour, the yellow building lay passive in the deeper shadow cast down over its façade
by the balcony running the width of the house. Immediately
over the vast door, hung far out to catch any traveler's eye,
hung a sign. On the oblong board a crude globe had been
painted, suspended between a sky filled with sun, moon and
stars, and a lashing sea, on which a sailing ship labored. The
name was painted across the top and bottom of the wooden
board: LOS SIETES MARES or: The Seven Seas.

As the sign over the door proclaimed, the building was an inn, and though in better repair than most of the houses of 1792 Acapulco, still, it remained a rough and ready place frequented only by stranded travelers eager to go elsewhere, or by transient sailors. The inn's customers came from all corners of the world, as the sign, swaying and creaking in the slight early morning breeze, suggested, and The Sign of the Seven Seas, poor as it might seem to many, silent and seemingly deserted in the dusk before dawn, was nevertheless, among the world of sailors of every nationality, quite famous. At that time, inns were few and far between; trade was just beginning with the new democracy formed under George Washington; the fast voyages by clipper ships from New York and Boston were still in the future. Yet at the Seven Seas almost every sailor could be sure that he would run into some companion long lost sight of, or hear, over his cup of *tequila*, rumfustian, or bottle of wine, tales of ships presumed lost, or of cargoes that had reached some other destination and some other owner than those for whom they had originally been intended. In short, months away from their own lands, any stranger was certain to find, within the walls of the Seven Seas, in its strange foreign setting, some unexpected link with home, wherever that home might be.

At half past three on a still morning, the evil-smelling narrow streets, never washed of litter except by the gusty downpours of the rainy season, echoed not even a late-returning footstep. The shadows cast by the moon had been blotted out, for the moon had long set. Even bold men did not venture out at such a solitary hour, for death could lurk in many ways in the streets of eighteenth-century Acapulco. In the black corners of street and hovel, an arm could strike death with a sharp knife or machete; a body be robbed, and no man, when the sun rose, be the wiser. Or a rich man foolish enough to step beyond the sheltering walls of inn or house could find himself bound and gagged and carried up beyond the confines of the winding streets to a mountainside where, starved and mistreated, he would be held for high ransom. Or, should a wayfarer be delayed until the town was silent, too often had he been found bloated and discolored from the fang of a snake that had lain across his path. To stir abroad after moon-set in Acapulco was therefore not even for the bold; only for the foolish.

Therefore until light came — for the streets were unlit by torch or lantern — no one stirred abroad. By four o'clock the birds in the trees of the square sensed the approach of dawn and awoke with a rising clatter of calls, shrill, cackling, and incredibly noisy. Cockatoos and other tropical birds joined in what soon became a deafening din, whistling in rising scales,

112

endlessly repeated; screaming in incessant downward glissandos; scolding on a single note at one another from the miniature jungle of leaves and lianas in the center of the square.

It was not long then before night dissolved like blue wood smoke. The little town seemed to shift within itself, as if turning over in its sleep. Soon women sauntered from the houses to fetch water, and children came from their pallets to sit yawning on the doorsteps. And with an iron crash and clank of bolts shot back and a great key turned, the door of the Seven Seas was thrown wide.

Pushing it open was a man scarcely higher than a child. His black hair stood in frowzled disorder just as it had been matted by his sleeping. His face at first glance appeared childlike, but a closer look proved it to be of indeterminate age, evil, bad-tempered, and with a shocking difference; one eyeball was entirely white, glazed and sightless, yet of a piercing horror so that the beholder could half believe that the dead eye could see.

What this creature lacked from one eye he made up with the one remaining. This good eye was as black as the other was white, and of a rare cunning. His young-old face seemed to hide many a foul deed, yet his coarse dirty fingers held a limberness and dexterity that made any who saw him put a protecting hand in a surreptitious gesture to their pockets where their weapons or their money lay.

The man with the dead eye pushed back the heavy door and stepped forward to peer on all sides, as if to sample the quality of the morning. He then glanced to the left, toward the high mountain range above the church where the first light had already barred the topmost peaks. By the strength of the sun the man evidently took knowledge of the degree of heat that there would be that day. He stretched, yawned broadly, showing strong white Indian teeth, and in the middle of his yawn was interrupted by a shout from inside.

"Modesto! Modesto! Where are you? You lazy thief and inferior pickpocket!"

The white-eyed man yawned again, though not with such relish, and was about to stretch once more when a heavy footfall sounded behind him and an imposing figure strode out to cuff his ears with a slap that sent him staggering forward, whining and whimpering. The man who now stood sniffing at the morning air was tall and heavy, nearly bald except for a fringe of fiery red hair that still clung to his head. His eyes, surprisingly, were as black as the one good eye of him he called Modesto, and thick lips over bad teeth hung loosely in a round face. The red-haired man's skin was congested and peony-colored, making his hair seem the redder, and he had a round paunch above sturdy knees.

"Why don't you come when I call?" he shouted. "Get back to the fire and heat up my coffee!"

The red-haired man leaned forward belligerently. The cuffed one bent away from him, half impertinent and half servile.

"*Bueno — bueno*, El Rojo," he whined, "I go. I hasten. I follow your every wish!"

El Rojo, The Red One, watched Modesto from sight, vanishing like a black crab into the airless dark interior of the inn. Modesto, or El Ciego, as he was sometimes called, The Blind One, had been El Rojo's servant for so many years that neither

114

master nor servant could remember when one had not ordered and the other obeyed. El Rojo, standing solid-legged before his door, looked quite competent to run even such a nefarious place as the harbor inn. There was no intrigue afoot in the whole of Mexico, or for the matter of that, scarcely in the whole of the Old World, that El Rojo did not know of and — more than likely — have a finger in. Powerful himself, he had friends in high places throughout Mexico and abroad. No man had attempted in years to get the better of El Rojo, for retribution, every man knew, would catch up with him wherever he might flee. Too many were in El Rojo's debt, for the innkeeper caused many to escape from justice, or had done some favor — not even sticking at murder — to help out a friend.

As El Rojo stood before his inn door, the shutters of the balcony above his head opened, and out over the iron railing flew a basinful of dirty water, barely missing El Rojo and splattering him before it fell into the muddy street. El Rojo turned with a roar and glared up at the half-opened shutters.

"Señor Osterbridge! Señor Osterbridge Hawsey! How many times do I have to ask you to look below before you throw anything out?"

A fair head jauntily adorned with a white nightcap was gingerly poked around the edge of the shutter, and a moment later Osterbridge Hawsey, tying the cords of his fine satin dressing gown about his waist, lounged out to the balcony. He was patting at his newly shaved face, and pulled his mouth down in a fairly sincere attempt at regret.

"El Rojo! My *dear* man! I could not be sorrier, really, I could not. You are perfectly right, as always, I may say. Of

116

*course* I should have looked. But so *distressingly* early — it never occurred to me that anyone might be abroad, almost before they had had time to get to bed, so to speak. . . ."

He leaned on the iron balcony, smiling down at the infuriated innkeeper with a soothing and seemingly candid charm.

"Good morning, by the by, El Rojo," he went on in a conversational way. "It does promise to be a most *charming* day, does it not? I rather fancied a dip in the ocean before the sun rose. My skin is so delicate, you know — " He straightened up, fidgeting the curls caught at the nape of his neck with a blue bow. "I should burn to an *ember* if I were not careful! These *tropics!*"

The fop rolled up his eyes in mock despair, and waving a languid hand, disappeared behind the balcony shutters once more. El Rojo, watching the brocaded figure vanish, gave a snort of impatience and sent another keen glance about the empty square. He was about to go inside when a movement or sound on the far side drew his attention.

The big man instantly became alert, squinting his eyes as if to pierce the dusk that still hovered over the town. Between the boles of the trees something moved, just where the street leading to distant Taxco cut into the right-hand corner of the square. El Rojo waited, watching.

It was the swing of a long grey cape and the reverberation of a rapid step, for now its owner came striding into view, turning to cut across the square and head toward the inn. As he approached, El Rojo's face cleared. A look of anticipation, almost of pleasure, crossed his red thick-lipped face, and his tense body relaxed. The figure was evidently that of a friend. In a moment the striding man leapt over the muddy street to gain the shallow steps that rose to the sidewalk, and advanced until he stood beside the innkeeper.

They made an ugly, yet a strangely well-assorted pair. The newcomer stood even taller than El Rojo, and his white skull was hairless, shaven to a grey bristle that barely showed over his head. His black brows hid deeply sunken icy eyes, and his nose showed the broken lines of a blow long ago received. A drooping black mustache trailed over his thin lips and hung below the corners of his mouth, and in his powerful hands he held a heavy leather whip, coiled like a waiting snake in his fingers. El Rojo's eyes lightened imperceptibly as he looked into the cold eyes of the man before him.

"It is a bold man, Señor Claggett Chew, who roams the streets of Acapulco after dark," he said, in grudging admiration. "Some even say, a foolish man."

Claggett Chew looked back at El Rojo with his strange unblinking stare.

"You know me, El Rojo. Am I then to be thought bold — or foolish?"

The voice, strong yet without inflection, was nevertheless such that El Rojo's eyes caught the shift as Claggett Chew's fingers tightened on the coiled whip. El Rojo threw back his head and laughed.

"I do enjoy my little joke with you, Señor Chew!" he said, "for, *por Díos*, you know yourself to be bold — overbold. There are many varieties of serpents, here in Acapulco, and some of them have legs, as you know." He shook his head chuckling, and as if marveling. "Have you then been absent all this night, with none to guard your safety?"

Claggett Chew loosened his fingers but not his gaze. "I am

able to safeguard myself," he replied coldly, "as well as my business." He began to move into the inn. "Besides, Simon Gosler went with me. He will be along later. I walk more rapidly than he." Over his shoulder he rapped out, "I shall have coffee, rumfustian, and bread here, in the fresh air, El Rojo!"

El Rojo, used to ordering and to being obeyed, smiled admiringly and turned at once.

"*Sí señor!*" he answered, and rushed toward the distant room where Modesto knelt, blowing on a charcoal fire. El Rojo bellowed at the top of his lungs, "Modesto! Thief and son of a thief! Why is the coffee not yet hot, inferior animal that you are?"

Modesto blew harder.

119

# CHAPTER 18

*I*N THE OWNER'S cabin Chris raised troubled eyes to Mr. Wicker's face. "*Claggett Chew?*" he exclaimed, unbelieving. "Alive? Ahead of us? But, sir — how? I thought — "

Mr. Wicker held up one long hand with a faint smile. "So many questions! One at a time, Christopher."

The man and the boy stood in the shade of the cabin facing the sunny brilliance of the sea beyond the window.

"You thought," Mr. Wicker began, "that Claggett Chew had perhaps been killed by a certain swordsman?"

"Yes."

" — Or that he drifted in his ship in an enveloping mist and sank at sea?"

"Yes!"

" — Or that the ship was dashed on a rock on some deserted shore and all aboard were lost and drowned?"

"Yes!" Chris cried. "Oh yes! Any of those! You mentioned his name some time ago, when I was practising being a rug. I thought you were thinking of old times; that I wouldn't have to be careful about him now." He paused, searching his master's face. "He ought to be dead. Why isn't he? Any other man would have been."

Mr. Wicker's handsome brooding face turned away.

"Just so, Christopher. 'Any other man' would have been, indeed. But you forget — Claggett Chew *is* no ordinary man. He has — unfortunately for us — powers beyond those of most men."

"He hasn't as strong a magic as yours, has he, sir?" Chris looked up earnestly. "Surely not that strong?"

Mr. Wicker continued to shake his head doubtfully. "It is hard to know exactly, Christopher. He has had time, now, since drifting ashore, to practise, to learn — who knows what of new and evil?"

Mr. Wicker strode away from the bright light and flashing water to take a quick turn or two up and down the cabin.

"Every puff of wind brings us nearer to Claggett Chew and whatever danger he may have in store," he began.

"But does he know of *us?*" Chris demanded. "Isn't there some way we can find out?"

Mr. Wicker stopped his pacing to ponder. "Yes, there is," he said at last. "I was going to show you. Today offers us the essential ingredients — sun and sea spume. Come, my boy, let us begin."

Going back to the window, hanging above the dipping sea, the magician took a small pouch from his pocket that Chris thought looked familiar.

"Didn't I have a pouch like that once, sir?" he asked.

Mr. Wicker nodded absently. "I believe you did — the very

same," he replied. "Now watch closely!"

Putting finger and thumb into the puckered mouth of the bag, Mr. Wicker drew them out, holding between them a fine clear stone as large as a hazel nut, sparkling and winking with fires of every color.

"A diamond?" Chris whispered.

His master agreed softly, and all at once an intense silence seemed to press upon the room, leaning against Chris's eardrums like a tangible force. The shifting, creaking sounds of ship boards, of lines and ropes high overhead, the sounds of footsteps and voices, faded. Even the wash and hiss of the sea around and below them seemed wiped out. Nothing remained, thought the earnest boy, but the black figure of the magician standing beside him, the — surely growing? — intensity of sunlight outside the cabin window, and the silence like a vast and swelling dome rising ever wider and higher above their heads.

The diamond, which held Chris's attention, was held out toward the window between the magician's finger and thumb. With a careful gesture Mr. Wicker opened the casement with his left hand, and instantly the freshness and power of the fine day rushed into the small cabin as if it were some golden bird with beating wings. For a confused second, Chris almost imagined he could see the glint of light on gilded feathers as the bird curved around, and fancied he heard the pulsing of the sweeping wings.

A smell of salt swept in after the wind, and a spatter of sea spray touched Chris's right cheek. He did not take his eyes from the diamond in his master's fingers, afraid that if he did some vital movement might be missed.

Slowly, Mr. Wicker held out his right hand beyond the window frame over the sea. His tall slender body was rigid, and Chris realized that the smallest unexpected jolt would loose the lightly held precious stone so that it would fall and be lost forever in the curling water.

Every sound was blotted out, and staring at the diamond, Chris could not be sure whether it was his concentration, the glare of the sun reflected from sky and water, or magic that made Mr. Wicker's fingers seem to disappear until all Chris saw was the flashing of the stone. Staring at it as he was, Chris thought that a large measure of the light of the sun and the

123

sea seemed to be drawn into the diamond, for it appeared to in- crease its size, then to gradually turn until it was spinning in the air. Sunlight and sea spume were drawn from the brilliant sky and whipping waves spinning around the hard core of the dia- mond in a delicate sparkling thread.

Around and around, larger and larger — Chris's eyes hurt from the flashes of sun and he felt giddy from too closely watching the circling ball of light. Then all at once the silence began to ease. Small noises began to cut through to his ears as if through a wall, and Chris again made out Mr. Wicker's still rigid hand, now palm upward, on which spun the ball of light.

With a motion so quick that Chris could not entirely follow it, Mr. Wicker flung the spinning ball toward the prow of the *Mirabelle*. It darted over the crests of the waves as if someone had caught the sun in a mirror, and raced the dazzling reflec- tion over the water. Far ahead of the plunging ship sped the shining ball.

The boy and the man watched it out of sight, ahead where water, sky, and light made a unison on the horizon, then both covered their aching eyes with their hands.

The cabin swam back into Chris's sight, blotches of black and blue and gold, and he looked at Mr. Wicker.

"I don't understand, sir. What does it do, the ball of light?"

Mr. Wicker sat down wearily at his desk, his face showing a sudden fatigue.

"It is magic that I use rarely, because its usefulness is limited." He sighed, then glanced up with his slight smile. "It has an especial quality, the Light-Ball, Christopher. Directed to where I want it to go by mental concentration, once at its destination it absorbs sounds. When it returns, we may learn something of Claggett Chew and his company."

"Like a recording tape and radio-directed missile combined?" Chris asked eagerly. Mr. Wicker permitted himself a chuckle.

"If you like, Christopher, though it is made of different elements — sea, light, and crystallized earth, which is the diamond." He leaned back in his chair as does a man tired to his bones. "We need not expect it back until noon. And in the meantime, please ask that I be undisturbed before two, for the truth of the matter is" — he smiled again — "that I am the radio-direction of our directed missile, and must continue to concentrate on its course. So go about your duties. Under no circumstances am I to be disturbed before two o'clock, and ask Captain Blizzard to take in sail, to lessen our speed. We are approaching land." He waved one long hand toward the door. "Leave me now, Christopher, and carry my messages most faithfully to the good Captain, but return at noon without fail."

Chris walked slowly from the room. He held to the latch of the door to prevent the wind that still planed in from the open window from slamming it to behind him. As he shut it carefully he could see his master's figure, relaxed and at ease now, in the chair behind his desk. It is therefore understandable that when he heard the instant click of the lock inside as he closed the door, he gave an involuntary start, for it was impossible for Mr. Wicker to have left his chair and crossed the room in that instant. Then Chris smiled, shaking his head at the powers of the magician, and went on his way up the companion ladder to the bridge, to give his messages to Captain Blizzard.

125

# CHAPTER 19

*J*UST BEFORE CHRIS reached the bridge to deliver his message to the Captain, a laughing light-footed Susan left the cook's galley. The sleeves of her dress were rolled up above her elbows, and she dusted flour from her wide apron. In her hand was a plate on which she carried a newly baked loaf of bread, a knife, and a pot of honey, for in the eighteenth century there were no means for keeping butter fresh on the long sea voyages. The smell of the crusty brown loaf mingled with the sun and sea air, and as Susan had surmised, David Russell had a free half-hour between duties. He was coming toward her even as she went out the galley door, and they turned, smiling, to face one another.

What a different young man Susan saw approaching her from the one she had spoken with months ago in Brother Balch's empty church! Or who had climbed an apple tree to avoid being sent away from Georgetown and his loved young lady. Or who had been discovered parched, starved, and near fainting, in the hold of the *Mirabelle*.

David Russell, always tall, had now, with the constant physical exercise necessary aboard a sailing ship — climbing aloft into the rigging, walking up anchor, hauling sail, or battling with broken shrouds in all weathers — grown and broadened. When he had left Georgetown he had been a pleasant-looking young man of nineteen. After several months of sun, wind, and sea, he had come into his full estate, and was in look and action a man. The expression in his face had changed. From that of a fun-loving, easygoing boy, he now showed all the character and promise that Susan had early recognized in him. The line of his jaw, browned by the tropic sun, was determined; the laughing eyes now held a deeper gravity and tenacity of purpose. The smiling mouth no longer showed a boyish softness, but the firmer marks of manhood and resolve. In the months of the sea journey his young body had toughened. Strength and vitality were apparent in his limber walk, and his hands and feet which had, in Georgetown, seemed a trifle too large for the rest of him, were now in proportion to the width of his shoulders and his added height. It was no longer a boy who came toward Susan, across the deck of the *Mirabelle*, but a man grown and assured.

As for Susan, leaning against the bulwarks waiting for him, she too had altered. David, looking at her with tenderness and pride as she stood in the sun, could scarcely recall the child who had stood beside him in the dim church and offered him the dahlia-red pin that had been the cause of all the trouble. The face lifted to his that afternoon had been soft, pretty, and a little empty. Confronting him now was a young woman whose character had developed during the tedious days and weeks, as had his own. From a fretful temper at being thwarted in her plan of elopement, Susan now welcomed the opportunity the journey gave her of proving the endurance of her feeling for David Russell. And she had taken Becky Boozer's advice to heart, filling the days while David worked his passage with whatever lessons Miss Teackle presented to her, working with a new gusto and earnestness that quite baffled her governess.

Becky Boozer had proved a sound balance for everything that Miss Theodora Teackle was not. Becky was cheerful and optimistic, refusing to see anything but the best of every situation; Miss Teackle, never satisfied, always either expected the worst, or looked forward to some contrarifying circumstance, being bitterly disappointed when she was not able to find it. Where Becky had a great sympathy for everyone — except possibly Miss Teackle — and saw any faults in friends or acquaintances reluctantly, Miss Teackle had no difficulty in seeing everyone's shortcomings with the greatest clarity, and as a rule, to the total exclusion of any redeeming qualities they might possess.

She had early crossed temperamental swords with Becky over Ned Cilley and General George Washington. Ned, Miss Teackle claimed, was a rough, uncouth sailor, not overly clean. This distinctly applied also, asserted Miss Teackle, to that dreadful parrot, who should not be allowed to perch on Becky's shoulder. Becky replied at first with politeness, but Miss Teackle's disparaging remarks continued with growing asperity, until the two women were not on speaking terms. Miss Teackle had said:

"That sailor Cilley: never was there a better name for a man, even if 'tis misspelled, for Silly he most certainly is!"

128

"Ned is no such thing!" Becky countered. "A more loyal and kindly soul never breathed; why — Ned would give his life for anyone on this ship, if need arose, so he would!" She shot a glance at Miss Teackle, who stood hugging her shawl in the breeze beyond the galley door. " — *Almost* all those aboard, likely," she amended.

"Humph!" shrugged Miss Teackle, returning to the attack. "Certain it is he would have few teeth to lose, along with it, for they are gone already, but for a straggler or two." She gave a look of malice toward Becky to see if this arrow had found its mark. "The sign of any gentleman in any walk of life is to be clean, at *least*." Then, seeing the sparks of anger in Becky's eyes as she lingeringly put down her rolling pin upon the floury board, Miss Teackle hurried on. "Upon my soul, that filthy parrot makes better sense than the man does, and sounds more like one than does Cilley himself." She nodded her head confidently. "One day that bird will be well mistaken for a soiled rag and tossed overboard, and good riddance!"

Becky turned slowly, her voice all honey, her eyes shooting flames.

" 'Upon your soul,' say you, Mistress Teackle! Have ye listened to yourself, ever? Take my advice — never do it, for 'tis not worth hearing, at any time." Drawing herself up to her full, imposing height, Becky came to the door. " 'Upon me soul,' says she! Dear woman, 'tis too plain from your talk that you have none, for it must have withered long years ago when you were just out of your childhood, and no man's memory can go back *that* far!"

She grasped the galley door, her ample rounded figure towering solidly above the bony frame of Miss Teackle who

now listened, pallid with outrage.

"I shall say a prayer of pity for your poor mother, my dear Miss Teackle," Becky informed her, "who had no better vittles to feed you with, it is plain, than pickles, vinegar, and every sour thing. Look at yourself and ponder a while on what you see, before you dare to point your skinny finger at another. Pshaw!" she ended, looking Miss Teackle up and down with infinite dislike and disdain, "Master Cilley is a better gentleman than you'll e'er have the good fortune to know, for like any gentleman or lady, he never knowingly hurts another." She thrust her head forward, at once menacing and triumphant. "And what does that make *you*, Miss Teackle?" she exclaimed and slammed shut the galley door in her opponent's flabbergasted face. Miss Teackle had not learned until then that Becky Boozer was famous for having the last, and best, word.

But Susan and David, meeting in the sun, had no misgivings, no wish for last words on any subject, unless it should be what

was uppermost in David's mind as he took Susan's hand and kissed it, accepting from her eyes and her smiling mouth her love and trust. Susan shook her shining head at him.

"You may not kiss the other hand, David my darling, or we shall lose this fine loaf and the last of the honey. I want you to try my bread of this morning to judge if there has been any improvement."

They sat down on two upturned casks, the plate and loaf between them. Cutting the fragrant still-warm bread, the young girl gave her companion a keen quick look.

"You are very thoughtful, for such a fine morning, Mr. Russell," she said, covering the anxiety of her words with a smile.

David looked up smiling, but his eyes were not as happy as his mouth.

"Let us try this delicious-looking bread and honey first," he suggested, "for my mouth is watering at the sight and smell of such good food made by the dearest hands I know!"

Susan smiled, cut the loaf and spread honey on the fine slice, and then watched David's face as he took the first bite with as much intentness as if her life depended on his enjoyment of it. But his expression instantly reassured her, for a look of bliss came over his face, and the young man closed his eyes, the better to savor such a delectable mouthful.

"Here — " he said at last, offering the slice dripping honey to her — "you try. There never was anything so good this side of heaven! What a cook!" He laughed as Susan leaned forward to take a bite. "No wonder I love you!"

His eyes grew grave again at his own words, and they ate in silence, a bite for David, then one for Susan, unaware that Becky Boozer stood watching them from the galley door, General Washington on her shoulder, her roses and feathers gesticulating languidly in the balmy breeze.

When the two had eaten their fill of bread and honey, Susan put the plate by, and together they went to lean against the ship's side, Susan's hand in David's strong brown one. Susan looked up at him, shading her sea-colored eyes with her other hand when the shadow of the sail above them shifted. "Come now, tell me, David," she begged. "You have something on your mind, and troubles and misgivings are made easier when they are shared."

She gave him a smile of confidence which for once David did not return. He looked down at her seriously, his two hands now enfolding her small one in a tightening hold. At last, after searching her face for many silent moments, he seemed to find in it all he sought, and spoke.

"I have been considering something for many weeks, but

132

the time seemed not come, until now, to speak of it. Now I can no longer keep silence."

He drew Susan closer to him. "Susan, my own love, we have done as your father wished these many long months, and it will be many months more — perhaps even more than a year — before we see home again. If" — he hastily added — "it so please God that we return safe to our homes once more."

He bent his head to look down into the lovely face turned up to his, the wide eyes troubled now, reflecting what Susan saw in his.

"I asked you once to marry me," David said, "and you did agree then, Susie." David paused. "Events were so disposed that our marriage was deferred. Now I ask you again, for we have the means in our power to carry out our wishes — will you be my wife, Susan? I love you with all my heart!"

Susan's eyes filled with tears, of love, of happiness, and an unease at the future that she could not dispel.

"Oh, David! You know I will! It has never been otherwise in my head or my heart! But how can we, so far from home? There is no Brother Balch here, and no church — "

"No," David answered with determination, "but there is a perfectly honest way. If he will, Captain Blizzard, as captain of this ship, can marry us, if he agrees to it."

Susan's face shone with a sun of happiness more vivid than the strong tropical sun that was rising slowly toward noon.

"David! Darling! Why did we not think of that before! Of course he can!" Then her face clouded suddenly and she dropped her arms from around David's neck and hung her head, looking away from him out over the sea. "I do not think

133

I should, David, much as I long to be your wife," she said. "My mother wanted me to wait until I was eighteen —"

"And when will you be that?" David demanded, holding her closely to him. "Think a moment, darling — when will you be eighteen?"

Astonishment was written over Susan's amazed young face. "Why — in two months! I had lost count, this voyage is so long, and one week is so like another." She laughed excitedly, grasping David's arms with her firm young hands. "I don't think my mother could object now — do you? But perhaps I had better ask Mr. Wicker. Let us go and ask him now —"

As she turned, Chris ran past, on his way to help furl sail, and overheard her last words. The young girl was stopped short by Chris's careless words, called out over his shoulder as he sprang up the mizzenmast.

"You can't see Mr. Wicker until two o'clock, Susan! He has left strict orders that on no account is he to be disturbed until then." Seeing her desolate face, he added sharply, "He meant it, too. It's important. There may be troub —"

The boy bit his lip, but though he had stifled the words "trouble ahead" Susan's face creased into worried lines. She drew back, to feel David's protecting arm about her, as together they stood watching Chris clamber up the mast.

"David! There is something wrong ahead — I feel it," Susan whispered. "Trouble of some kind. Perhaps we should go ahead at once with our plan, as long as Mr. Wicker is to be left alone until two?"

She looked up. David returned her look.

"I must do my part now to help take in sail," he said. "Then we shall speak to Captain Blizzard."

# CHAPTER 20

*A* LONG THE GLEAM-
ing scimitar of a beach
beyond Acapulco a curi-
ous procession was mak-
ing its way. The sun had barely risen; a freshness still moved
in the air that would soon be dissipated as the summer heat
increased. Nevertheless, although the sunlight scarcely threw
a shadow worthy of the name, the leader of the group, a gan-
gling figure on donkey-back, was holding a green parasol over
his head. Osterbridge Hawsey, would-be gentleman, of fashion and otherwise, was on his way to his morning dip. One
long leg trailed an inch above the white sand; the other was
crooked nonchalantly over the front of the saddle. In his right
hand he held a pair of lorgnettes, through which he examined
the totally empty beach, in the other he held the ivory handle
of the scalloped parasol. Now and again he glanced pleasur-
ably at the swinging tassels that hung between the scallops
along the border of his sunshade, that kept rhythmic time with
the deliberate plodding of the burro. This animal, head down,
followed along behind a tiny Mexican boy of five or six, who

guided the donkey's nose by a red silk string.

Following Osterbridge Hawsey trudged a dark-dressed Mexican woman, her head and shoulders draped in the somber folds of a *rebozo*. On her head she carried a swaying neatly folded pile of fresh linen and towels for the "señor," wrapped in a gaudy fringed Spanish shawl.

Some little distance behind, splashing through the flattening waves where the sand was hard, Claggett Chew rode on a prancing black horse. The hard-faced man wore a three-cornered black felt hat, pulled over his eyes to shade them, and held his beautiful and high-spirited mount on a tight rein, so that the finely bred creature danced with annoyance at not being permitted to gallop.

Last of all came a lop-eared mule, twitching its tail at early morning flies and picking its dreary way in laggard fashion, paying no attention to the cries and beatings given it by its rider. This man was almost the most sinister of the three, and it was to be wondered how he had been hoisted onto the mule

136

back, for he had only one good leg; the other had a wooden stump below the knee. Moreover, he was humpbacked, and wore black patches over both eyes. Yelling and cursing at the indifferent mule, he showed yellowed snaggle-teeth which, with his lank oily hair hanging unkempt to his shoulders, combined to make him an exceptionally unsavory personage. At last, repeated beatings had the reverse effect; the mule, despondent, stopped altogether and for good. The humpback, his voice hoarse from his cries, with an angry gesture pushed back both eye patches to his forehead, peering out from behind them with two perfectly good, if evil eyes.

"Zounds! By my oath!" he cried to the obstinate mule, "son of El Rojo himself, get on! I dare you! Creature of Satan, as my name is Simon Gosler I shall get you to move on if it's the last thing I do!"

Slipping nimbly off the mule, the humpback caught hold of the bridle with one hand, tugging at it with all his might while he belabored the dozing animal with his crutch, which he had held before him on the saddle.

Cursing and swearing, as the sun rose inexorably higher, the cripple was dripping with the sweat of anger and effort when all at once the mule awoke. It pricked up its hung-down ears and gave a screeching neck-stretched bray in the direction of the dwindling procession far ahead. As if it had thereby sounded the trumpets of its charge, it tore the bridle from the cripple's hand with a quick twist of its head and made off down the beach at top speed, leaving the humpback purple in the face with rage. There was nothing for it, however, and after a while Simon Gosler began to hobble along the harder wet sand, his peg-leg sinking in too far every third or fourth step. Then he must needs stop, seize his knee with both hands, and muttering oaths and imprecations, haul it from the sucking sand.

Meantime Osterbridge Hawsey, examining the sandy slopes and dunes as if he saw them for the first time instead of every day for over a year, finally chose his bathing spot. The tiny Mexican boy, grinning widely at Osterbridge, who never ceased to astonish him, ran to the donkey's side to help his master alight. However, as the sand rose on Osterbridge's left side at that point, his foot was already on the ground and he straightened up as if getting out of an easy chair.

"Onofré — my parasol," he said.

Onofré, swallowing his laughter, grasped the parasol which he struggled to hold high enough over the head of the tall señor. Osterbridge shut up his lorgnettes, and without looking around, clapped his hands in a delicate manner. The Mexican woman, barefooted, came forward. Osterbridge waved a tapering hand.

138

"Onofré — go beat the bushes."

The small boy handed back the parasol. Osterbridge leaned his weight on one hip, watching the boy run up the wide beach to the shade of coconut palms and palmetto scrub. Picking up a piece of driftwood as he ran, the boy began beating the shrubbery and thrashing about in the undergrowth.

"*So* distasteful, venomous serpents," murmured Osterbridge to no one in particular.

Soaring against the crystalline blue of the Mexican sky rose the graceful coco palms, wearing their green crests of leaves like crowns, high above the other trees that crowded below them.

Claggett Chew had flung himself off his horse when Osterbridge stopped, striding up the beach to tether the restless animal in the shade of the trees. There he threw off his clothes until he was naked except for his smallclothes, or underbreeches. Paying no attention to Osterbridge who, now satisfied that no venomous serpents remained, strolled up into the shadow where the Mexican woman had left his dry clothes and towels; Claggett Chew strode into the water farther down the beach. He went in as if to swim were a duty and no pleasure, but once in, he moved out beyond the rolling breakers with powerful strokes.

Osterbridge, far from undressing, kept on a great many clothes. He left on not only his smallclothes, but long cotton stockings, and a long-sleeved shirt, whose ruffled cuffs fell over his hands. The parasol paraded into the sea with him too, for Osterbridge's "dip" was exactly that. He ambled step by step into the water, and when he was in up to his chest, held the parasol a little higher and bobbed gently up and down, uttering delighted cries:

"Delicious! So refreshing! Too, too divine! Just like chilled wine!" and the like.

Onofré sat crouched at the edge of the sea, his black eyes shaded by his jet-black ragged hair, his face alive with humor and interest. Never, in all his long six years of life, had he seen or imagined anything quite as strange or as unpredictable as the Señor Hawsey. To swim — yes, that was good. The other señor swam well and seemingly understood the water. But this one — all dressed up! What customs were these? And with a parasol! *Un paraguas!* Wonder on wonders!

His mother could not explain it. Nor could the priest, who merely shook his head at the mention of any of the foreign gentlemen, and crossed himself. No, they were passing strange, and Onofré never took his eyes from one or the other, afraid that something new and unexpected might escape him.

So it was he who first saw the motion, distantly on the water. Claggett Chew was far out beyond the crash of the surf, in deep water, and it was Onofré's keen sight that saw the triangular fin cutting the sea. He sprang to his feet with a cry, but before he could call out a warning, *"Ahí un tiburón!* Look out — the shark!" Claggett Chew had thrust his hand to his belt, and taking a deep breath, had dived under the advancing menace.

Onofré jumped up and down on the sand trying to see better, and Simon Gosler, tardily approaching, put a grimy hand over his eyes to watch. Maria, Onofré's mother, began to pray, crossing herself, and Osterbridge, carefully holding his sunshade, retreated gracefully into shallow water.

But it was all over in a few seconds. The great sea tiger

rolled, showing its back, and then Claggett Chew rose to the
surface, putting a bloody dagger between his teeth as he swam
lazily back to shore, coasting in on a breaker. At sight of his
grey-white skin, as the tall man rose from the foam with shark's
blood staining the knife in his mouth, Maria turned her face
away and drew a fold of the dark *rebozo* across her eyes.

Coldly triumphant, Claggett Chew, his eyes glinting with a
hint of power and excitement, walked haughtily to where his
clothes lay on the beach. Simon Gosler, exhausted by his long
walk, limped panting, after him.

"How goes it with you, Captain?" he called out. "That
were a close call — too close for comfort. Did the son of Satan do you any harm?"

Claggett Chew did not look around but continued to pull
his clothes over his wet body.

"He did me no harm, Simon. Rather he did me a favor —
I was vastly in need of exercise this morning. My striking arm
has had little practice of late; the foolish fish did not even give

me a good fight, and I am afraid will never attempt another. See — " he pointed a long sinewy arm out to sea — "his companions of the deep battle over him!"

The water churned where the dying shark lolled, as a sea rabble fought over the no longer dangerous corpse of what had once been a feared and deadly gladiator. Osterbridge Hawsey, still paddling in the sea, called out in his turn.

"Claggett! Oh Claggett! Bravo! Very well done!"

Claggett Chew did not even glance at the fop, but threw himself on cool sand where the shade of the coco palms moved in pointed patterns over the beach. Simon Gosler sat down heavily a few feet away, at a respectful distance, but within close earshot, and waited for what his master might say. After a few moment's silence, Claggett Chew spoke, as if to the sea more than directly to his henchman who sat nearby.

"Did the Indian runners bring reports after I left?" he enquired, as if idly.

Simon Gosler was evidently waiting for the question. His sly eyes glowed with cunning.

"Aye, Cap'n, that they did. I had stationed them, as I told you, a half-league apart down the coast for twenty leagues. When the ship was sighted, one carried the news to the next, and so on, until the last reached me."

"And — ?" asked Claggett Chew, making traceries upon the sand with the point of his dagger. Simon Gosler's eyes winked with malice.

" — And 'tis a merchantman, making slow headway after taking in sail."

Claggett Chew frowned, his icy eyes hidden under the bushy black crags of his eyebrows, so startling in the pallor of

142

is face. No tropical sun ever seemed able to touch his skin into a healthy glow.

"Furled sail, eh?" he muttered. "That I do not care for. I do not like the sound of it, Simon."

"No, Cap'n. I did consider that you would not. What does it betoken, think you?"

"I am not entirely sure," Chew returned slowly, "but I like it not. With this good breeze she should be making continued headway for the port." He paused, then leaning on his left arm, tossed his dagger in the air and caught it as it came down. "We shall sail as soon as dusk falls, Simon, to the little bay one league down. There the ship will be hidden from sight, but able to move out and overtake the merchantman so soon as she passes." He spun the dagger in his hand. "Our ship is old; we could do with a new one, Simon — and its cargo!"

Simon Gosler gave a cackle of anticipation and gusto. " 'Twill not be the first time you will have taken a new ship with all that is aboard her, Cap'n! And you say truly, for the *Black Vulture* is past her prime, fleet ship though she still be." He nodded to his captain.

Claggett Chew stared moodily at the sand, his thin lips pressed tightly together.

"Yes," he said bitterly after a pause, "our long drifting in that infernal mist seemed to have a rotting effect not only on the ship, but on all the crew save the three of us here this morning."

Simon Gosler's face drew down into hard lines. "Aye, that it did," he growled through his broken and yellowed teeth, "for where are they now, our crew? Died aboard from lack of food, killed in brawls on ship and on shore, or deserted to

143

vessels returning to known ports." He wagged his head dolefully from side to side. "Still, Cap'n, we are better off without every man jack o' them, if it so be they be not of our mind!"

Claggett Chew seemed to be comforted by Gosler's words, though his frozen vicious face betrayed no change of expression. Only his eyes, which he kept averted, lost a trace of their somberness. Simon Gosler, who knew his Captain well, sensed the change, and went on.

"That were a trip no man would believe — and indeed, to how many have I told it, as Osterbridge Hawsey has too, and every man smiles at what he terms our 'fancy.' " He spat expertly to one side, squarely hitting the seashell he had aimed at. "Aye," he said with a certain grim satisfaction, "had it not happened to me, by my oath I do believe that I should never have credited the tale myself!" He gave a short cackle of sour wonderment. "For whoever heard of a mist about a ship so thick no man could see through it, even though a wind blew. Nor one which did not blow away nor lift for ninety-seven days and nights? No." He wagged his ill-kempt head. "It is not to be wondered at that no one believes us. I shall never understand that journey to the end of my days. Nor how it was that the good *Vulture* ever came safe ashore."

Simon Gosler shifted his position where he sat on the sand beside his master, hauling his peg-leg to an easier resting place. Claggett Chew, absorbed either in distant thoughts or else in reliving those months of horror, said nothing. In a bit, Gosler made a gesture with his clawlike hands, their ragged filthy nails at variance with the neat powerful fingers of Claggett Chew.

144

"How did we ever live through those weeks of rot, tell me that, Cap'n?" he demanded, though it was plain he did not need an answer. "Men going mad from lack of food and water, as we drifted on. Fighting to eat the very rats in the hold!"

Claggett Chew spoke with the closest he ever came to amusement.

"Speak for yourself, you old scavenger! How did *you* manage to survive?" He raised his head to dart a piercing look at the man sitting near him. The evil face, covered with a week-old stubble of dark beard which accentuated the downward lines of the unwashed face, the greasy sparse hair, seemed to fill Claggett Chew with a mixture of revulsion and satisfaction. He dropped his gaze at once but went on speaking.

"You gave up your hoarded gold piece by piece, did you not, you foul miser?" He flicked out the hand holding the dagger and pricked Gosler playfully with the point of it, making still another rent in the already ragged clothing. "Eh? Buying rats at a ducat apiece, and a mouthful of rain water for five pieces of gold? Eh? Eh?"

He prodded his crony again and Simon Gosler yelped and edged farther away. Claggett Chew had not finished, however.

"You manage, do you not, you unwashed fraud? You always manage to survive, come what may. Is that not so?"

"Aye-aye, good Cap'n," whined the cripple, "Zounds! I do my best!" His nasal voice rose, explanatory. "Well do you know I had saved that money many a year, denying myself every pleasure — "

Claggett Chew snorted with an approach at humor. "And denying yourself clean linen too, or even free water to wash with, all those years, in case it should be charged to you!" The broken-nosed man was obviously enjoying his goading of Simon. Simon Gosler, eager to appease his master, whined in a servile way, rubbing his gnarled repulsive hands.

"Aye-aye, Cap'n. Just as you say. Denying myself all those things. But the money was mine. I could spend it as I chose. I chose to live!"

Claggett Chew looked up again with a faint trace of admiration in his indifferent face.

"That is why I have kept you by me all these years, Gosler," he said, "exactly that. That you 'choose to live.' You are like some battered tomcat who continues to outlive one mischance after another. You can always wriggle your way out, no matter what the trap." He rose, stretching. "I shall go back to the inn for some sleep, Simon, and later we shall board the *Vulture*. Assemble the crew El Rojo obtained for us, and see that they are at their places on board ship. Be there yourself, and we shall be ready at dusk to avail ourselves of a better vessel, and a new cargo."

Without glancing again at the cripple crouched below him on the beach, Claggett Chew swung himself onto his horse and, along the hard wet border of beach where the surf curled and flattened, galloped under the white heat of the sun toward the village of Acapulco.

Simon Gosler watched him go, and as he heaved himself to his feet, muttered aloud to himself.

"Aye, you can say you keep me for my ways of getting out of tight places, Captain Chew," he croaked sarcastically to himself, running his tongue over his lips, "but Simon Gosler knows better. Ha! What living treasure — and what *pirate*

146

treasure — does Simon hold the key to? Worth more than the ransom of a king! And worth more than the ransom of a pirate captain!"

At this remark the humpback laughed with high good humor, doubling over at his own obscure joke, slapping his good leg as he relished his own thoughts.

"Ha! A nation's and a pirate's ransom, no less, all held in the hollow of this hand — " And at these words he held out his bony, miser's hand.

He made a frightening picture, propped on his one good leg in the thin shade of Mexican palms, a black-coated man, his clothes grease-spotted and soiled, creased and rumpled; the hump on his back, false though it was and sewn to the inner lining of his coat, had by its weight over the years given him a stoop which was gradually making him into a true hunchback. His thin hair hung about his face from a bald spot on his head; the black eye patches were ready to be pulled into place at a moment's notice, if he thought the occasion served, and a blind man might gain a few pence by begging. Above all, the avarice and cunning so evident in his look seemed, on that fair sunny beach above the sparkling sea, disagreeably out of place. His crooked black body stood harshly against the sharp palmetto leaves and glistening sand, as with a long satisfied motion, he slowly closed his claw fingers over something he imagined he held in his dirty hand. His fist tight-closed, he swung it high over his head, shaking it triumphantly in the air.

"Aha!" he cried, "I, Simon Gosler, hold the great Claggett Chew here, in the palm of my hand! The palm of my hand! Knowledge is power!"

And so saying, the cripple hopped and hobbled off to his mule, standing quietly in the shade beside Osterbridge Hawsey's donkey. Soon the miser had it headed back in the direction of the inn.

When Simon Gosler seemed well on his way, the leaves of the palmettos near where he had stood rattled, and their fronds were pushed aside by a small pair of Mexican hands. Onofré's bright black eyes followed the departing black figure as he rode away, and the boy crept out of his hiding place to sit musing thoughtfully in the shade.

But Osterbridge Hawsey was ready to come out of the sea. He called to the waiting boy.

"Onofré! Onofré! My towel — at once!" And then, as if to himself, in the way he had, "How the sea winks, just there by the water's edge. As dazzling as a diamond, 'pon my soul! Oh — the *heat*. I shall be burned to an ember! Onofré! Onofré!"

The sun rose across the sky, and the waves flashed as if a shining ball spun over their endless rolling.

# CHAPTER 21

*A*S NOON AP-
proached, the *Mirabelle*,
under less canvas, moved
slowly forward. Off her
starboard bow the coast of Mexico lay scarcely a quarter-
league away, the long range of mountains wiped of color in
the heat. The hills rising behind the jungle that grew almost
to the water's edge shimmered and wavered to the eye in the
hot air, and the dying breeze, so fresh earlier in the day, fitfully
flattened and lifted the myriad greens of the coastal trees.

In Captain Blizzard's cabin two young people stood hand in
hand, while the Captain looked at them in meditative silence.

" — So you see," Susan was saying, "I am so nearly eighteen
that I feel my mother could not have minded such a slight difference."

She looked hopefully at Captain Blizzard, who stood solidly
in front of the young couple in his habitual stance, his hands
clasped behind his back, his three chins folded one on to the
other.

"Surely you see your way clear to marrying us now, Captain?" David urged. "Our voyage will be many months longer before we reach our destination — wherever that is to be, and months again before we are returned to our homes in Georgetown. Who knows what dangers may lie ahead? I should like to be able to take my rightful place beside Susan at all times, as her lawful protector."

Captain Blizzard nodded his head, his kindly eyes shining with sympathy.

"Indeed, I understand full well, and for my part, can see no objection to it." He unclasped his hands and reaching out, picked up the heavy brass-bound Bible which lay on his table, weighing it in his hand. "But neither you nor I may have the last word on the matter, for if I mistake not, it is not I but the owner of this ship, Mr. Wicker, who is Susan's guardian." He looked piercingly at David and then at Susan, as she stood there before him under the low ceiling of the Captain's cabin. "I should be lacking in loyalty, on my own part as well as on yours, if I agreed to a hasty marriage here and now without asking the advice of Mr. Wicker."

"Oh but — " broke in Susan. Captain Blizzard held up a short fat hand.

"There are always plenty of 'buts,' young lady, but the main 'but' is — as I'm sure Mr. Russell will agree — that if a marriage is worth entering into at all, then it should be gone into with solemnity and dignity, as a life union deserves, and not in haste and secrecy, with the bride in a cooking apron and the groom in a seaman's working clothes!"

His round amiable face broke into an irresistible smile as he ended, and Susan found herself joining him. She began to laugh, looking at her rolled-up sleeves and apron dashed

with flour.

"Captain," she said, "truth to tell, I had forgotten how I looked! You are right — neither my mother nor my father would approve of my entering into holy matrimony dressed as a cook, good cook though I hope I am!" She glanced up at David, who stood glumly beside her, and took his hand in both of hers. "And I am afraid, neither would my vain feminine heart," she added. Then, "Cheer up, my darling!" she chided, "it is not far to go until the time when we may speak to Mr. Wicker, and I am sure, will be able to persuade him. Tomorrow can be our wedding day, and I can in the meantime, make myself into a neater bride!"

David Russell, however, would not be wheedled so easily out of his disappointment.

"You are perhaps right, sir," he said to Captain Blizzard, as they prepared to leave the cabin, "but events have a way — for Susan and me — of complicating themselves on a sudden, and I am only fearful that some trouble, as yet unfore-seen, may prevent what we have waited for, so long and so patiently."

Captain Blizzard clapped the young man on the shoulder. "There is only one way to look at it, Mr. Russell," he said, "and that is to be sure that you are in God's care, and that He will make all things right in His own time."

David did not reply, and he and Susan went out into the shadow and coolness of the passage beyond the cabin door. Next to Captain Blizzard's cabin lay that of the owner, and David's hand moved toward the latch. It was a small, gentle, yet firm hand that held his back.

"Have patience, David, dearest," Susan whispered. "Not even two hours to wait — we can manage that." She smiled at him in the quiet of the empty corridor. "It will turn out well, David. The Captain is right. I know it will. It has to!" she said, and putting her arms about his neck she kissed him with all her strength.

David Russell returned the compliment.

# CHAPTER 22

*P*ROMPTLY JUST BE-
fore noon Chris went down
to Mr. Wicker's cabin. On
his way he passed Susan
and David, headed toward the deck, and they smiled greetings
to one another. Chris waited until the two were out of sight
and earshot, then he knocked lightly on the cabin door. He
heard the lock turn with a click inside, and Mr. Wicker's
voice call out, bidding him enter. When Chris did so, his
master was still sitting behind his desk, relaxed and at ease.
Chris closed the door and stood hesitating, staring at the lock.

"What is it, Christopher?" Mr. Wicker asked.

"I am trying to close the lock without touching it, sir, as
you just did," his apprentice replied, "but I don't seem to
have the hang of it, or else I need a magic formula that I
don't yet know."

Mr. Wicker rose from his chair, his face eased with amusement.

"Good lad! You never say 'die,' do you? Well, that is an
easy trick. Here — come and stand by me. There. Now

place your fingers against your right temple — so. Press hard. Harder."

Chris followed his instructions to the letter. He did indeed feel the small bone under his fingers where Mr. Wicker had indicated.

"Now — " commanded Mr. Wicker — "become your own hand turning the key, in the same way as you concentrate on changing your shape. Incantation 73, Book I."

Chris concentrated hard. In imagination his arm stretched out, longer and longer from his side, until, as he spoke inside himself the magic words, he felt his fingers touch the key, grasp it, and with a flip, turn it in the lock. As if to advertise his success, he distinctly heard the *click* as the bolt slipped home.

"Bravo!" cried Mr. Wicker. "See? It is the simplest of magic. I thought I had shown you that long ago. Try again a time or two."

Chris looked up at him. "What about the Ball of Light, sir?" he asked. "I don't want to hold that up — "

Mr. Wicker looked down, his face grave but his eyes amused. He shook his head.

"We have time, Christopher. It will wait. Now. Just once or twice more, to be sure you have the trick firmly in mind. No telling when such knowledge will be useful."

Chris did as he was told, and after practising several times, Mr. Wicker gave his shoulder an affectionate grasp and moved away to the cabin window.

"That will do, Christopher. You have mastered that very well, and it may stand you in good stead. It is a handy device, when one does not want to bother to get up and cross the room," smiled his master. "Now come and join me here, for I have other work for you to do."

The brassy light of noon streamed through the small panes of the window. The *Mirabelle*, nearly deserted of any following breeze, scarcely moved. The white-topped waves of the morning had changed to an imperceptible glassy swell. Chris went forward to stand beside the magician and Mr. Wicker held up his left hand. Looped in it was the magic rope with which Chris had practised so often. Mr. Wicker held it out.

"Here you are, Christopher. Make the easiest of all — a rope ladder. You need not bother to make it long enough to reach the water — it will lengthen itself." Mr. Wicker's face was alight with eagerness. "A most convenient thing, that rope," he went on. "It is a valuable part of my equipment," he commented.

Chris took the silky loops into his own hands and faced about into the cabin, to have space enough in which to make the magic rope ladder. Pausing only the space of a breath, in order to recall the magic twists and turns necessary to make a ladder from what was then an inert piece of cord, the boy abruptly flung the rope the length of the room, holding the other end in one hand. Before the rope could fall below the middle air, Chris began the long-practised turns. Doubling back on itself, he guided the rope into the form of a ladder. The magic line wove back toward him, rung by rung, until at last he had a double rope hook left to hang over the sill of the cabin window. Mr. Wicker's face behind him expressed his thorough approval.

"Splendid! Splendid! Very well done, my boy. There we

155

are. Now hang the hooked end over the sill. Then down you go to the water's edge to bring me back the Light-Ball to unravel. We shall discover what, if anything, the sensitive strands have recorded and retained."

Chris hung the magic ladder out over the ship's side. At this hour the crew would be eating their midday meal, and, as Mr. Wicker had planned, none were about to see Chris clamber down to the sea, or wonder at what he was doing.

After carefully testing the ladder to see if the rope hook he had made would hold his weight securely, Chris swung himself to the sill, and reaching out with one foot, found the top rung. Grasping the rope sides, he began to go down slowly.

As he had made the ladder he had counted the rungs that it had seemed possible to make — no more than eight. When he had gone down six rungs, therefore, he glanced below him to see how much farther down he had to go. He was barely halfway. He took one more step and then tipped back his head to look up at his master's face above him, looking small and isolated, where Mr. Wicker hung out the window to follow his progress. Mr. Wicker waved a hand.

"Go on! Go on!" he called softly. Chris put down a foot. That was the eighth and last rung, but, as his master gestured him on, he put down a searching toe. It touched another rung. Nine. When there had been only eight! Then Chris had to smile at his own lack of faith, and put down one foot after another with growing confidence. Every time, his feet found the rungs which he knew had not been made.

Well, he thought to himself, Mr. Wicker *did* say, "it stretches." It certainly does — and thank goodness for that! he chuckled to himself.

156

In a few moments he saw that he had reached the surface of the sea. Above him towered the white sides of the rocking *Mirabelle*. The ship moved steadily ahead, dipping and rising like some graceful bird. Chris swayed and rocked with the ship on his rope ladder, and he crouched on the final rung to look about him for the ball of light.

It was not hard to find. It lay on the sea, flashing and spinning within reach, a circle of radiance.

Gingerly, Chris put out his hand, wondering how to carry it back. Then, remembering that Mr. Wicker had held it on his palm, Chris slipped his hand under the sparkling object, lifting it up out of the water.

It rested on his palm, giving his hand a sensation as of a constant mild electric shock, as well as a tickling feeling as it continued to spin on itself. Chris admired it for a moment, and then the problem of going back up the ladder asserted itself. Problem it really was, for now he had not only to be completely steady, meeting every swing of the ship with a counteracting swing of his body to keep the ball from rolling off his hand, but — without taking his eyes from his precious prize — he could hold on only with one hand.

He had reckoned without the help of the magic ladder. If it had stretched itself to fit his needs, so too, could it fold back into itself, and Chris found that he had only half the journey back that he had expected.

Still, that was quite long enough and far enough. Gradually, carefully, he went up, and his relief was enormous when he could let the spinning ball of light pass from his hand to that of the magician, who leaned down to take it.

After that it was only a moment before he stood once more

safely inside the cabin, coiling the magic rope into a neat circle, now that for the moment its work was over. The dusky cabin, to its farthest corners, was illumined by the light from the gently spinning ball. Chris watched as Mr. Wicker took up a ruler from his desk, and using it as a spinner uses the distaff, plucked the end of the fine glimmering strand from the top of the ball. He began to turn the ruler with one hand, winding off the thread of light as he turned.

Chris leaned forward, resting his hands on Mr. Wicker's desk as he bent toward the glowing thread, wispy as a spider's web. Then, in the silence, grew the sound of surf upon a beach, and there, in the owner's cabin aboard the *Mirabelle*, came the sound of a man's voice.

"Zounds! By my oath! Son of El Rojo himself, get on! I dare you! Creature of Satan, as my name is Simon Gosler I shall get you to move on if it's the last thing I do!"

Chris and Mr. Wicker exchanged looks, and then both returned their gaze to the delicately unwinding thread. Chris had no need to hear Simon Gosler's name. He would never forget that whining voice, first heard a year ago. Now, it seemed, farther in the past than that. But Chris's recollections were interrupted by the sound of someone clapping his hands, and again, the humming, spinning Light-Ball gave back what it had recorded many miles away. Osterbridge Hawsey's high-pitched voice came petulantly into the cabin.

"Onofré — my parasol!" And then, "Onofré — go beat the bushes!"

So it continued, with both man and listening boy as still as if frozen into their positions, the magician seated at his desk, the boy leaning forward with his weight on his hands, as into the ship's cabin came the voice they had waited for, and the information they had half expected to hear.

# CHAPTER 23

CHRIS RAN TO THE bridge as if he had wings on his feet. The final words spoken on the beach near Acapulco had resounded in Mr. Wicker's cabin. The Light-Ball, the sounds which held its gossamer thread gone, had disintegrated in a burst of radiance and mist, and the diamond at the core had rolled onto Mr. Wicker's desk. For a moment or two Chris and the magician had stared at the stone, taking into themselves all the ball of light had given them of disastrous information. At last Mr. Wicker had sighed, picked up the diamond, and looked at Chris.

"So, my boy, you heard how it is to be, ahead of us." He shook his head. "I was afraid of something of this sort, and more than ever regret the presence of the three ladies on board." He rose, shrugging his shoulders. "Well, it cannot be helped now, that is abundantly clear, and some plan of escape must be made for them. Let us see what can be planned, Christopher, for the time is short."

The magician and his pupil talked together in low tones, and after a while Mr. Wicker nodded.

"Yes, this is best. So — summon the others at once, and then be off with you, and may good luck and God's protection be with you, lad!"

Chris understood what he had to do, and his heart beat with excitement. This, he thought to himself as he ran, was more like it! This reminded him of the exhilarating times he had experienced on his first voyage aboard the *Mirabelle!* Would any other time — this time — equal it for excitement? he wondered. It was hard to imagine how, but something was beginning, that much was certain. He tore up to the bridge and, breathless, gave his message to Captain Blizzard and Mr. Finney.

"Fast as you can, please, sir, to Mr. Wicker's cabin! You and Mr. Finney both, sir!"

Dashing down to the deck he sprinted along one side and down the other looking for Amos and David. He found them, with Susan, in what was now Becky Boozer's galley. Schooled, now, to danger and sudden change, Chris did not blurt out his message before the two women, but beckoned David and Amos aside.

"Hurry! Mr. Wicker expects you both in his cabin — soon's you can get there! Say nothing — just go!"

With a bland face which he had trouble wiping of the excitement he felt, he smiled at Susan and Becky. He stood in the galley doorway, his body blocking the sight of Amos's and David's disappearing figures, as they ran toward the owner's cabin. Becky looked around, half concerned.

"Ye're mighty out of breath, Chris, so ye are. What is it this time, answer me that?"

Chris gulped and tried to look innocent. "Not a thing, Becky, except that I'm hungry again. You must have given me too small a lunch."

He grinned at her indignant face, the roses and feathers on her huge bonnet shaking with annoyance.

"Come now, boy," ejaculated the exasperated Becky, " 'tis bottomless ye are, and no mistake! Here — take this extra loaf made by our Miss Susie, and this piece of ham, and get out of our sight!"

But Chris persisted, for he was taking food for no immediate hunger.

"What about a flask of wine and water, Becky? How shall I wash all this down — "

" — 'thout a kiss from my Boozer!" put in General George Washington. Becky had to smile, and reached to a shelf behind her.

"Here," she said, "I had just filled this for Ned, who is to relieve Abner Cloud at the helm any time now. I can fill him another. Take it, boy, and be off!"

She thrust the leather-covered bottle at Chris, who threaded his belt through a ring at the bottle's neck, and breaking the bread into convenient chunks which he stuffed into his pockets along with the ham, he waved jauntily to Becky, blew a saucy kiss to Susan, who laughed at him, and ran off.

Only one sailor sat high on the crosstrees as lookout, and Chris, putting his fingers in his mouth, blew a shrill whistle. The man looked down, Chris beckoned, and when the sailor reached earshot, Chris gave him the message Mr. Wicker had told him to say. This took the man on a brief duty below deck and left the *Mirabelle* for a short time without lookout. It also

allowed a boy with a long rope coiled over one arm to slide
down another until he hung, swaying, just above the sea near
the prow of the ship. With rapid turns and flicks the rope
became what Chris knew so well how to do — a small rowing
boat. Jumping into its solid shell and grasping the two ends of
the rope, which instantly became oars, Chris with one long
pull had the little craft racing over the sea far ahead of the
tardier *Mirabelle*. The magic dinghy darted around a point of
land that hid Chris from the view of any aboard; then he could
rest and take breath a moment as he looked about him.

He knew what he had to do, but Mr. Wicker had had to
leave it to the boy's ingenuity as to how the task was to be
done. Time, of which there was now so little, was the main
factor. Light, brilliant at that hour, too clear, was also something to be fought, for every object on sea or land showed up

in the sun with terrible exactness. Chris knew as he rested, breathing fast, that unseen eyes might be taking stock of him from some part of the jungle and he would never know it. The sun had only an hour since passed noon; the heaviest heat of the afternoon lay ahead.

This, Chris hoped, might be on his side, for both animals and humans alike, in the tropics, slept out the hottest hours of the day. Chris put a hand to his neck. Once more Mr. Wicker had hung about it the little leather bag Chris had worn a year before. In it, he knew, were what Mr. Wicker termed "odds and ends of magic," and, together with what he knew and had been taught, Chris felt confident that he could face almost any situation into which he might be flung by some unexpected turn of events.

To Chris had been entrusted the dangerous commission of finding out all he could of the lay of the land; the position of the waiting pirate ship, the *Black Vulture*, and any last-minute plans that might be made by Claggett Chew. Though Chris had wanted to take his friend Amos along with him, Mr. Wicker had considered the mission one which might be better accomplished by a single person.

Though it was not the first time that Chris had gone, solitary, on a difficult job, still, rocking on the glaring sea alone, the boy felt a target for enemy eyes, or gun, or poisoned dart. He therefore resolved to take on a less noticeable shape than his own, and headed the magic boat for the shelter of some rocks. These stood well beyond the nearest deserted beach, rising from the sea far out from shore.

Behind him, as he gained the sudden shadow of the broken promontory, lay the heavy silence of the hour. Even the sea seemed muffled in the heat, its roar subdued. Just as Chris rowed his boat out of sight of the jungled coast, his heart skipped a beat. Not only had he had the eerie experience we all know, the feeling of having been observed by someone unseen, but more than that, his quick young eyes had caught sight of a branch swinging back into place on the otherwise motionless beach.

Who? What? Chris felt prickly with abrupt perspiration of nerves and heat. Peering through a crack in the towering rocks that were acting as a screen, he could see no living thing on the beach anywhere. The violence of the sun on the white coral sand hurt his eyes, but look and listen as he would, he could see or hear nothing.

Putting a part of his bread and ham into the leather pouch, which he knew from past experience was waterproof, and tying it and his bottle of watered wine together, he clung to the rock, coiling what had been a boat into its usual form, which he tied like a belt about his waist. He smiled as he remembered how he had once asked Mr. Wicker if the pouch and the rope would remain with him if he changed his shape, and his master's smiling reply. "Of what good is magic, Christopher, if it cannot adapt itself to new forms?" So now, shaking off his fears at having been seen, the boy took a deep breath, said a magic formula at breakneck speed, and with a splash, a porpoise plunged through the sea in the direction of the village of Acapulco.

One moment later, a wet Mexican boy called Onofré, whose curiosity was difficult to satisfy, clambered around the crags where he had thought he had seen a tall boy, and looked, astonished, for the boat that had moved so quickly over the sea.

# CHAPTER 24

*HE FACES OF THE* men gathered about the desk in Mr. Wicker's cabin were solemn and anxious. Mr. Wicker stood silent, waiting for everyone to be assembled.

David and Amos arrived first, and stood a little to one side, as was fitting, since they were the youngest. Then, with a surprisingly light tread for so large a man, Captain Blizzard came in closely followed by Mr. Finney. The first mate of the *Mirabelle* closed the door of the cabin behind him, and all stood looking expectantly, if gravely, at Mr. Wicker, who faced them for a moment in silence. At last he said:

"Gentlemen, I am sorry indeed to call you here on what is a serious matter." He looked down at the map spread open on his desk top, then he gestured to chairs nearby. "Be seated, Captain — Mr. Finney; David. Amos, you stand here behind me where you can look over my shoulder. Draw your chairs close, gentlemen, so that we may be able to study this map — "

Chairs scraped over the floor boards as without a word the three men drew up to the desk. Mr. Wicker himself sat down facing them and folded his hands, looking at them quietly one by one.

"What I had dreaded, Captain Blizzard, has now come to pass," he began. "We are not yet out of the way of our old enemy, the pirate long wanted by the law, Claggett Chew."

Captain Blizzard and Mr. Finney started back in surprise and exchanged astonished looks.

"What!" exclaimed the Captain, "has he not yet been hanged, nor found the traitor's grave he richly deserves? How can this be?"

Mr. Wicker shook his head impatiently. "That is something that perhaps we shall never know. Certain it is, however, that I have indisputable knowledge that he is not only close by, but intends seizing this ship and all upon her at dusk this very day."

Alarm and consternation were evident on all faces except that of Amos, who, sensing a fight and added excitement, grinned from ear to ear, but was wise enough to say nothing. Captain Blizzard recovered first from his surprise and leaned forward over the map to question Mr. Wicker.

"Have you knowledge of how he intends to make this seizure, Mr. Wicker?" he asked.

"No," Mr. Wicker looked back at him, "beyond knowing — you know better than I, Captain, having had previous experience of it — that Claggett Chew will stop at nothing to achieve his own ends. He undoubtedly knows that we are unarmed, while he, we need scarcely speculate, will have a crew of cutthroats and brigands who will make a shambles

167

of the *Mirabelle* and murder our loyal crew without a qualm."

David broke in at this point, his face white. "What about the women, sir?" he demanded. Mr. Wicker swung around to face him.

"Exactly, David. What about the women? This is why I was so reluctant to take the responsibility of having them on board, but the damage is done, and here they are." He threw out his hands. "I have asked you all here that we may consult on what to do, for time is running out, and a plan of action must be made at once."

Captain Blizzard spoke. "You have a plan yourself, sir?" Mr. Wicker nodded absently. "Then let us hear it before we present any other."

Mr. Wicker continued to look at the map before him, and turned it so that the men in front of him could see it more easily. He put one forefinger on a spot off the coastline. The three men and Amos leaned forward, their eyes on the finger.

"At this spot," Mr. Wicker began, "the *Mirabelle* sails at this moment." The finger moved forward to trace the indented line of the shore, where bay after bay fretted the land. "The coast we are following is most irregular, as you see," he went on, "while here" — he indicated a deeper bay than the others — "is where Claggett Chew proposes to hide his vessel, the *Black Vulture*, in order to sail out after we have passed, and overtaking us, make us an easy prize."

Four pairs of eyes followed this closely. Captain Blizzard looked up.

"And your plan, sir?" he urged.

"My plan," said Mr. Wicker regretfully, "is to turn tail.

The *Mirabelle* is not as fast a ship as the *Vulture*, but time is still in our favor. If Claggett Chew expects us at dusk, we still have a few extra hours in which to turn back, and during the night, make good headway out to sea. I have sent Christopher ahead to see what he can discover, but should we turn about now, he will still be able to overtake us. There is no fear of Christopher's being left behind."

He stopped and looked from face to face. Captain Blizzard sat leaning on one plump elbow, pulling at his underlip with thumb and forefinger as he pondered. Mr. Finney continued to study the map, but David Russell spoke up eagerly.

"Sir!" he cried, "I have another plan." He hitched his chair closer in his excitement. "You say that Clagget Chew's ship is faster than ours. Then it might be that no matter what way we turned, we should never succeed in shaking the *Vulture* off. Now, suppose that we should employ a ruse? First, take the three ladies off in a longboat with two sailors to protect them, together with stores and water. Then, as you said, turn about, and sail ahead in such a way that the pirate ship would catch sight of us before dark, but not too soon to overtake us. The *Vulture* would start in pursuit, and as soon as darkness comes, the *Mirabelle* would make a wide half-circle, doubling back again, picking up the ladies, and continuing on past Acapulco." He looked earnestly at Mr. Wicker. "What do you think of that as a plan?"

Captain Blizzard's face cleared, and he slapped his palm down on the desk.

"I for one, like it well, Mr. Russell. This the *Mirabelle* is capable of doing without too much danger of being overtaken. How say you, Mr. Wicker?"

Mr. Wicker dropped his eyes and shook his head. "By rights it should work. The plan is well designed. But it will not be successful," he stated with certainty.

Captain Blizzard's face, as well as David's, clouded over once more.

"You are afraid of the discovery of the ladies on shore?" the Captain wanted to know.

"But the shore is uninhabited," David broke in. "They could hide at the join of jungle and beach."

Captain Blizzard put in his word. "Truly, sir, I do think the risk of discovery very slight, if any exists at all. The Mexicans, we have heard, are not unfriendly. Given the slower speed of the *Mirabelle*, and the little time we have at our disposal, I must admit this seems as good a plan as comes to mind. I cannot better it," he asserted.

"For my part, I agree with the Captain," Mr. Finney said. David looked proud, and leaned back in his chair, waiting for the final decision.

Mr. Wicker kept looking at the map, as if he did not like to look elsewhere, and continued to shake his head.

"I can only say, Captain and gentlemen, that though the plan seems a good one, it will not prove successful." He sighed. "However, there is a great element of risk in whatever plan is accepted. I see I am outnumbered. We can do only the best we can. So, please God, all may yet end well."

He rose, turning his dark shining eyes on David Russell.

"Are you willing to risk the care of Susan, together with Miss Teackle and Becky Boozer, to Ned Cilley and Abner Cloud?" he asked. "They are the two most trustworthy members of the crew, and would be good fighters if need arose. Your youth and energy will be needed here on board to replace them, else I should have suggested that you be one of the party." He glanced about once more. "Do you agree to this, Captain, or do you offer any other suggestion?"

Captain Blizzard, getting up from his chair, shook his head with decision.

"No, sir. This seems entirely wise and satisfactory to me."
He paused, as if seeing Amos for the first time. "What about
the boy, there? How about letting him go with the ladies
too? He shoots well, and will do his part."

"Please, Mr. Wicker, sir!" Amos begged, "leave me go
along with Miss Becky and Ned!"

Mr. Wicker considered him, one hand on his shoulder.
"Yes," he said, "this is very good. Amos too shall go ashore."
He turned again to the Captain. "Very well, Captain. All is
agreed and decided, but" — and he looked slowly at the three
faces before him — "I want it to be remembered in the future
that I like it not, and have serious misgivings. Still, so must
it be. Mr. Finney, I bid you go and warn the ladies that in
one quarter-hour they must quit the ship for a few hours.
You, David, find Abner Cloud and Ned Cilley, and see to it
with them that the longboat is well provisioned and has ample
water. Also guns and ammunition. We must be prepared for
the unexpected. As for me, I shall clean my own guns, and
then join you on the bridge, Captain, when the ladies go
ashore."

The three men filed out, followed by Amos, and when he
was once more alone, Mr. Wicker clasped his hands behind
his back and strode up and down his cabin with bent head.
Pulling up short before the racks where his guns were laid he
muttered:

"I do not like it. I do not like it at all!" and stretching out
his hands, took down the first of his two guns.

# CHAPTER 25

*I*N THE TORRID damp heat of the tropical afternoon, Acapulco lay torpid. The streets were as silent and empty as if night reigned. Not a soul stirred. Sleeping peons lay in shady corners, buzzed over by lazy flies as the sleepers snored the heat away; dogs were stretched dozing under the coolness of stairways or under shrubs in the square, and even the raucous birds scarcely murmured to one another, so oppressive was the heat.

The Sign of the Seven Seas was as quiet as everything else, its doors open wide to lure any breeze inside, its shutters closed once more, this time against the battering gold fists of the sun instead of the stealthy evil fingers of the night.

Along the shore, at the beach where, only a few hours before, Osterbridge Hawsey had enjoyed his gentle dip, a porpoise cruised along the top of the sea, leaping and plunging in the freshness of the water. Then, as it leapt, catching sight of the nearby bell tower of Acapulco's church, the big fish dashed to the shadow of rocks near the shallower water, and in a moment, a wet white curly dog climbed over the shoal and shook itself thoroughly, once on dry land.

It looked a sorry sight, as bedraggled as a white rat, its curling hair plastered to its small body. But the hot air of midafternoon dried the little creature before it had trotted far, and then it was proved to be a very silly-looking dog indeed. Not exactly a poodle, and not exactly a Maltese, white woolly curls covered its body but deserted its short legs, leaving them spindly and fragile-looking. Its ears flopped over its face, and it had a wet black nose the size of a coat button. As for its tail, it curled over its back in a very saucy manner, entirely bare except for a dab of white fur on the end which bobbed as the animal tripped along, giving the poor thing a most ridiculous appearance. Just before it reached the end of the beach it stopped beside a pool of sea water and peered at the surface. Its reflection was well mirrored in the still water, and the dog's jaws opened in what one could have sworn was a laugh.

Laugh it was, for Chris eyed his disguise with hilarity and approval, turning this way and that to see how the tail curled over and how the ears flopped forward.

Some dog! he thought to himself. Well, I'm mongrel enough to suit anyone, and perhaps silly enough to catch the fancy of a silly person — dear Osterbridge Hawsey! It will be fun to see and hear him again, but this time I hope I'm not found out by his pirate pal. He shook himself, getting used to his new coat and to being on all fours, and thought, Here goes! Whereupon the dog trotted up the beach to the shady path that led from it into the streets of Acapulco.

The white dog paused when it reached the square to get its bearings, hoping that no real dog would wake and come up to

make friends, for a real dog would soon discover that it knew nothing of dog language, and might raise a clamor or start a fight that would betray it.

The animal glanced to right and left. To the right stood the church, and diagonally across from where the curly dog stood, it could see a sign above a door which heralded an inn. This, thought Chris, would do as a starting place as well as any other, and accordingly he went leisurely across the square toward the open door. As he reached the border of the square, however, he stopped under the wide leaves of a banana to reconnoiter.

No one was in sight; nothing moved. Reassured, the boy as a dog came out of his hiding place, ran up the tile steps to the raised sidewalk, and skirting the wall of the inn, put his nose around the door.

Silence. Darkness. Distant snores. A strong smell of wine, dust, and savory cooking that had been richly flavored with garlic and spices.  Hm-mm! thought Chris, and he edged in a little farther, his eyes becoming used to the dusk of the interior.

The room into which the white woolly dog stared was some forty feet long and twenty wide.  An alleyway ran along the outside of the inn at the left, and a series of high windows, now shuttered, gave on to this space.  Through broken chinks in the shutters Chris could see glimpses of tumbling vines and flowers, so that, even though it was an alley, the outlook was not unattractive.

In front of these windows on the left of the room were three long tables, while a smaller fourth was set apart and at cross-angles, closer to the door and the window near it.  This table Chris rightly took to be the one reserved for the inn's wealthier customers, for there was more air, more to see, and better chairs around this Spanish table.  Along the other tables stood no chairs at all, but much-scarred benches on either side.

Up the right wall of the room a stairway rose, disappearing into somberness above, and beyond its foot, at the far end of the chamber, a doorway made an oblong of sunlight and color, opening to a partly covered patio.  In the patio Chris could make out the side of a well, and see the haughty struttings of a handsome turkey cock, preening himself before his quite indifferent turkey hen.  A low cackle of geese and chickens droned in from this open sunny place, and Chris could hear the faint splash of a fountain.  Over his head, peacefully upside down, leaf-green lizards held to the ceiling with their tiny feet, waiting patiently for flies.  Now and again there was a streak of motion as one made a dart for an unsuspecting mouthful.

Seeing the room to be deserted, Chris, every inch a stray dog, dared to go forward.  Somewhat timidly, still unused to his four-footed shape, he came around the corner and ran silently in to investigate the room. To get a better view, since he was now so close to the ground, he leaped up to one of the chairs, and put his forepaws on the top of the first, smaller, table.

His eyes were immediately drawn to the surface of the table, this being the serving place of the notables. The wood was teak, and had more than probably at one time been a part of a ship, long ago wrecked and washed to shore, for the surface was weathered and rubbed as wood is that has been turned by waves and polished by sand. But what interested Chris were the countless marks, names and initials, deeply carved into the wood. Looking closer, he made out one or two, crudely chipped from the surface, it seemed, with the point of a knife or dagger. Others were done with great care as if there had been a lifetime in which to form them:

JON WETTEVRE
RIIP, HOLLAND
ARTVVR 1663    DIEGO VAS    RAFAEL FERNANDEZ
LISBON
1567
PASCHE GIDE        Rch. BURNISH
SALT ASHE                              1787

Then, hastily scratched, as if with the stone of a ring:

PLEASE HELP ANNE CA —

The rest had not been completed.

Chris looked at the names and dates, trying to imagine what the men who had carved them had looked like, what had brought them to the inn, or where the wood of the tabletop had been before it had been put to its present use. He felt a shiver of pity and dread at the one woman's name with its unfinished plea for help. Where had she been, and what her distress? In what year, and how had it ended? He would never know, and for the rest of his life he was to puzzle over the table at the Seven Seas.

Time was passing. The dog looked about him from his vantage point. Below the stairway stood — most surprisingly — a marble baptismal font. It was carved with saints' heads and winged cherubim, supported on a pedestal of twisted stone. Then Chris noticed the wine stains dripping down the edge of the font. So the brigands who frequented the inn scoffed at the church to the point of using a baptismal font for their grog!

Chris shook his head and, tired of his canine shape, went over to the shadow inside the door to the courtyard where, crouching against the wall, he took back his own form. This rested him for a moment. He was grateful for the brief respite, and as he straightened his arms and legs, which felt as if they had been forced into a size and a pattern too cramped for them, Chris saw a sliver of afternoon light glint on something that winked from a dark corner. It lay on the far side of the door. His curiosity overcoming his caution, he leaned over the bright open doorway and picked up the object.

It was a gold Spanish doubloon, but even as Chris slipped it for safety into the leather pouch about his neck, he heard a sudden sharp indrawn breath, and a voice almost beside him called out:

"*Quién allá?* Who is there?" and as Chris, his heart thumping against his side, changed back into his disguise as the white dog, the crablike silhouette of Modesto darkened the doorway immediately above him.

# CHAPTER 26

*F*OR A MOMENT Chris cowered back against the wall, trying to press himself out of sight of the man towering above him. For both to the dog that he seemed and to the boy he really was, Modesto was a frightening sight. Had Chris retained his own size he might have been as tall as Modesto, or even overtopped him. But as a small dog, Modesto towered high and black above him in the doorway, his dead white eye almost seeming to glow in the shuttered dusk of the inn room. His one good eye darted from side to side, searching out the moving shadow that had startled him.

All at once he caught sight of a pale blob of something near his feet, and bent down to stare. Chris, hoping for the best, jumped to his four feet, wagging his absurd tail in the best canine style, and lolling his tongue out in an expectant way, looking up into the fearsome face thrust down toward his with as trusting an air as he could muster.

Modesto was confounded, but only for a second. Evidently a small white dog was not what he had expected to find, and with an oath he straightened up, ignoring Chris and going forward with nimble speed to look under tables and in every corner, still unsatisfied.

Chris, taking courage, came after him, and when Modesto paused, baffled, scratching his untidy head and still shooting looks on all sides, Chris made so bold as to jump up playfully at him to see what sort of a response he would get.

The response was immediate and painful. Modesto's bare foot shot out, catching the white dog in the ribs, spinning him through the air. He fell with a thud, and got slowly and sorrowfully to his feet. Then, as if for the first time realizing his power, with a rapidity which excelled even Modesto's movements, the white dog dashed across the room, gave Modesto a piercing bite in the calf, and whirling in a streak of white, ran for the open door behind Modesto.

With a yell of fury and pain, the one-eyed man was too quick for it. He lunged out, diverting the dog's dash for freedom with his arm. The dog had to swerve and double back, and in that instant Modesto was after him.

There then began a chase around the four tables, the benches, and the chairs. Modesto was screaming with pain which was more hurt pride than hurt calf, and the longer he was obliged to chase the dog, the angrier he became. Oaths filled the air, together with the clatter of first an overturned chair, and then a tottering bench, which went down with a resounding crash.

Stirrings and annoyed voices could be heard all over the inn. The peaceful hour of siesta had been thoroughly and completely ruined. As the white dog, beginning to pant, made a scurry for the door leading out to the patio, the infuriated figure of El Rojo suddenly blocked that opening, shouting in his turn at Modesto to know the cause of such a commotion. Still hopping about and grabbing for the agile dog, Modesto called out:

"Be careful, señor! The scurvy creature has bitten me in the leg! He may be mad from the heat, and I shall die of the madness too! Catch him, and help me to wring his neck!"

El Rojo lumbered into the chase, and one long arm swept out to catch at the dog as it tore between his legs, the heavy figure of the big man ripping out a handful of white curly fur.

Chris was tiring badly, yet he did not want to rush from the inn, for once out he would never be able to get back — at least not in his dog form, which was a convenient disguise. He looked at Modesto, with his dead white eye and shock of black hair hanging above the raging black eye, and at El Rojo, his red face more than ever congested from his efforts, both coming gradually toward him with arms outspread. Chris backed up, step by step. He was watching first Modesto, and then the red-haired man. With a sickening sense of hopelessness he felt the hard cold column of the baptismal font against his back. Beyond it to the left lay the doorway, but Modesto stood in front of that escape. Away to the right lay the door to the patio, but El Rojo blocked that exit.

Chris wriggled into the small space behind the column of the font, considering frantically what he was to do.

"Now we have him, señor!" Modesto screamed excitedly.

"I shall break his neck with one hand!" returned El Rojo. "I am sick of having my siesta disturbed!"

The cornered dog looked desperately from side to side, its

ribs heaving. El Rojo, with his arms spread wide, made a motion to snatch the little animal, when, quite how neither Modesto nor his master could see, the little dog appeared to lean with all its strength — which seemed far greater than its size — against the stone column. The dog braced itself against the wall, pushing outward on the pedestal. To the unspeakable amazement of master and servant, the stone font shifted, swayed, hesitated, and toppled outward, the heavy marble top with its saints and cherubim rolling onto El Rojo's foot as the whole crashed to the floor with a thunderous din. In the second of consternation caused by this unforeseen move, and the bel-

low of pain from El Rojo, the little dog had slipped past Modesto's hand, and with the last remnants of its energy, had whisked around the corner and up the stairs.

El Rojo screamed with agony, hopping about on one foot while he clasped the other injured member in both hands. His oaths were such that even the lizards scampered to the other side of the ceiling, where they once more became immobilized.

Meanwhile the dog, turning to the left at the top of the stairs, saw a narrow space under the shutter-door of a room, and without time for thought, squeezed itself, exhausted, underneath.

# CHAPTER 27

ANYONE INTERESTED in the study of faces and expressions would have had material for thought as the longboat pulled away from the side of the *Mirabelle* in the white glare of the afternoon.

Miss Teackle occupied the best place in the stern of the boat, a black umbrella held rigidly over her disapproving and disquieted person. Her long pale face, made the longer by the tight, flat hair that framed it, was as compressed with displeasure as the lines of her thin mouth, pressed to a hard narrowness. Her bony body was encased, more than dressed, in an uncompromising black gown, utterly devoid of either style or charm. It set off to bad advantage her sallow complexion, which neither the sea air nor Becky Boozer's good food had cleared or colored.

Susan, unhappy and somewhat frightened, sat next to Miss Teackle. She had left her parasol behind, and a leghorn straw hat with a wide brim and a crown circled with a falling blue ribbon shaded her skin from the penetrating rays of the sun.

Small traveling cases lay at the women's feet, and Susan's eyes, resolutely holding back the tears she fought, strained to stay on David's face for as long as she could see it.

Becky Boozer alone looked cheerful and composed, sitting at one side (which weighted the boat considerably in that direction), her colossal bonnet shading not only her face but most of her huge body, its roses and plumes waving and dipping a farewell to the ship and a welcome to the shore.

Ned Cilley and Abner Cloud had difficulty in pulling the boat, for it was intended to be manned by more than two sailors, but they bent their backs under the sun and heaved at the oars in the clear blue water. This, as the two sailors widened the distance between themselves and the *Mirabelle*, changed from a dark blue to a deep blue-green. Patches of clear jade then showed, where the sand rose toward the shore, and paled as the boat approached the beach.

In the very prow of the boat, pulling on an oar as best he could and doing his part, sat Amos. His round dark head was uncovered to the sunshine, and he was stripped to the waist for the row in. Young as he was, a year less than Chris, his body was strong and muscular, and he had grown on the voyage, bidding fair to become taller than his friend.

General George Washington, perched on Becky's shoulder in the shade of her hat, eyed the *Mirabelle* and then the growing height of the jungle as they drew closer to shore with a certain measure of approval. At a movement from Susan, he began to chatter, shifting from foot to foot on his human perch.

"Pretty face! Pretty — how about a kiss? I need a kiss or a flagon of ale to sustain me, so I do!" but he did not succeed in bringing a smile to any face excepting Becky's. Now and again she looked down at the wicker basket at her feet, and once bent to lift the checkered red and white cloth that covered it. Looking underneath with an expert's glance, she seemed relieved, settling back again in her usual relaxed and happy way.

Instead of gazing back at her friends on board the *Mirabelle*, at the black-garbed figure of Mr. Wicker, standing between Captain Blizzard and Mr. Finney on the bridge, somberly watching the boat grow steadily smaller as it crossed the little bay, Becky faced, with obvious curiosity, toward the beach and the high band of green where the jungle stopped and the beach began. She was evidently glad at the prospect of feeling land under her massive feet once more, and as the breakers near the beach could be felt and heard, she turned to Susan. She ignored Miss Teackle, who as pointedly ignored her.

"Feel, dearie!" she exclaimed, with the enthusiasm of a young girl, "them waves lift up this heavy boat as 'twere a leaf! Sure, and we'll enjoy all the fun of the fair as we go in — the swings and that!"

She spoke to rouse the girl, whose expression she understood, and to distract her thoughts for long enough to help her govern her emotions. To anyone who did not know Becky her remark seemed merely one of careless interest but as she had hoped, it distracted Susan, who took her eyes from where they had wistfully held to David's, and saw how close inshore they were.

"I hope they will not overturn us, for I do not know how to swim, Becky, do you?" she said. Becky laughed and threw up her hands in a kind of resigned horror.

"Saints preserve us!" she cried, "no more do I, but I do believe and pray that if we should be flung into the sea, I should float like any cask, so I do!"

"So do I!" echoed General George Washington. Becky and her bird broke the spell for Susan, and she could not hold back a smile. Miss Teackle turned her head away with a sniff.

"That bird!" she scoffed to the empty sea. "Dear General Washington would shudder indeed if he knew what bore his name!"

The breakers humped their blue backs and hissed as they gathered speed to battle with the shore, from which they forever arose only momentarily vanquished before they began the assault again. Miss Teackle clutched her ugly bonnet to her head with one hand, her umbrella, weaponlike, in the other, and uttered a piercing cry.

At the cry, Ned Cilley, Abner Cloud, and Amos feathered their oars and looked around. Seeing how near they were to the land, and feeling the giant muscles of the sea lifting up the boat as if it weighed no more than air, they gave one last mighty pull and shipped their oars. The three then turned about in their seats, ready to leap ashore when they should beach.

Becky was about to give a whoop of joy as the craft rushed in toward the beach and the foam, but she recovered herself in time, and clapped a hand over her mouth to stifle such an unladylike sound.

With a grinding thud and swirl of white water, the longboat was beached, and Amos and Abner instantly sprang waist-deep into the water alongside to haul the boat to safety before the next on-rushing wave — already curling forward like a grasping hand — could swamp the boat. By their combined efforts with each succeeding wave floating the boat a little farther, they were able to drag the craft with its passengers high enough so that the women could step onto dry land.

Becky was nearest, and should have got out first, but Miss Teackle pushed past her. Miss Teackle put out her hand for support, but Ned Cilley, who had been about to offer his gnarled fingers to Becky, bent down abruptly to examine something in the sand just as Miss Teackle stepped out, and had it not been for Amos's quickness, she would have fallen on her face on the beach. Ned straightened up with an expressionless face, but there was an unholy twinkle in his keen blue eyes which Becky caught and answered in kind as she was ceremoniously handed out.

Susan jumped lightly last of all, swaying a little on the solid ground after so many months on board a tossing vessel. Amos climbed back into the boat to bring out the few parcels, and when he went up the beach with them, found that the ladies had made a slow progress toward the shade. Miss Teackle led the way, her umbrella erect above her head, though she waved Abner on in case there should be wild animals, crabs, or serpents in their path. Behind her came Susan, once more looking and feeling a prisoner. Last plodded Becky Boozer and General Washington.

When they were grouped at the edge of the jungle in the shade, the longboat drawn high up upon the sand far below, Ned Cilley addressed them.

"I has orders, ladies, from Mr. Wicker and Captain Blizzard, so I have, and this is what they did caution us to do."

He glanced over his shoulder at what seemed impenetrable forest behind him. "They did say to me that for us to remain on the beach was not safe, and so my orders is to make a resting place for us just inside the trees and shrubbery, so that we don't all stand out like furrin objeks upon the beach." He motioned to Amos. "You, Amos, take this knife and come with me. We'll clear a space for the ladies, and you, Abner, keep your gun handy while we work."

Even Miss Teackle, though she would never have admitted it, could feel the authority in Ned Cilley's voice. Susan looked, for the first time, less drawn, and as for Becky, she beamed with pride and affection.

The man and the boy, working fast and hard, cleared a small space near the top of the beach, leaving a protecting fringe of palmettos to screen them from the sea should any boat approach.

When all was ready the women picked up their various bags and necessaries, and moved over to sit on the cleared sand. It was Susan, looking about her, who cried:

"Why, look — there's a path, a well-worn path!"

And all at once what had begun to seem easy, in the space of those few words, was easy no longer.

# CHAPTER 2 8

*THE ROOM IN WHICH* Chris found himself was the front bedroom of the inn. He lay, to all appearances an exhausted dog, panting on the cool tiles of the floor. In a moment he noticed that the room was high-ceilinged and airy, and as his ribs began to heave less quickly and his heart to pound less fast, he looked about. The tall windows were shuttered, and he surmised that it was these that opened on to the balcony above the inn door. Along the wall, near the shuttered door which had allowed him a refuge, stood a high carved cupboard. Evidently the room had no closet for clothes other than this. A chest of drawers and a chair stood near the windows, and a small table and straight-backed chairs took up the center space. Together with a sofa, they gave the room the appearance of being partly a sitting room. The huge black wood bed was pushed with its head against the right-hand wall, and as Chris wearily turned toward it, he felt, before he saw, the eyes of its occupant on him.

Osterbridge Hawsey, reclining on a pile of pillows, perhaps to give him the illusion of coolness even if none existed, was looking at his unexpected visitor with an increasing interest. The noise of the chase below had evidently roused the fop from his nap, as it had everyone else, but he had not bothered to move from his comfortable position to find out the cause, and now waved a tapering hand at the little dog.

"Tut, tut! Who asked *you* in?" he said to the dog. "Are you the cause of that *frightful* din downstairs? If so, you are a horrid little thing. Stand up! Let me have a look at you."

This was just what Chris had hoped for, and tired though he was, he threw all his energy and ingenuity into trying to charm Osterbridge Hawsey. For he knew that if he could please Osterbridge, who was spoilt and willful, he would be safe as long as he could remain with him.

So at Osterbridge's command he jumped up, his absurd tail curling over, the pompom on the end switching from side to side as he wagged it. He lifted his flopping ears as far as they would go, and stared back at Osterbridge. To his enormous relief Osterbridge burst out laughing.

"Why — what a ridiculous-looking object you are, to be sure! Where in the world did you come from, and what *can* be your parentage? I never saw anything so silly or saucy in all my life. Come up here, little one — up — up!"

At this moment heavy running steps pounded up the stairs, and after pausing momentarily at the top, as if uncertain, turned to Osterbridge's door. A sharp knock followed, together with Modesto's voice.

"Sir! Señor Osterbridge! We are looking for a dog to kill! He caused El Rojo's big toe to be broken and created a terrible confusion. And he has bitten *me!*"

With a flying leap Chris bounded on to the bed and dived under the sheet, head foremost. Unfortunately his tail remained outside, just under Osterbridge's chin. The fashionable gave a shriek of amusement and could scarcely speak for laughing, but was finally able to get out a few choked words.

"Go away, Modesto, go *away!* There has been enough noise already without your adding to it! Kindly take my deepest sympathies to El Rojo for his toe — " He broke off to laugh, as much entertained by the thought of the big man hopping about holding to his foot, as by the blissful ignorance of the little dog who imagined himself entirely out of sight.

"Is that dog — that son of Satan — a white dog — in there by any chance?" persisted Modesto, getting down on his knees to apply his one good eye to the space under the door. Osterbridge instantly lost his temper, pushing the telltale part of Chris that remained on view under the sheet.

"*Modesto!*" screamed the outraged Osterbridge, "how *dare* you spy on me from under the door! Son of a beggar without a name! Find Onofré at once and have him bring me up a pitcher of water and a cooling drink of limes. If you ever peer at me so again, I shall run my rapier through that wicked black eye of yours, that I can promise you!"

Modesto withdrew with alacrity. "*Santa María* protect me!" he cried. "Not my good eye, Señor Osterbridge?"

"Your *good* eye!" replied Osterbridge with finality.

Outside, Modesto rubbed his chin in distress, and touched his one good eye as if to reassure himself that it was still there. He limped away, muttering to himself, and when his feet were to be heard clumping down the stairs, Osterbridge drew back the sheet from where Chris hid, head down and tail up. At

193

this sight of the dog at close quarters, and when he turned, the speaking expression of gratitude on the animal's face, Osterbridge began to laugh again, but lowered his voice cautiously when he spoke to the dog.

"You have given me the best laugh I have had in months, in this godforsaken place, and I thank you for it. It is as refreshing as snow would be in this heat — why, that's what you are, a veritable snowball, and that is what I shall call you."

He began to stroke his new pet, and to show his appreciation, Chris licked his new master's hand and wagged his tail furiously.

"When Onofré brings me my drink of lime juice and water, he shall give you a cooling drink too, poor little thing," Osterbridge promised. "Where *is* the boy? Oh dear — everything takes so long in this country. *Mañana — mañana* and the next day — it's always to be the day after that." He sighed. "What it is to be marooned in a strange land. Ah me!" He looked down delightedly at his new plaything. "You will entertain me vastly, I can see that already!" Osterbridge assured the newly christened Snowball. "Why — just to see you puts me in a good humor — only — heavens! have you got fleas, I wonder?"

Horrified, Osterbridge began to search, and Chris had difficulty in bending his head so as to hide the tiny leather bag that hung at his neck from the fop's probing fingers. It was not, after all, what a dog would ever possess. To avoid its discovery, Snowball jumped down from the bed and sat looking expectantly at Osterbridge. Osterbridge took the hint.

"Very well, we shall go for a walk as soon as Onofré has brought my drink — for I am as thirsty as you are, Snowball.

And I must get dressed again. Oh *dear* — clothes off —
clothes on — clothes off! What a tiresome business and what
a despicable climate! Do you swim, Snowball? We shall find
out tomorrow."

As he spoke, pulling on his clothes, there came a sudden
rapid patter of feet running up the stair. Osterbridge Hawsey
flung open his door in time to see a door at the opposite end
of the corridor also swung wide, and Claggett Chew in his
doorway, his face black with fury. The pirate strode forward

two great strides to catch the arm of Onofré as the boy reached the top step.

"Well, boy!" he snarled in a grinding voice, "where are you off to so fast?"

"I had something I wished to tell my master, señor!" Onofré gasped, out of breath from running.

"You shall tell me instead!" Claggett Chew spat at him, twisting the arm of the little boy in such a way that the child cried out.

"Señor! If you please — my arm!"

"If *I* please, Onofré! Keep your arm whole and tell me your message, or have your arm broken and keep your information to yourself." And he gave an added twist that whitened the boy's face under his dark skin. Osterbridge, his face livid with his own rage, called out, and Chris poked his Snowball nose around the door jamb to follow what went on.

"Claggett!" Osterbridge's voice rose in defiance, "drop that child's arm at once. His message is for me, not you, whatever it may be!"

Claggett Chew did not relinquish his hold on the boy, and his eyes sparked with venom when he looked at Osterbridge.

"The message may be for you, but you have developed a habit of intercepting information that is meant for *me*. So I intend to hear this also, do you see?"

He bent his head, wrenching Onofré's arm and the whole light body of the child about, so that Onofré half fell to the floor.

"Very well, boy. Give me the message!"

Onofré's breath was coming in shallow panting gulps but he said nothing. All at once Osterbridge spoke.

"Tell him, Onofré, or he will break your arm. I shall not be angry. Hurry and tell him!"

"Pardon me, Señor Osterbridge. It was for you alone — "

The boy gave a sob from the pain of his wrenched arm. Then he took a deep breath. He turned his head slightly in Osterbridge's direction, and as he half lay on the floor at Claggett Chew's feet, directed his words to his master, not Chew.

"With your permission, señor — " he began.

"Get on with it, little scum!" growled Claggett Chew, becoming impatient.

The boy had been speaking in Spanish up to that point, but now, half fainting, he broke into tolerable English, as if he wanted his message to be perfectly understood by the master for whom he had brought it.

"Sir," he whispered, "Simon Gosler's Indians have surprising a small *grupo* of strangers in the forest — they a net throw over them — even the big woman and the one who is not so

197

*bonita.* There are two sailors, and a boy with dark skin. They are to be walking here. Simon Gosler wanted to hiding them for himself."

Osterbridge listened, incredulous, and as Onofré's head slid forward on the floor, all he could find to say was:

"Onofré! You speak English! Why did you not tell me?"

"The señor never asked," Onofré replied with a wan smile, and fell forward in a faint.

The two men uttered quick oaths. Claggett Chew dropped Onofré's arm and strode to the top of the stairway, while Osterbridge ran to his page boy. The two men, always at odds with one another, met sharply at the top of the stairs, and glared for a second into one another's eyes. Then Osterbridge bent down to scoop Onofré into his arms, and Claggett Chew continued to stamp downstairs and out of the inn, walking with long forceful strides, almost running; coatless, and without a hat.

Osterbridge laid Onofré on his sofa and knelt down with a goblet of wine. Onofré began to open his eyes.

"Here, good lad, drink and rest. He shall not hurt you again, I promise you!" Osterbridge said. And then as Onofré's color began to creep back into his cheeks, Osterbridge whispered: "When you feel well enough, in a few moments, you shall tell me what you did *not* say!"

# CHAPTER 29

*O*STERBRIDGE *HAW*-sey's room seemed all at once overpoweringly close. The heat of the whole town and countryside seemed to concentrate itself within those four walls, as Chris realized what the Mexican boy Onofré had said. With the battering blow of shock he heard that his friends had been so soon discovered and so easily made prisoner. To remain in his disguise as a dog was extremely tiring too, and yet he felt that for a little longer his best course was to remain hidden in this way, able to see and hear a great deal of what went on, and what was yet to take place.

He had also seen, with amazement, that Osterbridge Hawsey and Claggett Chew were more nearly enemies than friends. Perhaps their long months of being mewed up together, as well as their differences in the past, had combined to set them at odds. Or Osterbridge, tired of dull days away from the gay fashionable life he preferred, had turned to intrigues against Chew to create excitement.

Chris, sitting close to the sofa where Onofré rested, so that should the boy speak, he would miss no word, wondered if Simon Gosler, as Onofré had hinted, was also attempting to get the better of Claggett Chew for his own ends. It all seemed very involved, and although Chris was heartsick for Susan and Becky Boozer, to say nothing of Amos and Ned Cilley, he stifled his desire to go to them at once in what he felt to be, in the long run, the wiser course. For, he reasoned, Claggett Chew would return with news, or Onofré would again be sent out to obtain fresh information. In each case they would return to the Sign of the Seven Seas, and from where he was he could discover where his friends were to be taken and what was to happen to them. The waiting, he knew, would be long and nerve-racking, but he must stick it out if he was to help them to escape with safety.

Osterbridge Hawsey went from the room and returned shortly afterward with a bowl and pitcher. The bowl he filled with cool water and set on the floor for Snowball, and although Chris found lapping an awkward way to drink, it was better than nothing, and he was grateful for the refreshment which he had badly needed. Osterbridge refilled the wine goblet and offered it to Onofré, putting a dampened cloth on the boy's head. In a few minutes the little page sat up, rubbing his arm and smiling wryly at his master. Osterbridge looked at him with concern.

"How do you feel now, Onofré?" he asked.

"Well, señor. No big hurt." He shook his head. "Onofré hangs head that the message not given to the señor alone."

"You need not be ashamed, Onofré. No one could have known that Chew knew what you were doing for me. You have been very clever up to now." Osterbridge Hawsey narrowed his eyes. "But never forget, Onofré, Claggett Chew is extremely clever — more than you, and — I am afraid — more than I. We must be more than ever careful. In fact, you may have to bring me news at some other place than here, for now that Claggett Chew knows what you are about, your usefulness to me is almost gone. Perhaps you have a friend — "

"No — no, señor! Please! It is Onofré who knows better than others where are all the hidden paths. It is Onofré who must serve you!"

Osterbridge smilingly patted the child's head. "You are loyal, Onofré, and that is something that no amount of gold can buy. We shall have to proceed with caution, step by step. Now, tell me what you did *not* say to Señor Chew!"

Onofré glanced at the door, still open to the corridor, but the hallway was empty, and no one was near but the little white dog. Onofré's eyes lit up at the thought of his information.

"Señor, Señor Chew no find the peoples taken by Simon Gosler unless Gosler wants them found. He with the hump has robbing Señor Chew's coffers been. The coffers from the silver mines of Taxco, these many months. Never big sums, easy of missing, but every week so much and so much. With a part of the silver he has been paying my peoples from down the coast — not Acapulco peoples but the savager peoples who live alone farther away. It is these ones who know how to catching animals with nets, and these ones who know hiding places no one else can find."

Onofré's eyes were round and bright with all he knew, and with the effort of putting it all into the English he was so

proud of knowing how to speak.

"Simon Gosler and his Indians also put net over fine young lady. Face and hair and all of her *muy bonita*. Gosler think he get big moneys for all these peoples, especially young person."

Osterbridge seized Onofré by the shoulder. "Ransom, Onofré? Is that what he plans?"

Onofré nodded hard. "Sí, señor. Moneys. Many moneys before he gives back all the peoples." Onofré hesitated, swallowed, and then blurted out, "Is more. Under a high crooked palm tree on faraway beach near swamp, Onofré has seen he with the hump bury chests from Taxco." He smiled. "Señor Gosler bury them all alone, so no one see" — he grinned up widely into Osterbridge's leaning face — "except Onofré. Onofré not like to be in dark-night with serpents and batthings. But he wonder why Simon Gosler so tired all day, and so follow to see."

He paused, watching Osterbridge with his round intelligent eyes. But his master's face was intent with listening. Onofré went on.

"Señor Gosler drag chests one by one behind donkey, over sand and dunes, in quiet of night. Onofré see him bury eight iron boxes. Have silver in. Maybe gold. Onofré cannot open."

Osterbridge heard to the last word and yet still stood, clutching his page boy's shoulders as if hearing the echo of the words. With a jolt, suddenly coming back to himself, he let his arms fall, and turned to walk up and down the room, thinking.

"So *that's* what he has been at!" he exclaimed. "I might have known. No wonder he has seemed so content, here, all this time! He has been storing up treasure! Perhaps he means to steal the *Black Vulture,* and slip away!" He pounded his fist into the palm of his left hand. "Villain! Villainous, sly, evil, slinking villain! Somehow I shall fool him — the old miser. Rob him of every crumb of gold and filing of silver, and let him weep his ugly miser's tears of rage!" He spun around before Onofré and Snowball, who watched him unblinkingly as he paced, sputtering, back and forth.

"What about the ship these people came from, Onofré?"

Onofré shook his head sadly. "I do not know, señor. Onofré cannot see anywhere — "

Osterbridge mused. "So the ship got away, or meant to return." He paused. "It must mean to return, and the travelers imagined that they landed on a deserted part of the coast. They will certainly wish to open parley with Claggett in order to buy back their passengers — "

Onofré shook his head vigorously. Osterbridge looked at him, puzzled.

"What do you mean, 'No,' Onofré?"

"Señor Chew mean to take the ship. Onofré heard.˙ On beach. His ship is all used up."

"*That* it most certainly is!" Osterbridge snorted with disdain. "A more ramshackle, filthy — " He broke off. "But Onofré — then if he meant to seize the ship, he would take everything on board her, as well as all the gold. Simon Gosler's captives would have nothing with which to buy themselves free — Claggett would have it all!"

Onofré looked solemn. "Sí, señor," he said.

Osterbridge's face was grim. "Then the poor unfortunates are doomed!" he cried. "Doomed as I am, to a living death here, out of the spin of the world, in this beautiful backwash of nowhere! Or else they will be killed to get them out of the way!"

The fop, shaking off the languid airs with which he had been cloaked by the boredom of months, seemed to both Onofré and to Chris, who sat observing him, a new man. He looked limber, instead of listless, forceful instead of feeble, and interested instead of inactive. He looked down at Onofré who gazed up at him, wondering what was coming next.

"I am tired of Claggett's fighting and robbing and murder, Onofré! I do not know who these wretched people are, but I, Osterbridge Hawsey, will put an end to Claggett Chew's destruction if it is humanly possible. Let me see! Let me see!"

He struck his forehead with his closed fist as if to pummel ideas into his head, and then struck his fist into his other hand.

"I have it, Onofré! Go as fast as you can to Simon Gosler. Find where the captives are being taken if you can, but take care that you are not seen to spy. Then — when he is no longer near them, so that he will not suspect that you know their hiding place — run up to Simon Gosler, or one of his Indians. Make it seem that you are only just delivering a message from me. Say that I invite him and all his followers to a big *fiesta* here tonight. Tell him there is to be unlimited wine and food for all. I shall also invite the crew of the *Black Vulture* for these are all followers of El Rojo."

Osterbridge Hawsey's eyes shone at the prospect, not only of excitement at last, but the hope of getting the better, for once, of Claggett Chew.

"I have little left with which to pay for such frivolity," he went on, tossing his fair head, "but I still have a jewel or two" — Osterbridge smirked at his own cleverness — "and with these I can buy as many hours of drunkenness as I may need to help the captives to escape, and somehow, to prevent their being pursued by the *Black Vulture*." He laughed aloud at the picture. "Imagine it, Onofré! Just you — a six-year-old — and I, Osterbridge Hawsey, routing two such tried and true villains as Claggett Chew, master-pirate, and Simon Gosler, miser and crook! That will be a great day, and worth living for!"

He turned a transfigured face to the Mexican boy.

"You understand it well? Repeat it to me."

Onofré repeated his orders exactly. Osterbridge Hawsey was satisfied.

"Good. The *fiesta* is for tonight, here at the inn. When dusk falls. And if you can manage to get a message to the

poor people — do so, but do not do it if you risk being seen, for Gosler or his men would kill you without mercy. I know them. You do not. Go, boy. Good fortune go with you!"

Onofré slipped out and down the stairs as silently as a brown feather, and Osterbridge put on his coat and with it, his languid air. At the door of the room he wheeled and snapped his fingers at Snowball.

"Come, Snowball!" he ordered. "We shall give our instructions for a great quantity of wines and spirits to be brought in by El Rojo — " he smiled suddenly, the languor gone again — "to amuse poor bored Osterbridge!" he said. But as he moved to the stairhead he recollected something and turned once more.

"No, Snowball! I think I shall have better service from El Rojo if you are not along. He *has* got a broken toe due to a little white dog, after all!" He laughed softly. "No — go back and wait for Osterbridge. So. I shall shut the door. And see that you do not slide under it again!" he warned.

With his usual graceful walk, Osterbridge Hawsey sauntered down the stairs, looking the picture of fatigued boredom, calling as he went, "Señor El Rojo! *Dear* man — where have you got to? I have had *such* a lovely inspiration — "

Chris, impatiently waiting for his new master to disappear, was eager to change his shape to that of a bird or a fly. He wanted to regain, with all speed, the *Mirabelle*, wherever she might be. Once he had advised his friends on board, and seen them safe ashore to help with the rescue, he could return by evening to take part in the *fiesta* and to help liberate Simon Gosler's captives. It was vital that he should not be gone long.

And with a terrible pang of fear he realized that all he had to count on to save the lives of his dear friends was the light in the eyes of one Osterbridge Hawsey.

# CHAPTER 30

*T*HE NEXT FEW hours seemed like months to Chris. Changing his shape to that of a sea bird he flew off the balcony of the inn, rising high above the white walls, the tiled and thatched roofs, of Acapulco.

At first he felt insecure in his new shape. Changing from a four-footed creature to that of a feathered one was tiring in itself, and flying, when one is not used to it, is as hard as any other work which one suddenly must do — and do well — for the first time. He wished above all else to be unnoticed, therefore a sea bird was the best disguise.

He could scarcely wait to be high in the air, for even before he would dash to the *Mirabelle*, wherever she might be sailing, Chris felt his heart could not be at rest until he knew where his captured friends might be. Spiraling higher and higher above the town, the coast soon lay below him. This, he thought, was splendid! For now he could get an idea of the whole lay of the land.

The bay of Acapulco was broken into, he now saw, by an

irregular jut of coastland in rough shape like a boot turned inward. As he faced inland, balancing on the hot currents of air, the bay spread in a great curve to his right, while the craggy coast dropped sheer from the mountain heights, to his left. Beaches began once more in the distance on either side, and as he rose even higher, he saw an inland lagoon behind and beyond Acapulco to the west. The mountains rose, marching to the interior, on the right side of this lagoon, and swamps opened almost to the sea on the other. Something moving, far up on the mountainside, caught his eye. A white dot, then a black one, and last a flash of moving red and black.

Hats! And Miss Teackle's umbrella! With a surge of relief and joy, Chris swooped forward with all his might in the direction of the tiny moving dots.

He could now see which way they must have taken. In order to hurry them beyond Claggett Chew's reach, Simon Gosler must have mounted all his prisoners on mule back, taking them up on secret trails from the beach where they had landed. They had evidently followed a trail parallel to Acapulco but far above it, skirting around the rugged precipices until they were now out of sight of any spies the pirate might send.

The lagoon, Chris noticed as he scudded over, dipping low to acquaint himself with what lay far below his friends, was wild and desolate. Taking a moment's rest on the branch of a dead tree, Chris was startled into flight when a log beneath him in the water rose ponderously to the brackish surface and snapped at a turtle. Alligators! And a second later, writhing across the lagoon, Chris saw a snake whose markings his father had long ago taught him. Snakes too! Chris felt a shiver arrow

209

down his spine, for it could only be across this confused waste of swampy water and boggy jungle shores that he could bring the captive party, if he was to get them out at all.

Lifting on his wings high above the water he had a brief difficulty in rediscovering the group. Coasting back and forth along the mountainside he smelt, before he saw, the smoke of a fire. Following the scent, he discovered a small ledge of perhaps twenty feet in width where the mountain trail ended. Behind it, well hidden by interlacing trees, he could make out the black mouth of a cavern, penetrating into the rocky hillside. Mules were tethered nearby, and bundles were scattered at the entrance to the cave.

Alighting on a tree as near as he dared, Chris peered down

through the leaves. The first thing he saw was Ned Cilley and Abner Cloud, their hands bound behind them, seated on the ground back to back. Much nearer to him, nearly below the tree where he sat perched, Amos lay at length, his hands also bound. No sign of Miss Teackle or Susan, but a vigorous voice from inside the cave could be heard saying:

"Undo me at once, you villain! What a way to treat a lady, 'pon my soul! How am I to care for my young lady, and cook her aught in this godforsaken reach of land, if my hands be tied? Fie on you!"

So Becky, at least, was unharmed and as lively as ever. Chris gave an interior smile of relief. Then he looked quickly around. Whatever men had been sent up with the party were inside the cave. Hastily, Chris fluttered into the brush near Amos, and there gratefully took back his own shape. He longed to stretch his arms and legs but there was no time for that. He bent forward and whispered.

"Amos! Don't turn your head. Can you hear me? Wiggle your feet if you can but don't answer!"

Amos, after an instant's stiffening from amazement at the sound of his friend's voice, wiggled his bound feet with far more vigor than was strictly necessary.

"Amos — I'm just behind you — six feet back in the bushes. Roll back as far as you can — I don't dare step out — and I'll try to cut you free. Take it easy, but hurry, before they come out of the cave!"

Amos rolled and pushed with his feet until he lay on his side with his bound hands behind him, against the bushes. Chris, meanwhile, had put his hand into the neck of the leather bag, and his fingers closed over a knife he remembered. Sharper than an ordinary knife, this magic knife blade, Chris knew from past experience, would whirl when pressed against any object, cutting deeply, even through metal. However, only its keen cutting blade was needed now, and Chris laid it lightly on the stout cord that held his friend. As he did so he whispered once more.

"Amos! Pretend to be still tied! Stay as you are, and if anyone wants to know why you're over here, say you wanted to be in a cooler place. Maybe the guards will sleep. If so, then untie the others, but ask them to remain as they were until I can get back. Osterbridge Hawsey is going to try to help you all, and tonight he will try to get the crew from the pirate ship, as well as all Gosler's men, drunk and asleep. I'll get back somehow — with help. Have you heard all this?"

Amos nodded his head.

"Good!" Chris whispered. "Try to tell the others. How many men are there to guard you?"

Amos's lips scarcely moved but Chris heard what he said.

"Six, and Simon Gosler. But Gosler says he's going back to talk to Claggett Chew. To get our ransom."

Chris pondered this, then he said, "I'm going to whistle now, and show my face, so that Ned and Abner will know that help is coming," and he gave a low whistle that sounded for all the world like the piping of the boatswain when the captain is piped aboard his ship.

It had an instant effect. Both Ned and Abner looked up, trying to locate the sound. Chris whistled again, and as their heads turned in his direction he parted the leafy branches enough to show his face for a second. He could say nothing, but he gave them a grin so heartening that the two men's hearts leapt up and they grinned back with hope and relief.

At that instant Simon Gosler hobbled out of the cave, darting suspicious looks in every direction.

"Did I hear a whistle?" he said. "What was that?"

There was a rustle of twigs, and a bird soared above the trees, winging its way toward the sea.

"Oh — just a bird," muttered Gosler. "It is uncommonly high from its sea haunts. Well — what are you doing over there?" he demanded of Amos, but before Amos could reply the formidable figure of Becky Boozer appeared at the entrance to the cave.

Not one whit intimidated by any man, much less Simon Gosler, and furious at their treatment and capture, Becky in

213

a temper was something to be avoided. With her brawny arms on her hips, her dress rumpled from her donkey ride, but her bonnet as firmly on her head as ever, she marched threateningly up to Simon Gosler. He backed away, almost seeming to shrivel, until had it not been for a warning cry from one of his Indian followers who belatedly came up the trail leading a pack mule, Simon Gosler might well have stepped back into the void. Becky did not budge as she watched the hump-back leap to one side and glance with a frightened eye into the abyss behind him.

"Afraid of a pore weak woman, you grubby, evil man?"

Becky sneered. "Here am I, weak as water, captivated the dear Lord knows where, and all of us starving for a bite of nourishment!"

She leaned forward, and Simon leaned away, his eye patches pushed up on to his forehead so that he fastened a look both uneasy and yet proud on Becky.

"Eh, woman, here ye be, and by the orders of Simon Gosler, no less! Make what you can of it!" he as sneeringly returned.

"If I did not know you to be all skin and bones and not fit to eat, I'd make soup of you, ugly little man, so I would!"

215

snapped Becky. "And in case I change my mind give me leave to unpack my cooking utensils and few oddments of food, to feed these good people with me!"

At the mention of food, Simon obviously pricked up his ears.

"Food, eh?" he said, smacking his lips. "Heh, heh, so you shall, my good woman — "

"Don't you 'good woman' me!" Becky shouted back. Throwing up his hands as if for protection, Simon finally moved away.

"Very well. You shall cook. But for us too. Six of us. The very best you have. See to it. And while I wait, I shall trot down the mountain for a word with an acquaintance of mine, Claggett Chew by name." He looked slyly at Becky. "See to it that you have a good dinner ready for my return, or you shall be tied up again. Well! What are you waiting for? There is your basket of vittles and bowls! Set to!"

Becky looked him up and down. "I need helpers, you dolt!" she said with infinite scorn. "I need those other ones to help — the tall thin one, and my own pretty lady. Bring them out of that dark place into the light, or you'll have no fine feast, that I promise you!"

Simon, looking over his shoulder at Becky as he went, nevertheless returned to the cave, bringing back Susan, now without her hat and her face all marked by tears. Miss Teackle also followed, more dour-looking than ever. The two women were followed by two Indians, who were joined by three more. The five men squatted on the ground where they could watch their prisoners.

As Simon Gosler was about to mount his mule for the descent to Acapulco and the ransom he felt so sure of, the last of the Indians came to the mountain ledge, leading the last mule.

"Señor! he called, "near the village I met Señor Hawsey's Onofré — "

"And what were you doing near the village, ruffian?" Simon snarled, vexed. "You should not have been anywhere near it — "

The Indian looked embarrassed and guilty. "Sí, señor. The señor did tell me, and it is true I intended to come straight along the path. But I had promised my sweetheart to see her after the hour of *siesta*, and you know how difficult women are when they are crossed — I felt I had to go, or she would have boxed my ears and gone off with that fellow Antonio — "

Simon sighed. "Always something!" he said in his nasal voice. "Very well. And Onofré?"

The Indian's face lightened. "Señor — Señor Osterbridge gives a big *fiesta* tonight at *Los Sietes Mares!* Much wine for all! Many good foods! You are invited, and all of us — "

He looked brightly around. Simon, at the prospect of free wine, food, and card games, was much tempted. He glanced shiftily from one to the other of the expectant Indians who, like children, waited to be allowed to go to the unexpected festival.

"There are the prisoners!" Simon said. "They must be guarded. Two of you should do. The other four can come with me — "

Cries of grief and chagrin filled the air as the Indians clamored around Simon Gosler, each one begging not to be left behind. Simon shook one grimy hand at them.

"Think of the riches we shall all have from the ransom these people will bring us!" he shouted, as the Indians clutched at his greasy black coat and frayed soiled cuffs. "Those who remain will have twice what the others have, who go to the *fiesta!*"

This put a different face on the matter, and the Indians began wrangling among themselves as to which should stay. Simon slapped them all to get their attention.

"We shall draw lots," he said, and taking up six twigs broke two off short, then turned his back to make the ends even in his fingers. Turning back again, he offered a twig end, one by one, to each of the now silent Indians.

Every man drew, and loud were the jubilant cries of those who held the long sticks and could go to the feast, but glum and silent were the two who must remain. These two sat down without a word, eyeing their luckier companions resentfully as the four happy men started off down the trail at a trot. Simon Gosler alone remained behind for a minute longer. He looked directly at Becky, and then at Ned Cilley and Abner Cloud.

"I shall be back," he assured them, "and make no mistake about your guards. They will have orders to kill any who attempt to escape!" And suiting the action to the word, he spoke in rapid dialect to the two silent Indians.

Their only response were slow smiles that uncovered their white teeth, and a thoughtful and anticipatory look at the prisoners grouped before them. Simon Gosler seemed entirely satisfied, and after a leering triumphant look at Becky, kicked at his mule's sides and disappeared around a bend of the path.

# CHAPTER 31

*HE LONG HOT DAY* was ending when Chris returned from his flight to the *Mirabelle*. The hour he had spent on board in Mr. Wicker's cabin, talking to his friend and master, and to the Captain, Mr. Finney, and David, now seemed a dream only half remembered. Briefly, feeling the terrible pressure behind him of not enough time for all there was to do, Chris had stood before the horror-stricken men as he told all he knew.

Only once was he interrupted in his tale, and this was when David Russell looked at Mr. Wicker's grim face, his own face white and drawn, and said quietly, "Sir, my most humble apologies, for you did say that my plan would not work and yet I pressed for its acceptance. Had I been wiser and listened to you, this dreadful thing would not have happened." Mr. Wicker had only waved a hand, as if the rights and wrongs of the plan were now of little importance beside the task of recovering their friends. Chris had continued his story, and when he had done, after a pause he added to Mr. Wicker:

"Sir, you shall do as you see fit, but I should like to suggest a way out. It is dangerous, but any way out will be, I am afraid."

"Speak, Christopher, for time moves, and you must return with all speed."

"Well, sir, our friends are, as I told you, on a mountainside just here — " He pointed to the map. "The trail to it goes high above the village. It could be followed by landing sailors at the same beach where we left them, and by trailing the mule tracks. If a rescuing party could do this, I could attempt to take our friends off, somehow, across the lagoon to the beach that you see *here*, on the far side of Acapulco. Longboats must remain well offshore, for the surf is high there, and the coast and tide dangerous. The sand is eaten out by the water, and it would be hard for the longboat to land. With the smaller dinghy that I have the use of" — here Chris and Mr. Wicker permitted themselves the ghosts of two understanding smiles at the mention of the rope boat — "I could perhaps by degrees get the captives off."

"You mean that those going up the trail would fight the guards and also any others who might come to the attack?" Mr. Wicker questioned.

Chris looked up from the map eagerly. "That's it, sir. They would offer a delaying action to keep the pirates or Indians occupied while I got our group off." He hesitated. "It will be terribly dangerous, getting them off that cliff, and the only way I can think of at the moment is by rope ladder." He shook his head at the prospect, and those about him nodded in agreement. "The trail ends at the cave, you see," Chris went on, "and the only way out is either down the trail or over the cliff. Since we can't count with any safety on getting out by the trail, it will have to be down the cliff."

"What about the swamp?" Captain Blizzard asked.

Chris swung about. "That too is very dangerous, sir," he replied, "but somehow it will have to be managed. Is there a moon? I haven't noticed — "

"Yes," Mr. Wicker said. "No longer quite full, but enough." He hesitated, and then, knowing that Chris would understand what lay behind his words while the others would not, he said to the boy, "I shall come ashore at the beach on the far side of Acapulco, Christopher, to meet you and our friends, and give you a hand. If I can, I will help to ferry them over the lagoon, or else I shall help to guide them through the swamp and jungle to the beach."

Chris felt enormously relieved, and looking the magician in the eyes, showed that he understood that Mr. Wicker's additional magic powers would be put to use in this emergency.

"Thank you, sir," he said feelingly, "we shall need all the help we can get, I'm sure of that!"

David broke in. "Mr. Wicker, sir, may I have leave to fight with those who go up the trail? Feeling as I do I can assure you that I shall do the work of two men!"

Mr. Wicker understood that the unhappy young man felt in large part responsible for the capture of his beloved Susan, and nodded soberly.

"Yes, David. That we can arrange after Christopher has gone." He turned to put his hand on Chris's shoulder. "I know you are tired, Christopher. I should like a word with you before you go — "

221

Captain Blizzard rose at once, holding out his pudgy hand to the boy.

"We are old friends, Christopher," he boomed, "and although this seems an almost impossible task, yet I have seen you do others equally difficult." He smiled cheerily, slapping Chris on the back. "I know you will be successful, but I wish you all the luck in the world, for we cannot return without our ladies and Ned, Abner, and Amos, that is certain. And we shall not!" he declared.

Chris grinned back as he shook the offered hand, feeling much heartened by the confidence Captain Blizzard had in him.

"I hope you are right, Captain," he returned. "I shall be glad when this night is over," he ended fervently.

One by one the three men left the cabin, pausing to shake Chris's hand and wish him well, as he did them, on their mutually hazardous enterprise. When Chris and Mr. Wicker were alone, Mr. Wicker went quickly to his sea chest, and opening it, took out several phials. Mixing certain powders and liquids on his measuring scales, he rapidly compounded a bluish liquid that in the deepening dusk gave off a faint phosphorescent glow. The magician poured it into a goblet of water and held it out to Chris.

"Here, my boy. Drink this quickly, for it will restore and sustain you during this difficult night." As Chris took the goblet from him, Mr. Wicker cautioned with a smile, "Do not expect it to taste good, my boy. But the effect is excellent, and you will be grateful for it." As Chris began to drink, making a face, Mr. Wicker went on. "It will not only give you added strength — and I am afraid you are going to need every ounce

this night, Christopher — but it will wipe out any need for food or drink, and this is as well, for poison is so easy to slip into either."

Chris put down the empty cup and sat down abruptly, putting his head on his arms on the magician's desk. Mr. Wicker looked down at his pupil with affection and pride.

"It works well," he said softly. "In a moment you will awake as refreshed as if you had slept the clock around."

Before five minutes had passed Chris lifted his head, yawned, stretched, and jumped to his feet alertly, crying:

"Sir! how long did you let me sleep, when there is so much to be done?"

Mr. Wicker put out a soothing hand. "Have no fear, Christopher. No time that cannot be spared has been lost, but rather, much gained." He went again to his sea chest and returning, put a small sponge into the boy's hand.

"Here, Christopher. Put this in your leather bag of 'odds and ends,' and without fail, wipe the tip of Claggett Chew's whip with this sponge. Mr. Chew will pursue his usual practice of tipping the metal wire at the end of his whip with poison, and this must not remain. This you must wipe off first of all — and from his sword — as soon as you get to the inn. Do not forget!" His piercing eyes, so dark at that moment that their blackness and depth held an overwhelming power, warned Chris as no words could have. Chris nodded seriously.

"I shall not, sir," he said.

"And do not forget that in your leather bag are various oddments of magic which will come in — shall we say — quite handy, when the time comes?"

His smile gave Chris a lift of the heart, almost making him feel for a passing second that all the dangers ahead could be easily overcome. But his master's final words washed away this hope.

"Never forget for a moment, Christopher," he warned, "that Claggett Chew is no ordinary man. Beware of him!" he cautioned. "He will try tricks we have no knowledge of — but the oddments of magic in the leather bag may help."

He strode over to the windows of the cabin which he flung wider to the softening light and westering sun.

"Now — be off with you!" the magician cried. "I shall help all I can. Good fortune and God's help be with us all!" Mr. Wicker called, leaning out after a steadily rising sea bird that was flying fast toward the setting sun.

# CHAPTER 32

EVEN BEFORE CHRIS reached the Sign of the Seven Seas he could see, as he flew over the square of the town that great excitement had taken hold of the people. The usual lethargy of the village was gone. Knots of men and women, children and dogs, clustered like dark grapes around the door of the inn. Fires had already been built on the beaches near the town, springing like shining feathers from the ground. Chris had been infinitely relieved to see, as he passed high over it, that the pirate ship had not been moved from its cove but lay silent and seemingly deserted. Uneasy at the length of time he had already been away, Chris considered trying to sink the *Vulture* by boring a hole in its hull with his magic knife. However, he decided he had not the time to spare. He would have to take a chance on its crew becoming sufficiently besotted with wine to be of no further hindrance to him or any of the *Mirabelle*, and so he continued.

Had it not been that dusk was almost upon Acapulco, and that the gilded light of the falling sun lay at full length looking into the faces of the early roisterers on the beach and those grouped about the inn, Chris's return, even as the bird he seemed, might have been more remarked. As it was, the shutters to Osterbridge Hawsey's room above the inn door were partially open. Hopping down from the balcony rail to the balcony itself to peer inside, the bird saw Osterbridge standing at the chest of drawers eying himself in a mirror. Engrossed in perfecting his appearance, Osterbridge never noticed a bird walking under his bed, and it was only when, in this favorable hiding place, Chris had taken on the shape of Snowball, that he began trying to gain Osterbridge's attention.

He thumped his tail and whined, sticking his black-button nose beyond the edge of the bed where Osterbridge could not fail to see it. Osterbridge instantly spun around and looked down, and seeing the rolling, guilty eyes of his pet, looking up at him half ashamed and half in fun, Osterbridge put his delicate lace-ruffled hands on his hips and pretended to look annoyed. His elegant fair head cocked to one side, he contemplated the innocent bright eyes of Snowball, who batted his eyelashes at his master and opened his mouth in a doggy grin, continuing to thump against the bed slats with his tail.

"So-ho, my friend!" said Osterbridge, "do not tell me that *that* is where you have been all this while, for I looked, not an hour ago. You *rascal!*" He stamped his red-heeled, silver-buckled shoe. Snowball pulled in his nose only to stick it out again a little farther, and give an enquiring bark.

"Sirrah!" cried Osterbridge, trying not to be delighted and amused, "by my oath, you are without a doubt the very silliest small dog that ever I had acquaintance with! Absolutely *no* telling where you have been, you sly rogue! Off with some

lady-canine, or chasing cats, or heaven knows *what* pastime!
Well," he bent down holding out his hand, "come along out,
you shameless creature! Osterbridge forgives you."

Snowball instantly wriggled himself out from under the
bed, shaking off the dust he had collected on his way. He
certainly looked like a none-too-tidy house mop when he
emerged, capering about Osterbridge's silk legs and satin-
trousered knees with every evidence of pleasure. Osterbridge
took his silver hairbrush up again and turned away.

"Very well — very well. So you are home again. Sit down
and behave yourself. You shall accompany Osterbridge to the
*fiesta*. I shall dress you up in just a moment — "

In a few minutes Osterbridge had placed the last beauty
patch on his cheek, tweaked the bow that held his hair, and
switched his full velvet gold-braided coat into position. Taking up an ivory-headed ebony cane, he swaggered up and down
the room while Snowball watched him with pretended admiration.

"Well, saucy!" Osterbridge enquired of his pet, "how do I look? Perfect, I am sure! Now — come here, and I shall tie your woolly topknot up with a bow."

Snowball, secretly gritting his teeth, allowed a salmon-pink bow to be placed on top of his head. It merely heightened his already comical appearance, and Chris knew he must look like a circus dog, such as some he had seen walking on their hind legs behind the clowns. But Osterbridge could scarcely contain his good humor.

"*Darling* Snowball!" he cried, "there has never been such an entertaining dog as you, upon my word! You are a picture, and one I hope El Rojo will not want to cut from its frame. Come, jump into Osterbridge's arms, for I should not want any harm to come to you —"

Snowball jumped up on the sofa as the first part of his leap into Osterbridge's protecting arms, when Onofré knocked lightly on the door and slipped into the room. Osterbridge's carefree look vanished at once, his face changing as he asked, sharply, but keeping his voice low:

"Well, Onofré?"

"All is good, señor," Onofré replied. "Señor Gosler already is below, and has left only two guards — Onofré counted those who came back with Señor Gosler."

Osterbridge gave a piece of gold to the boy. "Good! You have done even better than I had hoped, Onofré. How does one reach the captives?"

"The trail lies high on the mountain above the church, señor, and I am thinking that Señor Chew looks now for a way to carry the people off to another hiding place."

Osterbridge reached out to grasp Onofré's shoulder in an

unconsciously hard grasp, so great was his consternation.

"What are you saying, child?" he demanded, entirely forgetting Snowball, who took the opportunity to jump to the floor and back toward the window.

"Am saying that the Señor Chew has been seeing the mountain bit by bit in his long looking-stick — "

"His spyglass, Onofré? Is that what you mean?"

Onofré nodded. "Sí, señor. Looking-stick brings far things very close-by. Señor Chew found the cave in his look-stick, and also in the look-stick saw the señorita who is so *bonita*, with the setting-sun hair and the pale skin of flowers."

Osterbridge shook the boy to make the words come faster. "And? And — ?"

Onofré swallowed. " — And Señor Chew is on his way back here to get his sword. He holds his whip. Then Onofré thinks he will ask El Rojo for Indians not drunk, and will go up the mountain for the señorita."

Osterbridge bent down, intent. "But why — *why*, Onofré? Will he kill her?"

Onofré's face broke into a beaming smile. "Oh no, señor!" he said. "Onofré, hiding behind a rock, heard Señor Chew send an Indian to find the priest. He said he thought he would make the *fiesta* into a marriage feast, and marry the fine señorita!"

Staggered as he was at this fresh news, only then did Chris remember the poison on sword tip and whip end, and making a dash for it, with quaking heart rushed out of the door, heading for Claggett Chew's bedroom to do his work before the pirate should return.

# CHAPTER 33

*B*EHIND HIM CHRIS heard Osterbridge's distracted cry of "Stop him!" but a minute later he gathered, hearing no pursuing footsteps behind him, that Osterbridge Hawsey had held back the little Mexican boy to question him further on this new development on the part of Claggett Chew.

Chris's heart was beating wildly as he reached the door through which Claggett Chew had come to catch hold of Onofré, only a few hours ago. Not only was Chris shocked to know that Claggett Chew intended to marry Susan, beautiful enough to catch a pirate's fancy, but — how could one know? — with his errant knowledge and long memory, perhaps Claggett Chew knew Susan to be an heiress as well as a lovely woman.

The boy's heart beat unevenly at the thought of being caught by so cruel and heartless a man as Claggett Chew. Seeing him seize hold of Onofré at the stairhead seemed a year away instead of only that afternoon. At any moment the pirate might reappear. Somehow, Chris would have to secrete himself in Chew's room in order to cleanse the poisoned tip of the sword and the whip of their deadly and invisible charges.

The door was not locked. Under Chris's fingers, for he had had to regain his normal shape, the latch felt icy cold in the sultry air. With a hasty look over his shoulder to see if Oster-bridge or Onofré had followed him unheard, Chris lifted the latch and slid inside, closing the door and leaning against it.

The pirate's room opened above the patio at the back of the inn, but in spite of the smell of roasting meats, garlic, and frying fish that rose from the kitchen quarters close by, the sounds of bustle and the rumble of rolling wine kegs below, Chris did not take time to look out the window to see what was going on. His first care was to make sure that the large room was empty; when he found that it was, he next made a search for a hiding place in case he should be discovered.

This instantly presented itself in a high, wide hanging cup-board for clothes, such as the one that also stood in Osterbridge Hawsey's room, and accordingly Chris tiptoed over to turn the key to it and look inside.

Claggett Chew, unlike Osterbridge, did not possess many articles of clothing. A few extra coats, and on pegs, his knee breeches. On the floor of the cupboard stood several pairs of high boots, and leaning against the back wall of the cupboard, the sword which Chris sought.

Chris did not hesitate. The closet being a good deal higher than his head, he had no trouble in getting inside. First, he got out the sponge, and taking the sword by the hilt in the dim light of the cupboard, whose half-closed door now let in only deepening dusk, Chris thoroughly wiped the tip of the sword and edge of the blade. It was as he was about to re-place it that he heard the sudden heavy and unmistakable foot-fall, and almost before he had time to pull the cupboard door farther to and press himself into the depths of the wardrobe, Claggett Chew had come into his room. He kicked the door to, and evidently began to throw his clothes off in haste, after lighting a lantern that stood on the round center table.

Chris dared not move, for he feared that any smallest move-ment might make a scratch or a rustle that would catch the pirate's keen ear and cause his discovery. But by turning his head very slowly and very slightly, Chris could put his eye to a crack in the wood and through this slit, have an occasional glimpse of what Claggett Chew was doing.

To his surprise he saw that Claggett Chew was washing and dressing with care. He was dismayed when it came home to him that the pirate would open the cupboard for fresh clothes. Chris changed himself to a fly, and squeezing through the crack which he had been using, was able to observe Claggett Chew in leisure and comfort.

The fly crawled up to a convenient piece of carving on the cupboard door and sat there at ease, following, with its many-faceted eyes, the movements of the big pallid-skinned man as he washed his face and neck, and then his hands and arms, to the elbows. This he evidently considered quite sufficient, rub-bing at his shaven skull with a cloth. He was a cruel, ugly man, and his size, even in that large room, seemed too broad of shoulder and too high from heel to head. The flickering lantern light was alive in the new dark, and cast deeply drawn lines on the pirate's face that accentuated the brutality in it; the intelligence misdirected into such evil destructive ways.

All at once, while wiping his drooping black mustache, Claggett Chew stopped short and began looking keenly about. First to the window, over which he slammed the shutters, then, turning his body inch by inch, he examined the walls, foot by foot.

A sudden chill of fear iced Chris as he flattened himself as well as he could behind the piece of carving. He knew with certainty, as he watched Claggett Chew, that the man had felt himself to be watched, had felt the unmistakable sensation of having his actions followed by unseen eyes. However, not finding any false board through which he could be seen, his giant hand tapping the walls little by little, the baffled pirate shrugged his massive shoulders. Just as he turned away, apparently satisfied, by some eerie power of his own magic, he whipped back, reaching up unexpectedly to the very carving behind which Chris's fly body pressed itself.

Chris flattened himself into as nearly nothing as he could achieve. The powerful fingers of the pirate just reached as high as the carved scroll, and Chris saw their blunt tips — now enlarged, it seemed, to ten times their normal size, to Chris who had become so miniscule — as the groping fingers poked into every crevice. The finger-ends blotted out the light coming up from the room. They could so easily have snuffed out a fly's life without even being aware of it.

But the carving was just deep enough. Even by straining and probing, Claggett Chew's fingers could not quite reach into the little whorl of wood where Chris tried desperately to make himself one with the wood's curve and grain.

At last, reassured to some extent, Claggett Chew drew a chair up to the table near the lantern, and pulled a quill pen, ink, and sheets of paper toward him. On the floor beside him he dropped his long leather whip which lay beside his chair, coiled as a rattler ready to strike.

Now, thought Chris, was his moment, for Claggett Chew would undoubtedly take the whip with him when he left, as well as the sword. Mr. Wicker's last words rang in Chris's ears. Get to the whip he must!

The table below him was covered with a fine cloth which hung almost to the floor all around. As Chris was debating how he could hide under it and regain his human shape — a highly dangerous maneuver but essential if he was to use the sponge correctly — Claggett Chew put down the pen, got up and went to the door of his room.

That was all Chris needed. With his heart in his mouth, the fly flew down, darting under the table, and as Claggett Chew went to the head of the stairs clapping his hands to get attention, Chris became himself, hunched under the shadowy bowl of the draped tablecover. Outside, Chris could hear Claggett Chew calling out to El Rojo. Chris took up the sponge and stretched one hand for the whip.

"El Rojo! Send Modesto to me at once!" Claggett Chew shouted beyond the door. "If he cannot be sent, then it must be you, for I have important work that needs immediate attention!" And before Chris could get the tip of the whip pulled beneath the table, Claggett Chew had stamped back into the room and reseated himself.

At the closeness of the pirate, Chris, brave though he was, quaked inside, for the pirate had an old score to settle with him that Chris did not even like to remember, and should he be discovered there in this room, he knew he could expect no

mercy from a man such as Chew. The pirate's memory was long and his venom grew with the length of his remembrance.

Chris let the end of the whip slip from his fingers. It slid back to the floor with an almost imperceptible whisper of sound which echoed to Chris's straining ears like the roar of surf on a rocky shore. Claggett Chew was immersed in his writing, however, and paid no attention. His big booted feet stuck under the table a few inches from Chris's knees, as the boy knelt, bent double, under the low piece of furniture.

In a moment the limping drag of feet on the stair heralded the approach of El Rojo, and hearing the more rapid scratch of Claggett Chew's pen over the paper in the otherwise quiet room, Chris once more put out his hand, pulled the end of the whip with its vicious wire tip under the cover, and began to wipe the wire carefully with the sponge.

He had barely finished his work when a long muscular arm shot down, and Claggett Chew's fingers closed over the coil of the whip which he could never be long without. He swooped it up to the top of the table, and simultaneously El Rojo knocked and then entered the room.

"Señor!" El Rojo's voice growled, in bad humor from the pain of his toe, "at your service. I trust your commission will be brief, for Señor Osterbridge has given me much to do with this *fiesta* at a moment's notice."

"Yes," came Claggett Chew's cold voice in abstracted reply, as he continued to write, "it will be brief. There — " The pen was flung down, and with an impatient movement the pirate pushed his chair around, the toes of his boots hitting Chris's knees.

"Here, El Rojo, is a marriage contract to be signed by my bride!"

El Rojo evidently gave a start of surprise, and then began to laugh.

"Ho! ho!" His hands went up to hold his shaking paunch. "The señor is pleased to make merry! A bride! Here in Acapulco! *Por dios*, among the slatterns here, which one can have caught the señor's fancy?"

El Rojo's mirth was short-lived. Jumping to his feet so hastily that his chair overturned behind him, there followed from Claggett Chew the malignant *hiss!* of the whip and a cry from the innkeeper. Peeping out through the fringes of the table cover, Chris could see a curved scarlet line on El Rojo's double chin, and glimpsed the look of fury and amazement on his face as he put up a hand to the lash cut. Claggett

Chew calmly coiled the whip again. The tone of his voice was deadly, more cutting, even, than his whip.

"You forget yourself, El Rojo," Chew informed him. "You are, my good man, an innkeeper paid to furnish rooms and food and in no way licensed to laugh at your guests. When I say I have chosen a bride, let me make myself entirely clear: I mean exactly that. A bride suitable for Claggett Chew could never come from a filthy background such as this setting — " he waved a hand with infinite scorn — "this flea-bitten little village and this roosting place for the scum of the seas — this inn! No!" Claggett drew himself up. "My bride is of quality, as is only proper for me; of extreme beauty and youth, and an heiress to a considerable fortune. Fate has sent her here, and Claggett Chew never lets good opportunities slip by."

He looked the innkeeper up and down as if El Rojo were of even lower rank than Dead-Eye Modesto, and with a gesture of snarling contempt, Claggett Chew took a silver piece from his pocket, tossing it at El Rojo who, though white with rage, caught it from force of habit.

"There you are, for your trouble, El Rojo, in taking this paper across the square to the priest, where I shall presently bring my bride. When she is my wife, she shall sign this paper which makes over her fortune to me." He gave a smile that was more sneer than amusement, his eyes as flat and levelly evil as a snake's. "Very well!" he snapped when El Rojo, still stunned by his own emotions, did not move. "Very well, you may go!"

Wordless, swallowing, his mouth working, El Rojo, feared across the whole of Mexico, backed from the room, clutching in one hand the paper Claggett Chew had thrust at him, and the piece of silver in the other. Once outside the room and the door closed behind him, the sweat of an almost maniac anger burst out on El Rojo's face. Clotted red patched his face once more, and the big man stood trembling at the offenses Claggett Chew had given him. He looked first at the paper, and then, slowly, at the piece of silver. His huge hand opened, letting the coin roll to the floor where it spun into a corner. He muttered, choking:

" 'Roosting place for scum'!" he whispered, his thick lips quivering as he stood in the silence of the corridor outside the pirate's door. "My inn — the *Sign of the Seven Seas* — a roosting place for scum!" He looked back at Claggett Chew's door and then at the door of Osterbridge Hawsey's room. "You are right, *Mr.* Chew — it *has* become the roosting place for scum. I must have a spring cleaning, a thorough cleaning, and that, soon!"

Still shivering from outrage, the innkeeper, holding to the stair rail, made his painful limping way downstairs. No one heard his mutters, except perhaps a fly, and then a little white dog, who followed El Rojo halfway down the stairs and then sat, looking through the banisters at the scene in the room below. Chris knew he must wait for long enough time to pass to allow the *Mirabelle* to be at her appointed anchorage off the beach near the lagoon. And, for the safety of them all, it would be well for him to know how successful Osterbridge's plan was, and whether the feast would incapacitate the crew of the *Vulture* and the followers of Simon Gosler.

So it was that El Rojo never noticed either the fly or the dog so close to him. And anyway, whoever heard of a fly or a dog understanding what human beings find to say?

# CHAPTER 34

*HE SCENE THAT LAY* beneath Chris's eyes as he peered through the banisters was one he ever afterward remembered. The high-ceilinged long room was black with night excepting for dim whorls of yellow where fluttering candles or lanterns were placed on the tables, and threw a wavering scattered glow. The faint illumination threw into relief the brown-skinned sailors crowding the room, seated, packed tight, along the benches on both sides of the refectory tables, or standing in noisy groups. More intense shadows were cast by the figures of Modesto and his helpers as they came in and out from the kitchen. They bore trays laden with food and drink; their silhouettes were thrown upon the walls in giant brandishing shapes that seemed to bend menacingly over those below them.

Snowball peered down as Modesto and a dozen sweating boys staggered in with plates heaped with cooked pork, *enchiladas*, roasted chickens, steamed clams, fried *róbalo*, and sweet yams. The Indian-pirate crew provided by El Rojo to man the *Black Vulture* did not wait for the formality of individual plates, but reached dirty fingers into the bowls, stuffing their mouths and dropping gobbets of food on the tables in their greedy haste. Wine and *pulque*, the fiery drink made from the *maguey* cactus, in no time made themselves felt. The overheated room reeked of highly seasoned foods, wine fumes, and smoke. Unwashed bodies sweated in the close place on the hot night. The unshaven faces under rough hair shone with the greases of the feast and the perspiration brought on by the spices and heat of the food. Men chewed, gulped; spat out undesirable morsels on to the tiles; belched, and swilled down the wine set in great earthenware jugs before them. Sometimes, not waiting for a free cup — for there were not enough mugs to go around — they would tilt the crocks up to let a cascade of staining wine pour into their mouths and overflow down their chests to the floor. Over it all, outlining here a jaw line, there a crafty eye, there again a grasping hand, high cheekbone or beaked nose, moved the harried flapping orange of the tapers, transforming the scene into one of nightmare.

At the smaller table sat Osterbridge Hawsey, a half-filled beaker of wine beside him, aloof and clean in the midst of the noise and brawling. He was evidently eating nothing though pretending to do so, and drinking little, while encouraging all those about him to drink deeply, eat and be merry. Chris, looking at now this group, now that, noticed the keenness of Osterbridge's eyes. If any man seemed to lag behind in his drinking, Osterbridge would saunter his diffident way through the jostling, staggering crowd, and himself press wine upon his guest, joking him into yet another cupful. He would offer him the salt and the slice of lemon that took something of the burning from a swallow of raw *tequila* or *pulque*.

It seemed no time before the fiery foods and liquors put the celebrants in an uproarious mood. Chairs were snatched from under unsuspecting sailors about to sit down, and the sight of their heels in the air as they rolled grotesquely on the floor convulsed all those around. Wine was poured on the heads of others in mock baptisms, and then feats of skill began. Daggers were hurled at a mark upon the wall; there were even attempts at clumsy, bearlike dancing on the trestle tables, strewn with broken pottery and the remnants of food.

Osterbridge, watching with a faint smile and shrewdly assessing eyes, finally judged the time to be right. He called to Modesto to bring cards for the company, and in a trice games were in progress at every table, or even on the floor, for those who could not make a place for themselves or look over the shoulders of seated onlookers.

Osterbridge had placed Simon Gosler on his right, and he had called El Rojo to sit at table with them, to rest his aching foot and partake of wine, now that the feast was over. A game began between Simon Gosler, El Rojo, and the motley group around Osterbridge's table, while Osterbridge himself withdrew to lean against the wall. From this point of vantage he not only saw well, but could keep an eye on the effect of the drink on other merrymakers.

A short, heavy taper, as big as a man's fist, stood on the main table center and gave out an adequate light, flaring on the faces close-bent over the cards as they were flung down. Chris had a recollection that Simon was a good cardplayer but had been known to lose, and this, with his penny-pinching character, was unbearable to him. Not even the excess of

wine he had drunk that night clouded his brain enough to make him reckless in his betting. For a time his winnings grew on the table in front of him. The fitful light caressed and winked over the growing piles of silver. Then, whether because he tired, or simply that his luck changed, Simon Gosler's wealth began to dwindle and to rise ever higher before the broad beefy hands of El Rojo.

The candlelight made the innkeeper's shining face, flushed with drinking, into almost the color of wine itself, and his

fringe of red hair into filaments of copper wire. Across from
him, Simon Gosler's face with its hooked nose and draggling
oily hair took on lines of increasing severity and rising temper,
ill-controlled. El Rojo remained stolidly calm, playing his
cards with care but at a certain speed, while Simon Gosler
took longer and longer to make his moves.

The game at that table had finally come to a battle between
the two men, the other players sitting back to watch. Beyond
them in the main part of the room, the roisterers, as the eve-

ning progressed, had rapidly become sodden, and had fallen
asleep at the longer tables. Their drunken heads dropped forward among the litter of soiled cards and of wine dripping
from cups carelessly overturned. Some of the Indians lay
sprawled in snoring heaps upon the floor, arms and legs aban-
doned to slumber and fuddled wine-soaked dreams.

The room held a heavy uncomfortable silence as the sleepers
fell into still deeper sleep, until at last there was no sound to
be heard but the snap of the cards as Simon or El Rojo slapped
them down. Their companions, sensing the growing fierce-
ness between the two men, still crowded about the table,
watching every move with sleep-bleared eyes but saying nothing. Simon Gosler was wishing he had not begun the game,
and so lost the silver he loved more than anything else in life.
El Rojo was turning on Simon Gosler the pent-up feelings of
rage that the little white dog, first, and Claggett Chew later,
had begun in him.

The wealth before El Rojo grew, and at last Simon Gosler,
reduced to his last piece of silver, croaked out: "My one piece
against all of yours, El Rojo! One final hand!"

"Done!" growled the innkeeper. "Cut the cards."

The tension over the company was tight as a garroting cord,
and Chris, as Snowball, moved up to a higher step where he
could see better. There, he was lost in the upper shadow
and was even less remarked.

The cards slapped and flicked down, and all at once Simon
Gosler moved his fingers with a quick gesture as he put down
his final hand. Simultaneously there were sharp indrawn
catches of breath from all sides among the watching men.
Their black eyes swung from Simon's fingers, frozen above

the kings and queens in the center of the table, to El Rojo's face. The big man rose deliberately, wordless, and before the eye could follow it or Simon withdraw his hand from where he had attempted to change his cards, El Rojo's fist flashed up above his head and with a whistling thud, Simon Gosler's hand was pinned to the table on top of his cards. Up from the back of it shivered the hilt of El Rojo's dagger, and a bright red stain began to crawl toward the edge of the table.

What seemed to Chris minutes later, came Gosler's thin high scream of anguish as El Rojo, his eyes narrow, swept his winnings into his hand and barked out through his puffy lips:

"So — does El Rojo treat any cheat! Stay with your cards, infamous miser!"

In a second the audience about the table had faded away, some rolling to the floor to indulge in sleep, and one or two sliding from the room as silently as they could before other daggers should fly in flaring tempers or disagreements. Simon Gosler was left to whimper and moan as he plucked at the dagger in his hand by the light of the guttering candle.

Just then, Chris heard the door of Claggett Chew's room open, and his heavy resolute tread echo at the top of the stairs. Shattered and frightened by all he had seen, the little white dog found himself pelting down the stairs, only to be seized by the scruff of the neck at its foot by El Rojo.

"A-ha! My luck is in, in every way, this night!" he exulted, swinging the poor little creature high aloft. "Who has a dagger I can borrow? I have a score to settle — "

No one answered, and Osterbridge was running forward to stop the innkeeper when Claggett Chew's voice broke in behind them all.

"Throw the dog outside or in a cupboard, and explain what you have done to Simon Gosler," he demanded icily.

El Rojo did not turn around. "A good idea," he said, the color draining from his face with the hatred he felt for a man he had once admired, and opening a door under the stair, threw the little dog adorned with a lopsided bow into a dark airless place, locking the door on the outside.

"Did you deliver my message to the priest, Rojo?" Chris, bruised and shaken, could hear, muffled through the door. He could also detect the contempt in El Rojo's reply.

"No, pirate, I did *not*. The price for such a service is more than one piece of silver. I have been occupied by a most satisfying game of cards, and with nursing my foot. I am saving the strength of the other to kick someone. What do you intend doing about *that*, and where do you intend sleeping in future, for your room is no longer available for your use!"

"*This* is what I intend doing about it!" Claggett Chew replied, and Chris, straining his ear against the panel of the low door, could hear the metallic whisper as the pirate whipped out his sword. There was a sound of running feet, and Osterbridge's voice.

"Here — take my sword, Rojo! You shall not be defenseless!"

Then Osterbridge's light step echoed as he ran out the inn door, to the accompaniment of the ring and clash of blade on blade as the pirate and El Rojo fought, stumbling over the sprawling bodies of the Indians drunk enough to gratify even Osterbridge's highest hopes.

# CHAPTER 35

*HIS, OF ALL TIMES,* was the moment to dash to the help of his friends, Chris thought, hearing the heavy breathing, the sudden lunges and ringing parries, the half-completed ejaculations of the two villainous men fighting on the other side of his prison door. Chris knew that the moon would now be risen, and with Claggett Chew occupied, he stood a fair chance of rescuing the captives. Without these friends, he knew, he could never return to Georgetown.

But how to get out? Changing himself into a mouse, he investigated every inch of the closet where he had been flung. It was well made, for no smallest crack could he find large enough to allow even a fly to slide to freedom. Baffled, he changed back to his own shape, and then, frantic with haste to be gone, he remembered the trick of turning the key.

The key, however, was on the outside, and this presented new and untried difficulties. Still, Chris began to concentrate, repeating the magic formula. He was confused and distracted by the sounds of the fight going on beyond his cupboard door, and three times he made some small mistake of attention that meant he had to start afresh. On the fourth try, however, he could feel that he was losing himself, forgetting all sounds, all turmoil. In his mind he was putting himself outside the door stretching out his hand, touching the key, and with an effort that seemed to take an hour but actually took only a few seconds, he turned the key.

There was an audible *snap!* as the lock shot back and Chris held his breath in case either of the men he feared might have heard it. They apparently had not, for he heard their continuing shuffle of feet as they shifted position, and the unbroken clang and ring of steel on steel.

With one finger Chris pushed gently at the cupboard door. It swung outward for half an inch. Relief flooded the boy like a draught of refreshing water and he was about to change himself once more into a fly to soar out and away, when the lightning flitter of lizards across the ceiling caught his eye. There was no use in courting disaster. To be eaten by a lizard would be such a silly way to die! Yet Chris, unwilling to wait longer, changed himself again into a mouse, and quick as a blown bit of gray dust was out of the cupboard, past the laboring men, and into the cool night air outside the inn.

Never was a night sky more richly jeweled to a liberated prisoner's eyes, nor more welcome to see! Chris drew a deep breath, and then, with a leap, soared into the night in his guise of sea bird, dashing through the air toward the lagoon and then the mountainside.

So late, the fires along the beaches were no more than fading buds of crumbling fire; the village, with the festival over, was wrapped in sleep and silence. Osterbridge was nowhere to be seen, yet Chris thought he saw a small shadow moving along the way that led to the *Black Vulture's* cove, and a long, lean shadow, carrying what looked like a spade, hurrying down the far beach in the direction of the crooked palm.

Rising higher, Chris could see the dim masts and night-blue outline of the *Mirabelle,* standing off the beach he had so carefully described. The heavy surf there rose and fell and pounded, and a dim sheen of phosphorescence embroidered the line of the shore far below.

Making straight for the cave, Chris saw the glow of a fire and figures moving around it. Coming nearer, it needed only a glance for him to see that Becky had the situation well under control. Chris kept his bird's shape a little longer in order to see and hear unobserved, perching on a shrub near where Becky and Miss Teackle bent above a savory-smelling kettle.

To his amazement he heard Becky say: "Theodora, be so kind as to pass me the red pepper. So. Now, with your knowledge of pickles, do you consider that I dare add more to this?"

It took Chris a few seconds to realize that, as the saying goes, adversity makes strange companions, and that Becky and Miss Teackle, faced with danger, had forgotten their feud in their effort to get the better of their captors. The two Indians left to guard them were sitting close by the fire, smacking their lips and rubbing their stomachs in anticipation of the delicacy to come.

Knowing they could not understand English, Becky, though looking at them with great cordiality, said under her breath to Miss Teackle:

"Aye — they rub their stummicks now, they'll rub them better later, so they will!" And raising her voice she called to Ned, "Ned, me good friend, be you certain sure not to eat a bite nor a morsel of what I do serve these fellows, for unless Becky and Theodora here have no culinary art at all, this dish will win us our freedom, so it shall!"

Then Chris understood that Becky and Miss Teackle had concocted what would perhaps be the most famous stew of Becky's life, for while smelling most appetizing, it was so compounded that the effect would not be a happy one at all.

So it proved. Becky and Miss Teackle, who had a new gleam in her usually disapproving eye and was obviously thriving on the excitement, heaped the bowls of the two guards, who, kept waiting for their dinner, bolted the food like ravenous wolves.

It was scarcely down, however, before the red pepper and oil put in by Becky, the vinegar and pickles added by Miss Teackle, had their effect on the two empty stomachs. At first the men were aware of a vague discomfort, and slowed in their eating. Used to highly spiced foods, they did not at first think anything was wrong. The food itself soon put all doubts to flight. Pickles and pepper, vinegar and surfeit of oil, churned inside the miserable guards. Becky stood by with her hands on her hips as if eager to please and serve them, while watching every expression that crossed their faces. But when they began to clutch at their aching middles, and then to roll howling on the ground, both Becky and Miss Teackle threw back their heads and laughed until the echoes rang. With one accord they moved toward one another. The onetime enemies shook hands warmly.

"Eh! by me soul, Theodora, that there's the best afternoon's work that either you or I shall do for many a day!" Becky

declared, wiping the tears of laughter from her eyes. "I thank you for your addition of the vinegar and pickles, for pickles is a thing I do rarely think on, but 'twas the making of that stew, so it was!"

The two women fell to laughing once more. Miss Teackle finally stopped, gasping.

"My dear, Miss Becky," she said primly, though with a twinkle, "in a pickle we were, and it was a pickle alone that was needed to get us out!"

Then, amazed at her own joke, the two, so different and now united in their effort, laughed again. Susan, chuckling with them, had, with Amos, been untying Ned and Abner Cloud. Ned and Abner, stiff from their hours of bondage, rose rubbing their wrists and ankles, and in a trice it was the groaning guards who were bound with the very same cords.

Chris, while the women were congratulating themselves, had not been idle. After another look at Becky, he knew that her size and weight would never get down the cliff on even a magic rope ladder, so he had resolved to take her off first, on the back of a rope eagle. He knew about how much the eagle could carry, and while Becky's enormous size presented a desperate hazard, still, it had to be attempted. He had, therefore, taken back his human form, and behind the shelter of high grasses and leafy trees, made the magic turns and twists that created the spread-winged bird. Tying the eagle to a tree overhanging the abyss below, he went back to make himself known to his friends.

Great was the rejoicing and the tears of happiness when he was once more with his companions of old! Chris cut short the demonstration.

"We seem safe enough," he said, gathering his friends close about him, "safer than I had hoped. But we must work quickly, for Mr. Wicker always says we must be prepared for the unexpected. So — I am ready to take you off one by one" — he pointed to the cliff — "that way."

There were unbelieving cries and looks of consternation. Chris called for silence.

"Please, good friends, let's not waste a minute of time that is so precious! I'm going to start with Becky. You, Ned, and Abner, take the machetes of the guards and go a little way down the trail to stop anyone who may come from that direction. But," he called after them, "be on the lookout for David, for he will come that way!" He turned back. "Amos, you stand over the guards. Miss Teackle, I'll come back for you next. Now, Becky," he looked at his old friend and took her hand, "have you faith in me?"

Becky returned his look fondly, her plumed beflowered hat nodding her vigorous agreement.

"Aye, Chris, that I have," she replied with conviction.

"Then I must ask you to collect every ounce of it, for I shall blindfold you and take you safely to the *Mirabelle*. Will you trust me?"

Becky scarcely hesitated, but during her momentary silence Chris's courage quailed, that she might not agree. Then she squeezed his hand.

"Dear lad! I know that my master Mr. Wicker, and Captain Blizzard, and dear Ned, think the world of your ability, so who is Becky to doubt you? Where's your blindfold? I've not played at blindman's buff since I was a child!"

General Washington on her shoulder came to life to squawk Becky's own words back at her. "No man's memory can go back *that* far!" Becky laughed.

Hiding her eyes well with Ned Cilley's folded bandanna handkerchief, Chris took Becky by the hand and led her to where the magic eagle floated. For two hundred feet straight down, nothing lay below it, then came a fringe of rocks, and finally swampy morass. Chris closed his own eyes for a moment at the thought of settling Becky securely. He pulled in the eagle as near as he could, holding it close to the ground.

"Sit here, Becky," he said. "I'll be in front of you, and you'll be as safe — as — as — " He could find no word to describe how safe it would be, for he felt that of all things, safe it was *not*. Becky, obedient, sat heavily down on the eagle's back, and Chris climbed on to straddle the bird's neck. He was wondering privately whether even a magic eagle could lift such a double weight, as he pressed on the wings. Rocking a little, as if in protest, and quite slowly, the bird rose with difficulty into the air. Chris, his heart in his mouth as they began to move out over the abyss, cautioned Becky.

"Don't move, Becky! I'll tell you when we get to where we're going. Trust me!"

"Oh — I do, dearie!" Becky replied contentedly. "I understand none of it, but I trust you."

Far below, in the faint light of the waning moon, the pewter surface of the lagoon gave an occasional muted gleam in the blackness. The dark tangled mass of jungle at its rim appeared, fringing the lake and the beach, and at last to Chris's eyes came a sight of the *Mirabelle*. Taking no chances Chris circled far to seaward, out of sight of any sailors on watch, and brought the eagle back and down within two feet of the deck of the *Mirabelle*.

"You can get off now, Becky," he said, "but count to one hundred slowly before you take off your blindfold. I'm going now to bring Miss Teackle back."

Chris was already at the cliffside before Becky raised her bandanna, and clasped her hands with thanksgiving when she saw where she was.

# CHAPTER 36

*C*HRIS WANTED TO take Susan away with Miss Teackle but Susan Moffit was a stubborn young lady. Wildly happy at the thought that David would soon come up the path she refused to leave, insisting that Amos, instead, should go to safety. Chris therefore, willy-nilly, not wanting to waste time in arguing with a woman — always a lengthy and unsatisfactory process — bound both Miss Teackle's and Amos's eyes and hurried them onto the eagle's back. He not only wanted them to remain uncertain of their method of transportation, which was so unbelievable that Chris knew that to see and experience it more fully would frighten his friends, but also the height at which they moved was terrifying in itself. So for both these reasons he made sure that neither would peer from under their blindfolds.

Regretfully, and with many misgivings, he put Susan in Ned's care, and urged the magic bird forward as fast as its labored flight, under a triple weight, would go. Amos expostulated all the way, for he wanted to stay and fight, if need arose. But Chris pointed out that the sooner they were all aboard, the sooner the *Mirabelle* could make all sail to get out of the way of the pirate's clutches. This made very good sense to Amos who had no wish to delay the proceedings, and with Miss Teackle twittering like a sparrow in her excitement at the extraordinary evening through which she was passing, Chris guided the big rope eagle toward the ship.

The great rope bird's wings were far-spread. By touching the head to right or left, Chris could direct its flight, and by pressing on top of the beaky head, make the eagle go up or down. Evidently Mr. Wicker had seen to it that those sailors not with the rescuing party were not on deck, for Chris was able to bring the great bird down a second time unseen.

As he rose once more to go back for Susan, Chris saw below him, waiting beyond the crash of the surf, the longboat with its crew, ready to take off whoever should gain the beach. The *Mirabelle* rode at anchor without a light, under the high blue vault of the clear night. Time was passing, however, and Chris was well aware that it lacked little before moon-set. Then would come a time of total darkness, except for starlight. He wanted passionately to have done with his rescue work; he longed that they should all be safely gone. He felt a growing unease, for the night had gone forward almost too well. Chris no longer liked the feel of the very air about him.

As, high above the trees, he neared the dim glitter of the lagoon, Chris heard carried up to him distinctly, from far below, a gull's cry three times repeated. Instantly the boy, remembering how Mr. Wicker had once, in a now distant time, taken the form of a black-headed seagull, swung about, diverting the eagle down. In the deeper gloom at the edge of the

256

jungle he skimmed along the trees.

A forest had once stood there until the sea and inland springs had combined to flood the ground. Huge cypresses, *ceiba*, or silk-cotton trees, *marañon*, or cashew, still clung to life among more thickly crowding plants whose roots preferred the boggy ground. Chris moved patiently along, looking in the clouded light for Mr. Wicker.

He found him, nearly indistinguishable against the bole of a cedar tree many hundreds of years old. Chris brought the eagle up until Mr. Wicker could reach out and hold to the beak of the bird. His low whisper scarcely came to Chris, but the boy knew how well sound carries over water, and he strained his ears.

"Christopher! The magic bird can make no more than three trips of the same kind in a row! Bring Susan with you this time if you can. If not, then Ned and Abner, for you and I can manage Claggett Chew if need be, alone. We shall have to. Hurry!"

Chris wasted no time on words. "I shall, sir!" he whispered back huskily, and pressing on the back of the eagle, headed for the cave.

He found great celebration there, for David Russell had arrived safely but alone. Chris was nonplussed.

"Have you no followers, David?" he asked.

"I sent them back to man the longboat," David replied as they shook hands. "I did not want my idea of coming up this way to be the cause of lives lost other than my own. So I came without anyone. The path was not hard to find."

He had one arm about Susan, and the two clung together in a surge of joy and relief at finding one another unharmed.

257

Chris began to urge Susan to leave with David, but David refused.

"Ned and Abner are weary from their long hours of being bound, of being without food, and with waiting here on the trail," he said. "Do you take Susie and them, if you can, and I shall come when I am sure we are not followed."

At this, Susan became adamant, and the power of her refusal reminded Chris so much of her Grandmother Moffit that he had to smile, even though he was indignant at her obstinacy.

"If David stays, I stay!" Susan declared. "Hurry and take Ned and Abner. After that the three of us will regain the ship together." She stood firmly beside David. "Do not try to dissuade me, Chris," she said, almost defiantly. "David is to be my husband, and my place is beside him." Her fine eyes flashed and her cheeks were flushed as she put her hand in David's. "I would rather die beside him than live without him, so take our good friends at once. We seem safe enough here," she said.

Chris felt a pang at her words. "Oh! I do wish you hadn't said that, Susan, for it has been going too well to continue long! I hope you are right, and we must hurry, for the moon is setting," he went on. "Come on, Ned and Abner. We can do nothing with these two. I shall come back for them as soon as I can — "

His return to the ship with his two friends was soon accomplished but with it, the third and last trip the eagle could make. Letting himself down over the side of the *Mirabelle*, Chris transformed the rope from an eagle to a boat, darted over the water, and dashed far up on the beach. He then had

to take his sea-bird form for the return to the cliff.

Long before he reached it he heard the clash of swords ringing across the lagoon. He knew only too well whom he would find, and as he neared the cliff, he could see the tall powerful figure of Claggett Chew thrusting and parrying at David Russell's sword. He was effectively preventing David from heading down the trail.

Good swordsman though David might be, Chris knew that only one man was liable to be a match for Claggett Chew, and where Mr. Wicker might be at that minute none could tell. As fast as he could, Chris made the magic rope, which he had wound about his waist, into as long a ladder as he could, and rushing along the ledge, seized Susan firmly by the wrist from where she stood, paralyzed, unable to take her eyes from the battle between David and the pirate.

"Quick, Susan!" Chris called to her, "I'll cover David's retreat — he will go down after you. It's our only chance. Chew intends to marry you! You *have* to come!"

Susan, as one stunned, followed Chris to where he had secured the top of the rope ladder.

"Be brave, Susan. Shut your eyes, hold tight, and go down. I'll see that David comes at once."

"What about you?" Susan murmured between numb lips as she began, with a white face, to go down the ladder.

"Oh — don't worry. I'll make it!" Chris called back confidently, saying inside himself in a small voice: I hope.

As he ran back to guide David to the ladder, he saw that one of the guards had had his bindings cut by one expert flick of Claggett Chew's rapier, as the pirate, using his whip with his other hand, occupied David's attention for the moment essential to slash the guard to liberty.

"Unfasten your fellow, you stupid dog!" the pirate shouted, and the man, still groaning, stumbled forward to do as he was told.

Catching at what he thought to be an opening in Chew's guard, David, fancying that the pirate's attention was on the Indian, made a lunge. Chris, close behind, knew instinctively that Claggett Chew had given his opponent this false hope, for before the eye could blink, he had made a riposte. David gave a cry of pain and Chris saw the pirate's sword deeply pierce his friend's leg. Chris offered up a silent prayer of thanks to Mr. Wicker whose knowledge had foreseen this possibility. Had the sword remained tipped with its usual poisonous charge, within a few days David Russell would have been past all hope of saving. As it was, Chris wondered despairingly whether he could ever help the wounded man to safety under the harrowing circumstances which were their only chance of escape. As these thoughts filled his mind, Chris, in that second, came to David's side.

"Give me your sword!" he cried, "and you go back to the ladder! You mustn't leave Susan — I'll follow. Can you make it?"

David murmured a reply, and in shorter time than it takes to tell, Chris found himself with his back a few feet from the sheer drop of the cliff, fighting for his life against an expert with the rapier.

From the corner of his eye he saw that the two guards were now free. One was sneaking back toward the rope ladder, and the other was coming toward Chris, muscular hands outstretched. In the meantime, Chris had to be certain that Claggett Chew did not snatch his sword from him by twining his whip about it.

The boy thought that no matter how well he tried, his last moment had surely come.

# CHAPTER 37

*T WAS AT THAT* dreadful point that Chris remembered the leather bag at his neck. How to fight, watch the two wily Indians, and get his fingers into the mouth of the bag? But do it he must.

His fingers touched a capsule and tugged it out, maneuvering so that although his back was only a foot from the cliff edge, he had the two Indians to his left and Claggett Chew to his right. The rope ladder down which he saw David's disappearing head was close by.

At that moment he saw the first Indian raise his dagger to cut the ladder away. Chris waited no longer. He had no idea what the capsule contained, nor what would occur, but he threw it at the man with all the force he could muster. At the same time he crossed swords desperately with the pirate, who permitted himself a sour smile, thinking Chris to be so nearly vanquished.

The capsule struck a rock at the Indian's feet and exploded with only a faint sound. This sound, faint though it was, instantly affected Claggett Chew, for he seemed to understand it and rushed forward to drag the Indian clear.

He was too late. Two feet above ground Chris could see a brownish fog darkening the air. Claggett Chew dropped to the ground, so Chris did the same, wriggling forward at the very cliff's brink, while stones slipped from under him to rebound and echo in the void below. He reached the ladder top just as the Indians staggered back, holding their eyes and beginning to behave like madmen.

"The monster attacks me!" shrieked one. "Its talons kill me!"

"It tears out my entrails!" screamed the second. "Mercy! Mercy!"

Seeing nothing, Chris could only imagine that the powder in the capsule held the power of creating phantasms of unspeakable horror. Claggett Chew, even, was crawling away, making for the trail, down which he soon disappeared at a run. Chris, going down the ladder as fast as he could, knew the pirate had his reasons for leaving as he did, and surmised that he must know some other way to cut them off from the retreat they had planned.

As Chris continued down the seemingly endless ladder, he could feel David's uncertain descent ahead of him, weighting the ladder so that it held fairly steadily against the cliff. Above him, the terrible gurgling cries of the two obsessed Indians went on, and what was his consternation when, looking up, he saw them grappling with one another. Their frenzy was such that each had mistaken the other for the monster they thought was attacking them. Frozen to the ladder with horror, Chris saw and guessed the outcome, even as it occurred. Wrestling, striking, tackling one another, the two maddened Indians, in a final effort, were locked together, bending and swaying. One pushed, the other resisted but was bent backwards, and, neither letting go, both plummeted past Chris to plunge into the lagoon below. Chris thought of the snakes and the crocodiles, and as utter silence followed, without even the lap of water on rock, Chris felt sick and shuddered for Susan, too.

Thereafter he hurried on, to find Susan and David supporting each other on the narrow margin of bank above the lagoon. Susan was half fainting with fright at the battle, her escape, and then the terrifying death of the Indians, while David was in great pain from the severe wound in his leg. Chris wrenched off his shirt and tore it into strips.

"Here," he said to David, "let me bind that as well as I can to stop the blood. The Captain has medicines on board ship, once you get there."

He ripped the blood-soaked part of David's trouser off, and as he talked began to do quite a commendable job of bandaging.

"Somehow," he said, his fingers flying, "you have to hold on to yourself, David — and you too, Susan — to help me get you both to safety. The worst isn't over yet. The three of us need all the wits we can muster to get out of this as fast as we can. There. Is that any better?"

"Much," David said, his voice sounding stiff as if his jaw had been set against sound for some time.

"Think you can manage?" Chris asked solicitously, eyeing the young man in the dim light of the waning moon. David let his weight go on the wounded leg, stifled a cry, and replied:

"Of course."

Chris felt a surge of admiration for him. "Good for you! You comfort Susan. Look over that way" — he said — "away from where the Indians fell, and in a minute, we'll start across the lagoon." He remembered the flagon of wine and water he had taken from Becky — had it been only that morning? — and gave it to David. "Give Susan a drink of this, and you have some too," he suggested. "It will make you feel better, perhaps. Now — pay no attention to me — "

Chris could have saved his words. The two young people were busy with themselves. They drank a few mouthfuls from the flagon, and Chris, busy making the rope boat which had just been a ladder, heard David saying:

"How now, Susan! Do not make your Grandmother Moffit ashamed of you! No tears — no fainting spell! There is no time for such."

Susan, stung, drew herself up proudly, fighting against the dizziness and nausea she felt, and replied, "I am a Moffit. So my grandmother bade me remember, and in such a time as this, the Moffits are quite capable for whatever is to come!"

"Bless your dear heart!" came David's low voice, "of course they are!"

"How do you, David?" Susan asked, her anxiety for him wiping out all thought of herself. She put her arm around him in support. "Are you in much pain, darling?"

David's voice was too impatient to be quite honest, but Chris in his own heart, congratulated him on his firm tone.

"Not at all, Susan. It was a mere graze that drew more blood than it did damage. Let us speak no more about it — "

Chris now had the boat ready and was holding it steady.

266

"Quickly!" he urged softly. "Susan, will you get in first and help me give David a hand? David"—he went on—"I'm sorry to ask it, but I need your help on the other oar—"

They were in, and Chris pushed the boat off from the hateful cliff with his foot. The lagoon seemed almost blacked out, and only a fitful leaden sheen gave the fugitives guidance for the crossing. Chris motioned to one of the oars.

"We must pull our best," he said, trying to sound matter-of-fact. "I hate to have to tell you this, but the lagoon has crocodiles in it. We could easily run into one. Susan, please look over our heads and tell us how to avoid what may seem to be only logs!"

The three young people sat tensely in the little boat, David and Chris pulling as long and as hard as they could on the oars. All at once the boat rocked and shipped water, almost throwing Susan out. Chris felt that this was Claggett Chew disguised as a crocodile, coming up under the keel in an effort to upset them. Just then, with a roar, a second crocodile rose from nowhere to do battle with the first, and Chris reasoned in himself that this circumstance was too much coincidence — it could only be Mr. Wicker coming to their rescue.

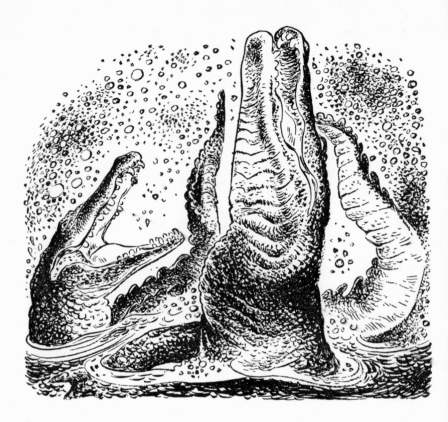

The boat shot on again, leaving the water behind it thrashing with the two scaly beasts who snapped their formidable jaws at one another and whipped about as they tried to beat each other across the eyes with their ponderous tails.

Chris, pulling so hard on his oar that his blood beat in pounding folds inside his head, was in a frenzy to get Susan and David ashore to go back to the help of his master, for Claggett Chew was a terrifying enemy and one with whom he did not want Mr. Wicker, wise as he was, to be left long alone.

The shore was reached at last, and as Chris saw David help Susan to the swampy ground, he handed David back his sword.

"Here," he said, "you had better have this to protect Susan. Just go straight ahead — you'll reach the dunes soon, and I will come as soon as I can, to help you reach the longboat." As the two began to move away Chris called softly after them, "Susan! Lend me your cape! Maybe I can fool Claggett Chew with it!"

Susan gladly took it from her shoulders and as his friends disappeared, Chris found a limber young tree of the right height. It grew in the opposite direction to that taken by Susan and David. This sapling he draped with Susan's cloak. It looked for all the world like a young woman with her head bowed into her hands in total despair. Chris smiled at his ruse, and then stood listening.

The lagoon was silent. A ghastly, night-drenched silence rebounded to Chris's ears, strain them though he would. The thrashing and splashing of the huge reptiles had stopped. There was not a sound. Who had won? Was Mr. Wicker all right? And if so, where was he?

Chris stood at the edge of the jungle, hidden in blackness now, for the moon had set, and only faint blue starlight filtered through the knotted vines and branches. As he stood listening, Chris heard once more the three-times seagull's cry, and knew that Mr. Wicker had arisen undefeated from his battle. The seagull seemed to be flying rapidly overhead in the direction of the beach where Susan and David would emerge, and Chris turned back into the jungle, intending to take his seabird shape and go quickly to rejoin his friends.

Ahead of him the starlight strengthened, it seemed to Chris, and he saw that Susan must have come back, or got lost, for she wandered a little way beyond him. Chris ran after her.

"Susan!" he called, "I'll help you!"

He had not even come up to her when the figure turned and straightened to its full height. With a sickening feeling of hopelessness Chris saw who it was. Claggett Chew had tricked him with his own trap, and had put on Susan's cloak.

Chris, running forward as he was, saw the long reach of the whip, and heard its serpent-like hiss even before he saw it. He swerved to one side, running on and to the left, beyond Claggett Chew.

Chew put his hand in his pocket, drawing out what seemed

to be glowworms, for the objects in his hand shone with a
light of their own. With two bounds the pirate, his white
face snarling in his rage, tossed the tiny glowing things ahead
of the running boy.

They struck the ground ten feet ahead of Chris. He saw
them uncurl themselves even as they fell. Once on the ground
they disappeared with incredible speed. Chris, racing hard,
too hard to be able to take some shape other than his own,
could not stop his headlong flight. In another moment he
had set foot on the ground where the strange grubs had been

thrown, and with a gasp, had fallen into the pit they had burrowed! He found himself with the surface of the ground well over his head, and still he continued to sink!

A shout of triumph came from Claggett Chew, and his whip hissed into the hole, cutting at Chris's hairline, so that he was almost blinded by his own blood that streamed over one eye. He knew that Claggett Chew wanted to scalp him, and he felt like an animal in a trap.

But the boy was not finished yet. As the whip flashed down a second time he grabbed hold of it, feeling the ground dropping from under his feet as the voracious grubs ate their way into the mossy bog.

Chris held fast to the whip with one hand, and neatly wrapped and knotted it about his waist. This left his hands free, and he thrust his left hand a last time into the leather bag, praying that there might still be one last particle of magic in it to save him from the pirate magician.

His fingers felt only seeds, yet help he had to have. He shook the seeds into one palm, closing his hand to hold them fast. He then began hauling himself to the top of the pit by means of Claggett Chew's own whip.

As he reached the top of the cavity, panting, he was met by a sword point. He knew well enough that the pirate would run him through if he did not act instantly. Taking good aim he flung the seeds at Claggett Chew's feet, and simultaneously rolled to one side, unrolling himself from the whip and also just beyond the reach of Claggett Chew's rapier.

In that second the magical seeds did their work. As Chris rose on the far side of the pit, he saw, to his utter amazement, enormous ferns springing from the ground, their curling heads

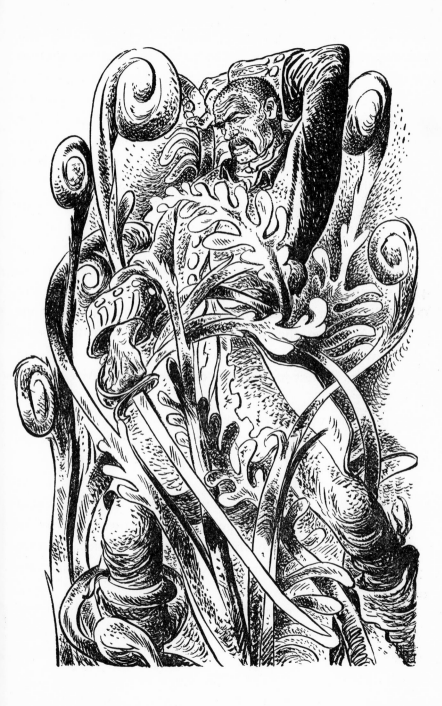

unfolding as they grew. With a sinister, winding, blowing motion, they curled about whatever lay near them, binding their tendril fronds about first Claggett Chew's boots, then his sword, then his arms.

The pirate gave a hoarse shout of rage and perhaps terror, and began to struggle with the enveloping plants. Chris did not wait to see how his enemy would fare, but took his bird form with relief. In no time he was high above the living nets of the jungle. Below he saw the *Mirabelle*, the longboat hauled aboard, lifting anchor and preparing to sail.

Only a tired boy, and a man scarred by the teeth of a crocodile, were watching for a certain cove as the *Mirabelle* passed. From the owner's cabin window, as the ship moved homeward beyond Acapulco, the two watchers saw in the growing light of a new day that the *Black Vulture* lay beached and ashore.

"Anchors do not lift themselves," commented Mr. Wicker dryly.

"Could just one rather thin man and a boy walk an anchor up?" Chris asked curiously.

"If they could not, a knife blade gives the same result," his master replied with a smile.

As the long tropic shore swept slowly past, Chris said wistfully, "I liked Osterbridge pretty well, there, toward the end." He looked up into Mr. Wicker's satisfied face. "What's going to happen to him, sir? Could you tell me, just this once?"

Mr. Wicker's eyes crinkled at the corners, and his mouth followed suit, but he did not look down into the earnest face lifted to his.

"Just this once, then, Christopher," he smiled. "If you look sharply, you will see the tag end of a second donkey under the shade of the trees. It is carrying Osterbridge's wardrobe." A ghost of a chuckle sounded. "Our friend is very shortly going to take to the Taxco road, heading, I rather think," Mr. Wicker said meditatively, "toward Texas. Or what will be Texas. Although he may care for the society of Mexico City."

Chris felt suddenly relieved, and with a lighter heart. His face cleared. "The society part sounds more likely, I think," he said. "I suppose Onofré will stay where he belongs, in Acapulco with his mother — " He nodded, echoing a reply that Mr. Wicker could have made. Then he smiled, as if Osterbridge could see him, across the expanse of water.

For it seemed to them both as the *Mirabelle* headed for home on that warm early morning, that someone bathing in the sea, under a parasol, waved a white handkerchief to the passing ship, and a little boy on the sand jumped up and down. But whether that was to see better, or whether it was from joy, neither of the watchers ever knew.

# CHAPTER 38

*I*'LL GO NO MORE a-roaming, a-roaming, a-roaming!" sang Becky, and Miss Theodora Teackle came up to the kitchen table to hum with her friend as together they put the finishing touches to as fine a wedding cake as anyone could ever hope to see. Becky shook her head in remembrance.

"Lawks, Theodora, upon me soul, there were times when I fancied we should never taste home cooking again!" she said. Miss Teackle gave a smile far less wry than it would have been a year before.

"Becky, 'twas our stew that set all right. You provided the pepper — as usual — "

" — But you provided the pickles!" chuckled Becky, and then, as they stood off to admire the result of their efforts, Becky added, " 'Twill be the prettiest and happiest wedding I shall ever see, that I know!"

"Barring, might be, your own!" suggested Miss Teackle slyly.

Becky smirked and hung her head. General George Washington in his cage by the kitchen window put in his bit.

"Sure an' I need a kiss from my Boozer!" he squawked. Becky rallied and looked pointedly at Miss Teackle.

"What about a possible Mrs. Finney?" she challenged. "Sure and you and Mr. Finney did seem to find yourselves marvelous good company all the way home!" Becky stated, her hands on her hips and her flowers and feathers fluttering with excitement.

Now it was Miss Teackle's turn to be coy. The tall thin woman was no longer even as dour in appearance as she used to be, for today she had ventured to dress in grey for the wedding instead of her usual black. She actually had the grace to blush.

"There now!" went on Becky, pretending not to notice, "all is ready. Are those boys washed and dressed yet?" She went over to the bottom of the stair that led to the attic room where Amos and Chris were making themselves presentable for the ceremony. "Come along, boys," she called, "or we shall be late, and that would never do!"

Feet rattled down the steps, and there stood Amos in a new bottle-green suit with brass buttons and scarlet waistcoat, and Chris in a blue suit with canary-yellow waistcoat and highly polished shoes. The boys carried their three-cornered hats under their arms in the best style, and as they slowly turned before Becky and Miss Teackle so that those ladies could see if their necks and ears were clean, a resounding knock sounded on the back door. There stood Captain Blizzard, Mr. Finney, and Ned Cilley, all in their Sunday best, with flowers on their coats. Miss Teackle led the way on Mr. Finney's arm, then

came Becky between Ned and the Captain, while the boys
followed after.

Amos lowered his voice to Chris. "You can shake your
head all you wants," he said, "but I *still* says that 'twas you
and Mr. Wicker that saved that girl and the ladies! All very
fine to let Mr. David take the credit! You forgets, Chris,
I've seen you in action — don't I remember!" Amos said
firmly.

"Well," Chris murmured back as they went along to
Brother Balch's church, "I can't stop what you *think*, Amos,

I just know how it *was*. David had a bad fight with Claggett
Chew. You know yourself that his leg wound kept him sick
a-bed nearly all the way home. He had to get Susan through
a jungle full of snakes and crocodiles, in spite of the pain —"

Amos shuddered. "Humph! Crocondiles! Never did like
such things! Guess Mr. David's plenty brave. Anyhow, Miss
Susan made up her mind to marry him long before ever she
left home." Amos smiled and shook his head. "Miss Susan's
like her grandmama. Mighty lot of spirit they got, both the
one and the other! She'll make a good wife to Mr. Russell,

279

and now he's a hero, Miss Susan's pa's only too glad to 'gree."

"Yes," Chris said, not without a feeling of sadness, "it has turned out well. Thank goodness," he added fervently. "Several times, back there, I didn't see how it *could*."

The church came before them, friends of the Moffits and the Russells already gathering in smiling groups. Scarcely were Becky, Miss Teackle, and their friends in their places than Mr. Wicker came down the center aisle quietly escorting a beaming Martha Moffit to her place in the front pew on the bride's side of the church. At a gesture from her, he sat beside her. Chris thought his master's finely chiseled profile looked sterner and sadder than usual, and as a rustle and the voices of the choir heralded the arrival of the bride, Chris saw Mr. Wicker's eyes on David Russell's radiant face. It came to the boy then, like a personal blow at the heart, that Mr. Wicker would have wished himself to be standing there, waiting for the prettiest bride Georgetown had ever known, to come down the aisle on her father's arm.

There seems to be one magic Mr. Wicker hasn't got, the boy thought to himself. I wish I'd had the power to change a girl's heart for him, but — once it's given — I guess no magic can do that.

Behind him, in the slave gallery, tears of joy ran on the cheeks of Uncle Borb and Aunt Abby, Jonah and Juno, who had bowed their heads in daily prayer for their Susie long after all others thought her lost at sea. The sun streamed in through the windows as it had one earlier time, only this time the church was not empty but garlanded with the smiling, joyous faces of Susan's and David's friends.

The ceremony over, Jonah called for the cake and carried it

280

to Colonel Moffit's house for the reception. What a feast Becky Boozer had ready for Mr. Wicker's friends! Bustling about, she bade them pull the table away from the window so that all should be accommodated with ease, and then, stirring in different pots, first this one and then that, her bonnet quivering with the pleasurable excitement of the day, she bade the company sit down.

"Ah dear!" Becky cried, wiping her eyes on a corner of the mammoth apron with which she had covered up her wedding finery, "such a beautiful bride! And such a handsome groom! Ah, dearie, I'm all of a tearful!" and Becky snorted and sobbed unashamedly. Ned Cilley threw down his knife and fork to run over and comfort her, standing on tiptoe to reach high enough to kiss her chin. Becky was at last sufficiently calmed to say that all was cooked to a turn.

"But," she said, her nose pink from her tears, "as for me, I'm that churned about from the excitement that I cannot eat a mouthful. I'm sure that poor dear Ned is too, but you must all have a taste, to keep up your strength — "

" — and spirits!" squawked General Washington from his cage. "Don't forget the spirits!"

"Aye, by me soul, the bird's fair human!" Becky cried. "Run, Amos, and set the spirits and ale upon the table, there's a dear. Now you all sit where you are — " she commanded, looking from Captain Blizzard's round red face to long-faced Mr. Finney who was gazing glumly at Miss Teackle, who as glumly gazed back. Becky smiled happily, for she knew their glumness was merely love, and let her glance move to Chris. It passed from him to Ned and Amos, as the dark boy slid into his chair, his face expectant. Suddenly her own face fell.

"Deed, upon me soul, I do not know if I have chosen aright to tempt appetites dulled by surfeit of excitement!" she said. Then, as they looked up at her brightly, where she stood before the fire in her outrageous hat, the firelight beating upon her with its own kind of benediction, she continued. "Still, I can only do me best. Come, Chris, help me take these few samples to the table!"

The table had had two extra leaves added to it to make it large enough for the additional guests, but it was scarcely big enough to hold all the variety of foods Becky had made to heap upon it. Meat and fruit tarts; bowls of thick cream; vegetables, braised and baked; roasts and fowls, fish and stews; cakes; open latticed tarts; puddings and fruit fools.

Ned watched the seemingly endless procession of plates and bowls, his face shining, his occasional teeth bared in a smile of greed. He glanced at Captain Blizzard who sat in his chair even more stupefied at the sight than Ned. Ned waited some seconds with commendable patience for his captain to make the first move, but when he did not, with a whoop that the boys knew of old as his usual signal, Ned cried lustily:

"By yer leave, Captain, sar!" and without further ado, speared a potato on his fork and a squab on his knife, plunging into the meal with tremendous and noisy gusto.

At this, all fell to, while Becky stood by anxiously, watching first one, then the other. Although Ned was certainly anything but backward, reaching in every direction for an indiscriminate choice of meats or sweets or cheeses, with great gulping draughts of ale, Becky urged him on.

"Keep up your strength, my poor Ned, for 'tis a hard life ye lead at sea. And you too, poor Captain, a-standin' on your bridge the livelong day. And you, Mr. Finney — food will cheer you up — have a pie? Theodora, you're too thin by half, take a duck. 'Tis only a wild one and will scarce make a mouthful."

So she encouraged them one and all, but as he began to slow up and look with less eagerness on the bountiful food, Chris caught sight, standing in the doorway that led to his study, of the figure of Mr. Wicker.

Chris did not have to be told. He rose, looking around slowly at the faces of his friends, silently bidding them, one by one, goodbye.

"Will you excuse me, Becky?" he asked.

"Of course, dearie. You will be back?" she asked, unaccountably uneasy.

"I hope so," Chris said, and as he walked away, resolutely not looking over his shoulder, he felt the sudden dismay in all his friends; their friendship, like strong hands, loosing him regretfully, unwilling to let him go.

# CHAPTER 39

*O*NCE *AGAIN, CHRIS* ran up the hill toward his house. Once again, as on another time, his magic knowledge had been wiped from his mind when Mr. Wicker had put his hand on his head. Once more he had taken off the clothes of 1793, for he had spent a year in Mr. Wicker's time with his eighteenth-century friends — and had put back his clothes of the present day.

"May I keep the memory of it all as I did before?" he asked. Mr. Wicker nodded. "And come back, perhaps? May I do that too?" he begged.

"Yes," said Mr. Wicker. "I shall need your help again, Christopher. Of that I am sure."

Chris's eyes lit up. "Can I count on that, sir?" he cried. "If I can, it will take out all the sting of having to go back — "

"Very well." Mr. Wicker smiled, his eyes unsmiling. "Count on it, Christopher. And now," he had said, leading the way to the door, when Chris had put on his own clothes, "thank you once more for your invaluable help. Thanks to you I was able to keep my word to Colonel Moffit, and bring his daughter safely home."

Chris grinned up at him. "It did Miss Teackle a power of good too, that voyage home, sir!" he said. As he had hoped, his remark brought a smile to his master's fine grave face.

"Cheer up, sir!" Chris made bold to say. "Susie's a pretty girl but she's too obstinate for you. Anyone that stubborn needs to be where she's going — to a big busy plantation where she'll have a lot to do!"

Mr. Wicker looked back at his pupil with the first genuine smile Chris had seen him wear in many weeks. Yet he looked thoughtful too.

"Perhaps you are right, my boy. Miss Susan very nearly got herself — by her obstinacy in Acapulco — a husband she would not have liked as well," he said. "So — fare thee well, boy. God's blessing go with you. When the time comes, you will return."

"I shall, I shall! I loved it — all of it!" he shouted back, but Mr. Wicker had already left the doorway of his shop, and there was Chris once more on Wisconsin Avenue at the close of a fine spring day.

The seasons are all jumbled up in my head, Chris thought as he walked home. Two long voyages and the heat in Acapulco. Now spring still here —

His mother looked up over her evening paper when he came in the door. "Have a nice boat trip, dear?" she asked. "You've been gone for two days — it must have been fun. I want to hear all about it." She looked so tranquil that Chris began to feel uneasy.

"Two days?" he said. "That — long? You weren't worried?" he wanted to know.

His mother held out her hand to pull him over for a kiss. "Oh no," she replied peacefully, "your friend Mr. Wicker is considerate. He telephoned to me to let me know where you were, and that you were all right."

Chris looked away, examining, as he had already countless times, the winking gold of a Spanish doubloon that was never out of his pocket. "Where did he say I was?" he asked, as if absently, leaning against her chair.

His mother touched with one finger, gently, a scar she had not noticed before, at his hairline along the top of his forehead. "Why — " she said — "at the hotel where you were. It had the most marvelous name. We must go there sometime."

Chris waited. His mother tickled the back of his neck, which he loved.

"*The Sign of the Seven Seas!*" she said, in her eager voice. "I want to hear what it looks like." She picked up her paper again. "I would almost never have believed it could exist, except that that's where the operator said the call came from. On the coast somewhere, is it?" she asked.

Chris was moving away to go upstairs. "Yes," he said, vaguely, spinning his coin, "on the coast."

"What did you mutter, dear?" his mother called after him sharply. "It sounded like 'magic.'"

Chris leaned back around the corner of the wall into the room again. "Yes," he said briefly, "that's what I did say."

His mother looked slightly puzzled. "Magic? Why magic? What magic?" She took up her newspaper but looked across at Chris's head, stuck around the corner of the door. "The telephone, was that it?"

Chris accepted the line of least resistance for a change. "Yes," he agreed. "The telephone."

His mother settled back again with a comfortable smile. "It *is* like magic, isn't it?" she said. "I've often thought so, myself."

"There's so much — that's magic," Chris replied.

But by then he was halfway up the stairs. His mother called after him again in the tone of voice Chris knew meant that she expected no answer.

"Aren't you glad you took your sweater, dear?" she said.

## END